Fixation

by

Katja Desjarlais

Fixation

Cover Art by *Diana Carlile*

The Wild Rose Press, Inc.
PO Box 708
Adams Basin, NY 14410-0708
Visit us at www.thewildrosepress.com

Publishing History
First Edition, 2023
Trade Paperback ISBN 978-1-5092-4535-2
Digital ISBN 978-1-5092-4536-9

Published in the United States of America

Leaning his elbows on his knees, Nichol set his phone on the coffee table. "So have you had a lot of problems with vampires where you work?"

"All the time."

He flexed his arms out and forced his jaw to relax before he cracked a molar. "You never mentioned that before."

"I work nighttime security, NK," Highsteaks stated, her voice bordering on exasperation. "What the hell do you think I deal with?"

Thugs.

Criminals.

Drunk college students.

His lips drew into a thin line over his elongating fangs. "The guy who caught you in the ribs," he growled. "Human or vamp?"

"Vamp," she replied, apparently oblivious to his souring temper. "You probably don't see a lot of them if you're rural, but they move really freakin' fast."

"What did he look like?" he demanded, his mind focused solely on her attacker, primed to run down the list of vampires still known to be residing in North America.

"He looked like goo by the time I was done with him. I told you a million times, I'm good at what I do."

He sat back in his seat.

A fucking vamp killer.

Of course.

Dedication

This book is dedicated to Dena, whose inadvertent JCS comment saved this plot. And because I'm petty and books live forever, I'm going to get the last word.
I'm not bad.
You're bad.
(And amazing, but still. Long live shovels and those heavy, heavy CanCan skirts)

Chapter One

"Where do you want me to leave the grocery order?"

Nichol Kaius glanced up at Bianca. "Just toss it on the table and I'll get to it before dawn," he muttered, turning his attention back to his monitor and minimizing the open browser tabs. "Could you let Jagger know a replacement vehicle is on its way Thursday? I'll need you and Molly to run a pickup into the city during the day."

"Of course, honey," the Former Tender replied as she straightened the piles of papers on the com room table. "There's no rush on the groceries. Make sure you get to bed at some point." She crossed the room and knelt at his side. "When was the last time you ate?"

With a grunt of annoyance, he slid his chair a fraction away from her. "Had a bag yesterday."

"Mmmmm-hmmmm." Her blue eyes narrowed at him suspiciously as she rose to her feet. "Well, I'll send Boy up with another before dawn. You look tired."

He waited until Bee exited the room before rolling over to the table and snatching the grocery list from the pile of papers now neatly, and incorrectly, stacked on his desk. "Why the hell are there seven different types of shampoo?" he yelled into the empty hall as he pulled his browser back up and began the increasingly tedious task of placing the grocery order for the haunt. Grumbling to himself, he opened his chat app.

587OriginalNK: what the hell is it with women and shampoo

When no response came in immediately, he continued to scour the online store's beauty department, checking off doubles of every hair product request.

"Hey man!"

Mickey's voice broke through his concentration, and he leveled his younger hauntmate with a dead glare, pushing away from the computer and crossing his arms. "What."

"Lis is ready to work on Rhys's tattoos," Mick replied as he ran his tongue along one fang, completely unaffected by his ire. "Are you able to monitor it?"

He glanced at the clock and frowned. "Put Boy on duty. I'm busy."

Mickey shoved a hand through his long blond hair and slouched against the wall. "No can do. Boy freaks Lis out and Rhys thinks it's best she's not jumpy when she's handling the sulfur."

His teeth grinding in frustration, he minimized his screens and rose to his feet. "Fine. Where are they?"

"Sparring room," Mick said as he strode behind him. "Louis's going to hole up with me and Audra in the common room until it's done so he can help me keep my walls up against the pain."

"Don't adjust the balance settings on the stereo," he growled turning down the hall and running through his mental to-do list, shifting two tasks to the next night's already heavy load. As he passed the weapons room, he called out to Dominic and Molly while they argued over his youngest hauntmate's reservations over the weight of a new handgun. "Start Molly with the pistol, then move onto the .45 if she can handle it."

He pushed the heavy door open to the sparring room. Lis and Rhys stood in the corner, Lis's hands on her hips and Rhys's navy eyes narrowed. Pulling the door closed, he glared at the pair. "What."

"He's being unreasonable," Lis spat, gesturing toward the sparring room hose. "Tell him no one dies from a little cold water."

"Thousands do," Nichol responded, lifting the hose and checking the nozzle while Rhys's anger visibly morphed to victory.

"See, baby?" Rhys grinned, pulling his shirt off. "Nichol, I'm going to need you to hose the sulfur out once it beads. And only after Lis is out of range of the spray."

He nodded and approached the couple while she huffed and grumbled under her breath, her words crystal clear to the vampires in the room. When she was ready, Rhys lifted a blade to his bicep and sliced deep along one gray loop. Nichol held back while Lis injected the wound with a yellow sulfur mixture, her free hand stroking Rhys's jawline.

Her words of frustration turned to reassurances and whispered encouragements as the sulfur bonded to the mercury Rhys had used to create the intricate tattoos crawling along his arms, the silver element now leeching into his body and poisoning his blood.

"You can rinse it out now," she said, kissing Rhys's cheek and stepping out of the way once she was satisfied with the number of yellow beads forming in the cut.

He angled the spray, keeping his attention on his brother's blackening irises. "How many rounds are you doing?"

"Two," she replied, her voice shaking slightly.

"Three," Rhys grunted, flexing his hands and locking his eyes on Lis. "We agreed on three, sweetheart."

By the time Nichol was rinsing the third injection from Rhys's arm, the trio was on the cement floor of the sparring room, Lis soaked and straddling Rhys's lap against Nichol's warnings and Nichol holding Rhys's snapping jaw closed until the last of the beaded mercury was washed from the wound.

"I'm good," Rhys growled, fighting hard against his brother's hold without grazing the woman sitting on him. "Let me the fuck go."

He eased his grip slowly, prepared to restrain Rhys if he went for Lis's throat. When his younger brother closed his eyes, wrapped his arms around his lover, and leaned forward to rest his forehead on hers, he got to his feet and turned off the hose.

****

Highsteaks1403: we like to smell nice and look pretty

Highsteaks1403: you aren't one of those bulk bin lye soap guys are u

Highsteaks1403: ??

Nichol checked the clock.

Two hours ago.

He ran a hand through his damp hair, momentarily regretting showering and changing after the sparring room.

587OriginalNK: Sorry. Had to help my brother with something

He paused.

587OriginalNK: What shampoo do you use

Highsteaks1403: you're back! (happy dance)

4

Highsteaks1403: This one

He opened the link in his browser.

587OriginalNK: at that price does it come with someone to wash your hair for you

Highsteaks1403: Ha! No. That position's open if you want it ;)

He frowned at the screen.

587OriginalNK: Better get back to work. I'll check in tomorrow

Pulling his browser to the forefront, he continued to check off the items on Bianca's shopping list, keeping one eye on the chat box where Highsteaks was typing and deleting. He ran the virtual cart through the haunt's household expense account and printed off the receipt before turning his attention to his overflowing email inbox.

Highsteaks1403: all right. have a good night NK

He kept the chat box open in the corner of his screen while he ran through the litany of emails, deleting the spam and firing off quick responses to vampires reaching out to the Kaius haunt for blood orders and Tenders. With their bloodslave quarters almost completely shut down thanks to the haunt's reintegration efforts for the unlucky humans who'd been collected throughout the years and Rhys's curated vampire companion trade no longer operating, a standard form reply was all the energy he needed to invest before he turned his attention to more pressing matters. He relegated purchase receipt emails into their appropriate folders and compared the balances against the expenses in each account, scribbling a quick note to remind himself to call a clothing company about a double charge during daylight hours.

He was two pages into his news alerts when dawn

arrived, sending a brief tremor through his limbs. Boy's careful footsteps arrived at the com room door, stopping until Nichol acknowledged him.

"Bianca send you?" he asked, minimizing his screen and swiveling his chair toward the mute vampire who inhabited the bloodslave quarters.

Boy nodded and walked in, handing him a bag of A-positive. He set the bag on the table until Boy made no move to leave.

"You fear Bianca more than me?" He picked up the blood and tore a hole in the corner. When Boy nodded and backed into the corner to wait, he leaned back into his chair. "Probably wise," he mused aloud, knowing any vampire stupid enough to disobey the mother hen of the haunt would regret it for weeks.

Bianca Schumann was trained to be a Tender—a vampire courtesan—decades ago, returning to the Kaius haunt recently as both an officially recognized Former Tender in the vampire community and Jagger Kaius's lover.

She was a whole lot of badass wrapped in a tiny blonde package, and he was glad to know he wasn't the only old vamp in the haunt who bent to her demands without a fight. "Goddammit. I forgot to swing by the common room and let Mick know Rhys was done."

He pulled out his phone and fired off a quick text to Mick, adding his partner Audra to the message to ensure one of them received it. Although his empathic brother was becoming better at blocking the emotions of his hauntmates, subjecting Mick to Rhys's pain was senseless when Louis' flat affect was there to cocoon him.

Gulping down the rest of the blood bag, he carefully

rolled the open corner shut before tossing it in the trash and grabbing a paper from the printer. "Could you slip this under Jagg and Bianca's door on your way?"

Boy stepped forward to take the grocery receipt, his blue eyes scanning the product list.

"I know," he grunted. "That's a shit-ton of shampoo."

He turned back to his monitor as Boy exited. Highsteaks no longer showed online, her icon greyed out. Closing out the chat window, he focused his attention to the multitudes of financial accounts the haunt maintained, examining the purchases and deposits for inconsistencies.

Kaius's bank account remained untouched, the last transaction still the large withdrawal the haunt leader had made six weeks earlier after his angry departure.

He pulled up the haunt's phone accounts.

Nothing.

Kai's cell remained unused.

It wasn't a surprise, but it frustrated him, nonetheless. Especially when he knew deep down this absence was different than the others. The haunt's leader had often disappeared for long stretches throughout Nichol's fourteen centuries, but this was the first time Kaius left on his own accord and not under the call of his own creator. The radio silence was deafening thanks to the increased pressure it put on him to keep the haunt together until Kaius returned.

If he returned.

He ran a hand through his hair, his teeth grinding as he set the computer into sleep mode and shoved his phone into his back pocket. Placing the dust cover on his keyboard, he ran a finger over the top of the monitor and made a mental note to wipe down his system at dusk. After a quick reorganization of the papers Bianca had straightened, he pulled the com room door closed and headed to his bunker.

The main wing of the haunt was quiet. With Louis, Lis, and Rhys the only other occupants now, the constant noise of the past two years was softened to a dull hum.

Unless he passed through while Rhys and Lis were still awake.

He hesitated at their door before he knocked, listening in for a moment as the couple whispered quietly to each other. The dim light coming from under their door flickered as Rhys made his way over.

He scanned his younger brother over quickly. "Everything good?"

Rhys held his bare arms out for inspection. The mercury tattoo Lis treated had changed slightly, its color a fraction lighter than the untreated markings. "Yeah. Thanks for the help down there. If you could make it for the rest of them, that'd be cool."

He nodded. "How often do you intend to go through this?" he asked, his mind flicking quickly through the images of Rhys's muscles rigid with pain while he held still for Lis.

"Once a week," Rhys replied, reaching up to scratch at the untreated arm before dropping his hand.

"Just let me know when and I'll be there," he stated, walking toward his own room and pulling his phone out. He flipped through the haunt's stocks as he stripped down, turning each item right-side-out before placing it into the laundry hamper Bianca had insisted every bunker room needed.

His was slate gray.

Louis's was red with yellow and orange flames.

Pulling on a pair of nylon board shorts, he flopped onto his bed and opened his chat app.

587OriginalNK: Night, HS

He rolled over and reached into his bedside table, rifling around until his fingers latched on to a small glass vial. He popped the cap as his phone lit up.

Highsteaks1403: shouldn't you be sleeping

587OriginalNK: shouldn't you be

587OriginalNK: in bed now so no lectures

He recapped the vial and set it on the nightstand.

Highsteaks1403: no lectures I promise. busy week this week?

587OriginalNK: always. Still on night shifts?

Highsteaks1403: ugh yes

He glared at his phone for a moment. Highsteaks had been working night shifts as long as they'd been chatting, well over a year now. After a few pushes for her to consider moving out of security and into a safer line of work, he finally dropped the subject.

It still pissed him off.

Which pissed him off more.

All he knew about Highsteaks came from typo-ridden messages and emoticons. Her anonymity—and her respect of his own—kept their conversations safe and light.

Her decision to work a job which placed her outside alone at night was none of his business.

Highsteaks1403: still annoys the crap outta you doesn't it

With a huff, he laid back and turned down the brightness on his phone.

587OriginalNK: Nopre

587OriginalNK: Nope*

587OriginalNK: they still making you work alone?

Highsteaks1403: yeah at least no ones around to annoy me

587OriginalNK: totally understand that

He brushed off the fleeting thought passing through his mind.

His phone number was definitely not on the approved share list for random women on the internet.

Highsteaks1403: gonna jump in the shower and try to sleep ttyl sweet dreams

587OriginalNK: u 2

He plugged his phone into the charging cord and set it beside the glass vial on his nightstand. After a moment of contemplation, he dropped the container back into the drawer, turned off his light, and rolled onto his back.

Chapter Two

Nichol ignored his hauntmates as he finished up an email to Kaius and sent it off, knowing it would go unread. He set his chat to silent and closed out the screen before Highsteaks could message him during the meeting, hoping to keep the evening briefing short so he could get on with his night.

"Nichol agrees with me," Audra stated, her arms and legs crossing away from Mick. "Right?"

Smacking Mickey's booted feet off the com room table, he rolled his chair up and leaned forward to address his younger brother. "Mickey, Audra can't get anything done in the bloodslave quarters while you're down there growling and glaring at every man in the cells. If you can't keep that shit tamped down, stay the hell out of there. Audra has work to do if we hope to reintegrate the last of them back into human society."

When Audra's cat eyes gleamed with triumph, he turned his attention to his best friend. "And Audra, you're a psychologist. You know damn well your interactions with Boy are a sore spot. From now on, I'll accompany you into the quarters when you're down there. All in agreement?"

While Mick and Audra grumbled their acceptance of the offer, he caught the slight narrowing of Boy's eyes.

"Since we're doing couple's therapy," he continued,

11

his voice clipped with frustration, "Jagger and Bianca. You two need to combine your emails into one. I don't care how you go about it, but I'm getting duplicate responses from both of you and double the notifications. Jagg, I don't give a rat's ass if you don't like the folder method Bee uses, figure it out and deal."

Bianca reached across the table, patting his hand before he could discreetly snatch it away.

"Dominic," he barked. "Molly's a grown woman. For the next two weeks, you're banned from her weapons training with Jagg. One of these days, she's going to sludge you, and I for one will be very fucking grateful. Now end that snarling, *stat*."

Louis snickered, his chair booted by Rhys as he and Lis joined the rest of the hauntmates around the crowded table.

"Sorry we're late," Lis said, sitting as Rhys pushed her chair in for her.

"We were fucking," Rhys explained nonchalantly, earning a sharp jab in his ribs from Lis.

"We were *not*," she hissed as the group listened in, the women glaring at Rhys with disapproval and the guys smirking.

Scooting his chair just out of Lis's reach, Rhys grinned over her head at Nichol and mouthed, "Totally were."

Mickey's barking laugh clued Lis in immediately, and Rhys's ribs received another blow.

Nichol banged his fist on the table, holding back significantly to avoid adding the ordering of a replacement table to his to-do list. "Here's where we're sitting. Eleven bloodslaves left in the quarters—"

"Ten," Audra corrected, glancing at Boy. "We lost

the last woman this afternoon."

He scribbled a quick note and continued. "Ten. Ideally, that would make two large resettlement missions if Audra and Molly can get five at a time prepped to go." He looked at the women in charge. "I want that place cleared out by month's end. Any who refuse will need to be transferred to another haunt. We are officially three weeks away from being out of the bloodslave business for good."

Met with grim nods, he turned to Jagger and Bianca, ensuring Jagg's attention was on his mouth while he spoke. "How are we keeping up against the government propaganda machine?"

"We're not," his deaf brother replied. "For every story we put out there, five pop up from the other side. Unless we start putting faces to the information, we're going to go completely under the wire."

Spinning his pen in his hand, he rocked back. "Whose faces are you aiming for?"

Bianca pursed her lips and crossed her legs. "Lis, Audra, and myself are off the table due to our public issues over the past two years. That leaves Molly as the female representation."

Ignoring Molly's exaggerated bowing acceptance of the role, he pressed on. "And the male?"

"I'm obviously out since that footage of Audra breaking me out of the Lincoln jail is still making the rounds," Jagger stated, pausing his humming and placing his hand on Bee's thigh. "Rhys and Boy, too, because they're holding spots one and two on the Vampire Enforcement Agency's Most Wanted. That leaves Mick, Louis, Dominic, and you."

Louis shook his head. "No way. I'm way too

forgettable. Not a good sales tactic to feature a vamp with the gift of blending into the background."

"Mick, you're in," Nichol announced, preparing to move on.

"Why me?" Mickey moaned. "Dominic cleans up better and has that whole deer-in-the-headlight-trust-me look going for him."

"Dom, you're in," he amended, knowing Mick was right. "All videos will be filtered through me before being put up. I want them shot inside in an unmarked room. Nothing identifiable. Mick, I need you and Louis to scan the vamp chatter. There are three missing women in Wisconsin, and still no lock on Chen or Dovidas. Compile the info and toss it on the table by tomorrow night. If those two are creating another Deviant army, I want to know, stat."

There was a general muttering of agreement around the table. No one wanted to be caught unawares again if two of their enemies were turning humans into half-vamped zombies known as Deviants throughout the vampire community. It was hard enough keeping negative vamp news out from running rampant. Hundreds of hive-minded zombies crawling through cities under the control of fanged assholes like Chen or Dovidas would only mean more work online and on the ground.

He scanned his notes, crossing off each of the covered items.

"Any news from Kai?" Dom asked, looking around the table as the others fell silent. "What?"

"We're operating under the assumption Kaius won't be returning," he stated, keeping his attention on his notes. "This may or may not be permanent."

The room went still as he verbalized for the first time what they'd all considered in the quiet of their own bunks.

He ticked off a few unimportant items from the evening's meeting list and shuffled them to a later date. "Dominic, I want you and Rhys to start hauling equipment out of the bloodslave quarters tonight. Boy will take care of eliminating everything in a controlled fire at the back west side of the property."

Rhys draped his arms over Lis's shoulders and nuzzled her neck. "Why the rush to clear out the quarters?"

"Streamlining," he replied. "I want this haunt ready to abandon and relocate with as little hassle as possible." When several of the hauntmates began to protest, he straightened his back. "There's no plan to vacate," he stated with a huff. "But there have been seventeen Deepfryings since…since we returned from L.A." An image of Rhys's charred body wrapped around Lis's while they burned on network television flashed through his mind. Try as he might to remember the outcome had been good, the visual still haunted him, as did his failures that fateful night to protect Mikhail from the pain of Rhys's burning. "That's an average of two a week. We have an escape route to Canada if we need it, and no way are we being held up by anything we can deal with now."

"How many successful extractions have there been?" Louis asked.

"None. One young haunt in Texas tried to pull a copycat of our mission and ended up wiping out the whole group." He glanced down at his list. The legalization of Deepfryers throughout the United States had been a blow to vampires, far more than the registration and tattooing laws. Glass enclosures outfitted with UV rays capable of baking a vampire in less than ten minutes were now everywhere and being put to use with little restraint. "I've counted those six under a single event." He pushed the list of names into the middle of the table. "We lost one ancient in Minnesota, but his second-in-command informed me his sire was, for lack of a better term, done and willing to sacrifice himself for the sake of buying his haunt time to run."

It didn't go unnoticed that every gaze flickered to Rhys before returning to the table.

Slapping his hand on the table to pull the haunt's attention, he sat back. "That's it. Get out," he announced, forcing a fangy smile. "I hate you all. Text me if you need anything."

The group filtered out of the com room; their moods more somber than they had been when they arrived. When Rhys moved to leave, he called him back. "Where's your strength sitting at?" he asked quietly to avoid being overheard by the others.

Rhys scratched at his arm, his black hair falling into his eyes. "Fuuuuck," he groaned. "Two? Maybe three hundred? It's a slower recovery than I expected."

Lis pulled him from the room, chastising Rhys's language as they strode down the hall and left Nichol alone.

Two or three hundred.

For a vampire in his seventh century, the strength of one half his age could be a death sentence in battle.

Cursing the Deepfryers, he woke his computer up and pulled out his phone to text Boy to come back. Scanning the financials absently while he waited, he looked at the balances without actually seeing them, flipping from one account to the next.

Boy came in quietly, his tall form crouched slightly in an instinctual preparation for attack.

The mute male was not of their bloodline, working as a servant for the Kaius haunt for as long as Nichol could remember. His past, his age, his abilities—all of it was kept behind the vacant blue eyes of the vamp known only as Boy.

And now was not the time for secrets.

"If we come down to a physical confrontation anytime soon, we're down to you and me until Rhys is up to par," he stated, swiveling his chair and staring Boy down. "Show me your rings."

Boy's eyes flicked to the corner, blatantly ignoring the question regarding the age markings encircling the ankles of all vampires like tree rings.

"Fine," Nichol growled, running his hand through his hair in frustration but refusing to disrespect the male's privacy. "Are you older than Rhys?"

A brief hesitation before he nodded.

"Me?"

Another hesitation, another nod.

"Kai?"

When Boy didn't respond, he swung his chair back to his computer. "Good enough." He closed out the financial accounts and opened a new browser window to begin his venture into the FBI Vamp Division's portal. "Make sure you keep fed and rested. I can cover whatever duties you need in the quarters if you have too much on your plate."

He held off opening his messenger until Boy disappeared down the hall.

Highsteaks1403: I hate I hate I hate my job SING WITH ME NOW I hate I hate I hate my job

Highsteaks1403: Where r uuuuuuuuuuuuuuuu

Highsteaks1403: my browser is acting up gonna delete reinstall and see if it speeds up

His fingers twitched over the keyboard.

His network was as secure as it got.

And—like his phone number—was not on the approved share list.

587OriginalNK: What happened at work?

Highsteaks' window indicated she was responding, and it was a long one. He followed the paths through the FBI security protocols while he waited. To avoid detection once he entered the main server, he activated his downloader to pull the recent information in small chunks and routed them into a folder on his desktop for easy access.

Highsteaks1403: chased a guy down on a security breach and the asshole doubled back and caught me in the ribs with a knife. barely grazed me but now i'm off the floor until i heal and get permission from the boss to return. and you know my boss is an absolute dick. typing with one hand now can't get comfortable

He read the message over twice, wiping his lower lip when his fangs lengthened involuntarily and sliced him.

587OriginalNK: This is why I suggested you find another line of work

Highsteaks1403: so not in the mood for you to start in on me

He growled at the screen, pushing himself away from the desk until he could guarantee he wouldn't come off as a complete ass in his response.

587OriginalNK: Anything I can do to help?
Highsteaks1403: :) that's better. no
Highsteaks1403: pain killers kicking in i'll message you later if you're up
587OriginalNK: k

He glowered at the screen, willing it to show him the extent of the injury so he would know precisely how exaggerated or understated the reported attack was. Opening a second browser, he hunted the national news for any information about an injured security guard until the clicking of Audra's heels stopped at his door.

"Are you able to come now?"

"Goddamnit, Audra," he grumbled to his best friend, clicking all but the FBI lines closed. "Yeah. Now's fine."

****

The glow of the computer monitor was the only light in the communication room when Nichol finally made his way back up from the bloodslave quarters. He crossed the room and read the program message on the screen, swearing under his breath as he closed out the window detailing the cause of the program shutdown mid-download.

On to tomorrow's list.

Ignoring the chat app's notifications, he scanned his emails on the way to his bunker. He quickly emailed out the inventory list he'd counted out in the quarters while Audra finished her discussions with the remaining reluctant bloodslaves.

Mick wasn't entirely in the wrong. Those men were more interested in her lips than in her words.

Heaving his door shut, he stripped down on his way to the shower, ensuring the clothing was righted and landed inside the hamper completely. He stepped into the shower spray as he turned it on, letting the initial run of ice water wake his fogged mind.

Four hours supervising the men in the bloodslave quarters.

Another three checking Boy's inventory and pulling the few items that wouldn't require demolition.

Forty minutes rationalizing his decision to exclude Dominic from Molly's weapons training with Jagger.

An hour combining Bianca's email with Jagg's and filtering their collective spam while the vampire was occupied in the weapons room and unable to argue.

Ten minutes calming Mick down when Boy inadvertently brushed against Audra in the hall.

And the final two hours taking his frustrations out on Boy in the sparring room.

He scrubbed the blood from his hair, briefly contemplating if three-hundred dollar shampoo could really be that much better than his three dollar bottle. While the water washed away the combined spatters of his blood and Boy's, he could feel himself tensing as thoughts of the next night's tasks began to run through his mind.

He toweled off quickly and pulled his shorts on, aiming for a few hours of rest despite the late afternoon hour. His phone notifications continued to light up as he plugged it in, turned off the lights, and dropped onto his mattress.

Restart the FBI probe.

Confirm the car delivery.

Order another dozen burner phones.

With a snarl, he yanked his nightstand drawer open and grabbed the glass vial. He popped the lid with his teeth, covered the opening with his finger, and tipped the liquid upside-down to coat his skin. Spitting the cap onto his bed, he licked the ancient blood off his finger, the slight high hitting him instantly. As his mind began to settle, he replaced the cap, tossed the vial back in his drawer, and opened his chat app.

Chapter Three

Nichol glared at the stack of boxes strewn across the com room table, his heaps of paperwork crumpled beneath them. "Goddamnit, Molly," he growled, opening the first package and separating the contents into neat piles on the chairs.

"Need help?"

He gestured toward the unopened boxes and handed Audra a small blade. "Don't cut yourself," he warned as he picked up a set of pink headphones adorned with glittery cat ears. "Who ordered these?"

"Those would be mine," she replied primly, plucking them from his hands. "Sometimes Mickey's depressing grunge music is a little too much."

Smirking, he continued to rifle through the order. "Pink cat ears?"

With a huff, she hid her smile behind her black and turquoise hair. "How are you holding up?" she asked casually, as though the question wasn't loaded with insinuation.

"Fine."

Her first box done, she moved closer to him and sliced open another. "You've been taking on an awful lot lately," she mused, passing a container of vinyl cleaner over for Dominic's pile. "You don't think you're stretching yourself a little thin?"

He dropped the empty boxes on the floor and began

filling them with each hauntmates' items. "Nope."

"See, now you're just being an ass," she stated, her hands on hips with the blade dangerously close to her leg. "I'm concerned."

Rolling his shoulders out, he stood up and eased the knife from her hand. Her cat eyes followed his every move, her mind analyzing his every word. "I told you not to attempt to psycho-babble me."

With an inelegant snort, she snatched the blade back and opened the next box. "That was before we were besties. I've been psychoanalyzing you every night since Louisville."

He side-eyed the one woman he considered his comrade. Her absence around the communication room had become noticeable during Rhys's imprisonment months earlier, back when her time became filled with the bloodslaves, and her tumultuous relationship with Mickey. "And what are your conclusions?"

"I think you're over-compensating for Kaius's absence by filling your role, his role, and then supplementing Kai's void for the others."

"Okay, Freud," he scoffed, breaking down the last of the empty boxes. He gave her a long, hard look. "I'm good. A few growing pains while we get some things sorted out, but nothing I can't manage."

She glanced down at her buzzing phone and frowned. "And you'll let me know if it gets to be too much." Reading the incoming text, she sighed. "I better get down to the quarters. Boy just broke up a fight."

He passed the lightest boxes to her. "I'll come with. We'll detour through the Tender quarters and drop these off on the way."

He hitched the heavier packages into his arms and

followed her down the hall.

"I better let Mick know I'm heading there early," she grumbled as they entered the suites. "Is this irrational jealousy so prevalent among your brothers a guy thing or a vampire thing?"

Setting Molly and Dominic's box beside their door, he rolled his eyes. "According to Bianca, our line carries an innate emotional immaturity making us both brutish and irresistible."

"She never said 'irresistible'," Audra laughed, opening the door to the suite she and Mick shared. "I'm going to grab my notebook and we can head down."

Nichol looked around the former Tender quarters. "Who's been sleeping on the couch?"

"Mickey."

Stepping aside to allow her to lead them out of the wing, he looked back at the sofa. "His choice or yours?"

She huffed, her heels clicking louder as she sped up. "His. Conversation over."

Making a mental note to check on Mickey before dawn, he followed her into the bloodslave quarters. Boy passed them on the stairs, his arms laden with various medical devices and tubing. Audra patted his back as he passed, earning a flicker of gratefulness Nichol couldn't remember having seen in Boy's eyes before.

Ever.

They approached the cells, Audra's eyes narrowing at the two men isolated into their own confinements. "Explain."

****

"Mick," Nichol called into the common room when there was a pause in the video game Mickey and Louis were playing. "Be in the communication room in five."

Without waiting for a response, he headed to his sanctuary and powered up his computer. Pulling a microfiber cloth from his desk drawer, he carefully ran it across the tower and monitor before turning his attention to the keyboard.

"What's up?"

Mick flipped a chair around and straddled it, drumming his fingers on the table while he finished up his task and contemplated the best way to approach the subject. "Why the fuck are you sleeping on the sofa?"

His brother's jaw tensed, his shoulders hunching slightly as his long hair fell into his eyes. "What's it to you?"

He swiveled his chair, rested his elbows on his knees, and attempted to draw from everything he'd witnessed Audra do over the past few years. "I'm concerned."

Mick's expression morphed from defensive to wariness. "Uh-huh."

"Just tell me what the hell's going on," he griped, one eye on the clock. "If it's normal relationship issues, fine. But if there's more to it, I need to know, and it needs to be dealt with."

Mickey rolled his eyes and leaned back. "It's nothing much. We're just different and figuring shit out. The makeup sex more than makes up for a night or two on the couch."

He nodded thoughtfully, as he'd seen Audra do countless times. "You're probably to blame. Apologize, make up, then smarten up. Whatever instinct you followed to place you on the couch, disregard in the future, as well as any advice stemming from Rhys or Dominic.

"You may consider Jagger's opinions, but would be wise to remember that he, like you, is also a dumbass." Counseling complete and crossed off his mental task list, he turned back to his computer and began the tedious process of breaking back in to the FBI servers.

"You really suck at this," Mickey finally stated as he stood. "I appreciate the effort, but really. Don't. This was awkward and uncomfortable. And I'm not sure if we're supposed to hug now."

"Touch me, and your arm will be ripped off and shoved up your ass."
****

587OriginalNK: how's the injury

Nichol continued to monitor his download program carefully while he waited for Highsteaks to respond. Her green icon went gray within moments, reappearing almost twenty minutes later.

Highsteaks1403: sore :(
587OriginalNK: where'd you go
Highsteaks1403: awww miss me? ;)
587OriginalNK: still having connection issues?
Highsteaks1403: hot and cold much?

He clicked on his search bar and typed in Highsteaks 'question.

What. The fuck.

He pulled up his chat log, reading back through their discussion from the afternoon.

He found the hot pretty fucking fast.

And had no memory of typing those words.

Highsteaks1403: nevermind NK i'll message you another time

Her icon greyed out again.

"Nichol, honey," Bianca's voice called. "Do you

want me to move these papers before the others arrive?"

He looked at the time and grit his teeth. "Don't bother," he ground out, closing out the download program. "The meeting will be quick."

****

Nichol's laundry was neatly folded on his bed, a small pink note from Bianca left on top reminding him to order in a suitable video camera. He plugged in his dead phone and fell face-first onto his mattress, his damp towel still wrapped around his hips.

The respite was brief, his phone lighting up within minutes as it charged.

Texts from two haunts in Northern Italy requiring a mediator for a land dispute.

News alerts for another missing woman in Missouri.

An email from a young haunt leader asking for assistance with a newly-turned vampire set to enter the Deepfryer at midnight.

But not a word from Highsteaks.

He rolled onto his back slowly, avoiding the fresh laundry on the edge of the bed. He reached instinctively into his nightstand drawer and popped the cap on the vial, wrinkling his nose at the chemical scent of the artificial preservative added to keep the blood potent. With the practiced flip of his wrist, he coated his finger, ran it over his tongue, and waited for the relief to hit.

Flirting.

Goddamn flirting.

He took one more taste of the blood and recapped the vial.

His conversation with Highsteaks from the previous afternoon scrolled through his head.

The veiled innuendos.

The loaded comments.

Snatching his phone from the nightstand, he opened his chat app and fired off a message.

587OriginalNK: u up

He closed his eyes and allowed the foggy warmth to move unencumbered through his mind and mute the constant pressure sitting in the base on his skull.

Highsteaks1403: yeah i'm up

587OriginalNK: you still pissed with me

Highsteaks1403: yup

587OriginalNK: it's been a real bitch of a night

Highsteaks1403: its 2pm

587OriginalNK: And I just got home from work

Highsteaks1403: wtf go to bed

587OriginalNK: rather talk to you

Chapter Four

"This is what Dovidas and Chen are after," Nichol murmured to Boy, leaning back in his chair to allow his hauntmate a better view of the computer screen. "Those vampires who aren't igniting in Deepfryers are jumping ship by the dozens. New turnings will be nil under these circumstances." He released the tension in his jaw as his molars cracked. "If Dovidas and Chen lay low long enough, they'll be the only vampires left in the U.S."

Boy's brows knotted as he tentatively flipped through the news reports and images of the rapidly increasing number of Deepfryings. Nichol brushed his hand away and pulled up a map from his desktop.

"The blue dots are the locations of known haunts as of six months ago. The red dots are the haunts who have contacted me about their relocations. Most have headed to South America, a few north to Canada." He zoomed the map in. "Yellow are unconfirmed moves, but whose contact info has gone dark within the past few months."

He printed off the image before closing out the map.

"Of the fifteen hundred known vampires who usually reside here, I'd place our numbers at seven, maybe eight hundred now if we account the stragglers and loners like Louis. Jagger and Bee have seen a noticeable shift in their pledged supporters. More are willing to do online attacks from remote locations, but none are volunteering to hit the streets." He looked over at Boy. "At tonight's meeting, I'll be posing the option of vacating the haunt permanently within the month. Do I have your support?"

Boy's long hair fell into his eyes while he examined the map without responding.

He pushed back in his chair and drummed his fingers on his desk.

His inbox had been lighting up for the past three weeks as Deepfryer usage increased, and haunt leaders began exiting the country. Desperate emails from younger haunts seeking advice, sage messages from ancients expounding the virtues of retreating and regrouping, frantic requests day and night from lone vampires looking to be brought into established haunts for protection. He answered each one diligently, researching the safest routes and closest safe-houses before replying.

Both the routes and the safe-houses were coming up in shorter and shorter supply.

"Got another text from Mississippi," Rhys announced, striding into the com room alone. "Remember Gillian? Her master is hauling ass through an underground into Mexico. She's meeting him in Panama and needs a passport, asap."

He felt his shoulders tense up. The mass exodus had exposed an issue most haunt leaders hadn't considered: the travel capabilities of their human companions. Requests had begun trickling in the week before from Tenders ill-prepared to cross international borders and unable to keep up physically to the harsh terrain the vampires were traveling.

"I'll need a week," he muttered, scanning his computer's bookmarks for his passport book connection.

"Make sure she sends me a proper photo and signature, and I'll express-post it once I get another passbook shipment."

Rhys spun a chair around and straddled it, reading over his shoulder and ignoring Boy entirely. "Better put in for another twenty orders," he suggested. "I anticipate a rush on requests when the younger masters begin getting their shit together."

"Have you managed to make contact with all your Tender sales?" he asked, following Rhys's advice and running the items through the Tender account.

"Don't let Lis hear you say that," Rhys grumbled, glancing over his shoulder. "Or Audra. Fuck, Nichol. It's like you want to get me yelled at. Yeah, I touched base with all of the women. Some have their documentation already, a few are insisting they aren't leaving, but a lot are in the dark about what their masters are planning."

He reached over and tugged the map away from Boy. "Put a 'T' in every location with a Tender and we'll try to track their movements as well."

Rhys's eyes narrowed as he began marking the paper. "These are the ones who've gotten outta Dodge?"

With a terse nod, he pulled out his list for the night and listened for his approaching hauntmates. "I'll need to meet with you tonight after the others go."

"No problem," Rhys replied, his attention on the tiny colored dots on the map.

He waited until the group was assembled, sizing each member's readiness while they chatted and jostled across the table. He read over his list, slowly crossing off all the issues that could be tabled for another night.

"We have one item to discuss," he began, pausing as his hauntmates settled. "Relocation. I want pros, cons, opinions, and potential issues. Go."

Arms crossed en masse as the group immediately went on the defensive.

"We aren't running with our tail between our legs," Mickey stated. "I say we hunker down, lay low, and wait this out."

"Rebuild would take years," Jagger added, looking at Bianca. "The logistics of our security, weapons, and intelligence systems alone would put us at a disadvantage for months. Longer, perhaps."

He nodded, noting both points.

"Where would you consider relocating to?" Audra asked, patting Mick's knee when he opened his mouth to protest the idea.

"That would be decided upon as a group," he replied. "Short term stops as well." He looked around the table and set the map in the middle. "There are approximately seven hundred known vampires left in the United States right now, with more leaving every week. It's one thing to be outnumbered. It's another to be alone. The time's come for us to consider cutting our losses and leaving the country."

"Cutting our losses?" Dominic echoed with a frown. "What exactly do you mean by that?"

He rocked back in his chair. "We've had a good run in the States, but if we have to go, we have to go. It's not our homeland, it's our host."

"It's my homeland," Dominic said slowly. "I was born here. So was Molly. Right, Moll?"

Molly nodded.

As did Bianca.

And Audra.

And Lis.

Rhys draped his arm over Lis's shoulders. "I don't think Nichol's suggesting we never return. More of an extended vacation." When Lis shuffled her chair away from him, he yanked her seat back and held it tight to him. "Just pointing it out, baby. Not agreeing."

His phone buzzed in his pocket. Ignoring it, he looked over to Boy. "Those of us old enough to see empires fall are rightfully cautious about remaining in hostile territory. If we step back and examine the larger picture further into the future, resettling and regrouping elsewhere is a reasonable consideration."

He swiveled to his computer and pulled up a second map. "Dovidas's goal of a Deepfryer in every country is quickly becoming realized. With North America home to half the world's known vampire population, the elimination of the species on this continent alone would create the perfect grounds for a rebuild."

Pointing to dozens of orange circles dotting the map, he angled the screen for the others. "If I was Dovidas—with Chen backing me—I would lay low for a century, sire a few dozen strong males, and build up a Deviant army. Then quietly eliminate any vamps who venture back onto the territory while establishing my children in key positions around the country. Sooner or later, humans will become complacent about vampires again, and when that happens, a stronghold will already be established." He crossed his arms. "If Dovidas wants to be the top dog, this is the only way he can do it."

"You think he wants to replace Kaius as the head honcho," Jagg stated bluntly.

"I think Kai fell into the position, and I think Dovidas is actively pursuing a takeover," he replied. "Since Kaius is MIA, the next natural targets are those sitting in this room. With the timing of Dovidas's communication with Senator Green, the Deepfryer implementation, and Fallon Derry's hate-on for him, I believe Rhys was intended to be the first assassination by Deepfryer."

Rhys's navy eyes narrowed. "I'm not into vamp politics."

"You carry the Kaius name and eliminating the great Rhys Kaius would have been the perfect warning of a regime change to every vampire watching," he stated, distracted by the incessant buzzing of his phone. "All wheelings and dealings aside, our haunt name alone has placed us as rulers since our feet hit American soil. Reluctant as some of us may be." He ran his hand through his hair. "Lis, Bianca, you two can attest to that."

Bianca sighed and leaned into Jagg. "Despite how cloistered you've kept yourselves, the Kaius haunt word is law in every circle I've run in."

"Yeah, well, that's Kaius, not us," Rhys argued. "I've never touched the vampire political arena. Neither has Jagg or Dominic."

Lis cleared her throat. "I only know what I overheard over the years, but Bianca can probably vouch for it. While Kaius is viewed as the final word in the U.S., Nichol is essentially considered the speaker for the king." When he grunted, Lis looked over at him apologetically and continued. "Jagger's name has been tied to a lot of unsolved hits carried out in Europe and Mickey was discussed as the driving force behind most backdoor human dealings done over the past two centuries."

She grinned at Mick as Audra kissed his cheek. "At the McConaughey haunt, rumors were Kaius's youngest had the strength and speed of a vampire five times his age." She glanced at Dominic. "Sorry, Dom, but the nickname I overheard for you was the Little Crown Prince."

"Little Spoiled Bitch is more accurate," Rhys interjected, earning a boot to his chair from Dominic.

With a quick jab of her elbow, Lis silenced Rhys. "You, honey, have women loyal to you and tied to the leaders of almost every other influential haunt in the world." She sat back and drew her arms around herself. "But that's just what I heard over the years."

Nichol leaned back in his chair. "And unfortunately, it's all true. Dovidas is gunning for our position. And he's using a more prolific species to do it. Take the night to think about all this, and we'll reconvene tomorrow at dusk to hash out the issues."

While the others filtered from the room, Rhys and Lis hung back. He pulled his phone out of his back pocket and began scrolling through the notifications. "Where's your strength sitting at?"

Rhys crossed his arms, his jaw tensing. "Maybe three hundred."

He placed his phone face-down on his desk. "Not good enough," he said, swiveling to face Rhys directly. "The sulfur treatments end tonight."

Lis stepped in front of Rhys defensively. "No way! That mercury is toxic, and we need to get it out of his system."

"What we need," he growled, turning his attention to his brother, "is you in top form. Those treatments are keeping you weak, and I need my second in prime condition."

When Lis began to protest further, Rhys grabbed her

hand, intertwining his fingers with hers. "Bypass me. Raise Jagg to second."

He dropped his forearms to his knees and hunched forward. "Lis, I need a minute with Rhys alone."

Lis reluctantly released Rhys's hand. "I'll wait for you in the common room," she called as she exited, pulling the door closed behind her.

"I wouldn't demand this if I didn't need it." He ran a hand through his hair and fought the urge to check his messages. "Hell, I'd be handing you the lead if I thought you'd take it."

****

Nichol released the suction on the dropper and lolled his head back as the ancient blood worked its way into his system.

Highsteaks1403: u sure? it's still pretty gross

He rolled his eyes. 'Gross' was relative.

587OriginalNK: just send the damn pic

He waited for Highsteaks to upload the picture of her healing injury. She'd made it through her first night back on rotation, but he wasn't convinced she was ready.

Highsteaks1403: here you go. getting better

He stared at the photo, forcing his eyes to focus on the laceration and not on the smoothness of the olive skin.

And definitely not on the swell of a hip in the bottom of the frame.

He mentally cataloged the image against other human injuries he'd encountered that had been untreated by a vampire mate's healing blood.

587OriginalNK: You're right. That's gross

Highsteaks1403: :D

Highsteaks1403: smartass

587OriginalNK: one of these days I'm going to train you to send longer messages so you don't buzz me every two minutes while I'm working

Highsteaks1403: i like distracting you ;)

587OriginalNK: yeah well I thought something happened

Highsteaks1403: awwww you were worried

He absently refilled the dropper and stuck it under his tongue.

587OriginalNK: maybe

Chapter Five

Nichol crossed his arms and rocked back in his chair. "There isn't a single vamp in Denver other than us."

"All the more reason it's possible," Mickey stated, mimicking his pose. "The city has no direct bad blood with vampires. Hell, they haven't even gotten around to assembling their Deepfryer. Audra drove into town today and checked. Having Denver declared a sanctuary city would give us a tight base and would give us control of who settled here and who didn't. With the right incentive for the mayor, we should be golden."

"How much will this incentive cost?" he asked, glancing at his phone as it buzzed intermittently.

Mickey pushed a sloppily penned paper toward him. "I'll open low, but anticipate ten million a year for the duration of the agreement after an initial investment of twenty-five million."

His brows rose. "Are we bribing or…"

Audra's long fingers flicked Mick's crumpled notes off the table and replaced them with her own impeccable diagrams. "This is an anticipated cost breakdown for negotiations," she said, pointing at a neatly drawn pie chart. "Jagger suggested we allocate eight million to the training and employment of fifty officers to essentially act as vamp-cops. They could patrol city borders, respond to complaints, and would answer to both the city and us." When he nodded his head slowly, she turned the graph slightly. "We should anticipate a million-dollar allocation to the blood banks, since we'll require their cooperation with the influx of vampires in the region. Another fourteen million for the establishment of vampire-safe homes to be rented out while new arrivals arrange their own shelter. The rent can be split between the city and us in good faith."

Tapping the chart, he leaned forward in his seat and quickly scanned the messages coming in from Highsteaks. "And this?"

"One million for incidentals, and another for school libraries." When he frowned, Audra's cat eyes locked on his. "That one is non-negotiable on your end."

Holding back a grin at Highsteaks' most recent emoji-laden text, he refocused on the meeting. "How do you intend to present this to the city?"

Jagger and Mick exchanged a look. "We figured we could have the meeting here," Jagg began slowly, sliding his chair to the side to allow Bianca to move in tighter. "We Fort Knox the hell out of this place and Bee can mediate alongside Mickey. A show of trust on our behalf."

"And if things go south, I'll razzle-dazzle the haunt's location from their heads," the haunt's resident hypnotist, Louis, threw in.

He could feel all eyes on him while he mulled over the idea.

Exposing their names.

Exposing their faces.

Exposing their haunt.

He folded Audra's notes in half methodically, pinching the edges to keep them squared as he did.

"Everyone here has 24 hours to text me their pros and cons regarding this suggestion," he stated, pushing away from the table. "I'll make the decision at midnight tomorrow. Now fuck off."

Waiting until the others vacated the room, he motioned to Boy. "Yay or nay?"

Boy pulled out his phone, his large hands fumbling to tap out a message. When he finished, he held it out.

—*Will check the back escape tunnel tonight and report on repairs needed*—

With a grunt, he turned his chair back to the computer and fired it up as Boy held another message in his line of sight.

—*The greatest victory is that which requires no battle*—

"Shut up, you mute bastard," he grumbled. "I'll take Sun Tzu's words as a yes, then."

Boy slipped from the com room, leaving him alone. He rolled over to the door, easing it closed before pulling his phone from his pocket.

587OriginalNK: wtf do you have against eggplants

Highsteaks1403: :D those aren't supposed to be eggplants

587OriginalNK: they're eggplants

Highsteaks1403: if it has a DICK it is a DICK

He reached into his desk drawer for his vial while he glanced over the previous messages.

587OriginalNK: I don't see how I was supposed to get "dick" from an emoji of an eggplant

Highsteaks1403: forget the damn eggplant. men are jerks

Squeezing the dropper onto his tongue, he rocked back, stretched his legs up onto the table, and glared at his phone.

587OriginalNK: Did you have a date tonight?

He refilled the dropper and brought it back to his lips, forcing his teeth to stop grinding long enough to ingest the liquid.

Highsteaks1403: another double date with my boss, his gf, and one of his loser buddies

He rolled out his shoulders and arched his neck back. A third hit of the ancient blood, and he felt the familiar fog slowing his mind and softening his souring mood.

587OriginalNK: so what did this guy do

Highsteaks1403: rude. grabby.

587OriginalNK: next time say no

Highsteaks1403: easy for you to say. ur the boss

587OriginalNK: tell him you have a boyfriend

Rolling over to his monitor, he began absently scanning for information on the Denver mayor.

Highsteaks1403: why don't U tell him I have a boyfriend?

Printing off a stats page on the mayor's political positions, he logged off and shut the computer down.

587OriginalNK: give me his number and I will

Highsteaks1403: :D he'll ask who I'm dating

587OriginalNK: I'll tell him it's me

Highsteaks went silent as he walked toward the sparring room to oversee the women's training regime for Jagger.

587OriginalNK: hey

Highsteaks' icon greyed. He stared at the small dot for a moment before he turned his attention to Audra. "Keep those damn elbows in when you jab."

****

Highsteaks1403: booze or drugs

Nichol opened his messenger app and flipped the lock on his bunker door.

587OriginalNK: ?

It had been eleven hours since Highsteaks had gone dark. Setting his boots in the corner of his room, he stripped down to his boxers, flicked off the lights, flopped onto his bed, and reached into his bedside table.

Highsteaks1403: which are you on

587OriginalNK: right now I'm on eight hours of sleep in ten days

Highsteaks1403: whatever

He ran his hand through his hair and growled in frustration.

587OriginalNK: what the fuck is your problem

Highsteaks1403: you're an eggplant

Setting the dropper aside, he brought the glass bottle to his lips and drained the remaining blood from the vial.

587OriginalNK: are you at home or work

Highsteaks1403: home

His thumb hovered over the tiny phone icon in his messenger app before he tapped it and unleashed the most offensive digital ringing he'd ever heard. Setting his phone on his nightstand, he lay back and closed his eyes as the ancient blood temporarily blocked his frenetic thoughts.

"Hello?"

The woman's voice was hesitant, hushed.

"I'm not a fucking eggplant," he grumbled into the dark.

There was a soft rustling of fabric as Highsteaks sighed. "You're definitely something," she said quietly. "Nice to finally hear your voice, NK. You sound as cranky as you write."

He grinned, the warmth of his high combining with the peculiar thrill of listening to Highsteaks speak after months and months of misspelled correspondence. "Yeah, well, you sound as exasperated as you write. But with proper punctuation." When she huffed into the phone, he put his arms behind his head. "So why am I a dick?"

"Because I can pretty much tell the moment whatever it is you're on sets in," she replied curtly. "You go from stick-up-the-ass arms-length to hey-hey-yo-baby instantly."

"I've never said 'hey-hey-yo-baby'."

"You know damn well what I'm talking about. Look, forget it. What're you up to?"

"Lying in bed wondering why the fuck I'm voluntarily talking with an ornery female outside of my required work hours," he grunted as he shifted position. "You?"

"Lying in bed wondering why I haven't hung up on you."

"How are the ribs healing up?"

She snorted inelegantly, earning a frown from him. "Nice change of subject. They're good. I'm on full rotation again."

He rolled onto his side and glared at the phone screen. "Tell me the name of the company you work for," he demanded, unimpressed she was being put back on duty so quickly.

"Tell me the name of the company *you* run," she retorted, a blatant reminder of the unwritten rule of anonymity the pair adhered to rigidly during their discussions.

With a huff, he flopped onto his back. "Fair enough. I was going to research their corporate policies on employees injured in the line of duty, but since I can't, I want you to review the procedures you follow to ensure there isn't a repeat attack."

She snickered into the phone and sighed. "Awwww, you worry about me, don't you?"

"List the procedures."

While Highsteaks began rattling off a litany of measures she took to ensure her safety, he could feel himself slipping further into the cocoon of the ancient blood he'd taken. The woman's voice became almost soothing as his mind abandoned her words in exchange for following the rise and fall of her cadence as she spoke.

"… so even when working alone, I have some form of communi—"

"How tall are you?" he interrupted, his waffling attention turning to the creation of a visual for Highsteaks' voice.

After a brief pause, she replied slowly. "Five foot six. You?"

"Six two."

"That's almost Yeti-sized," she teased.

"My younger brothers are Yeti-sized," he grinned. "I'm on the shorter side."

"I could still probably kick your ass," she stated confidently. "I'm pretty lethal."

"I would love to see you try."

Chapter Six

Nichol stood in the doorway watching his hauntmates with a mixture of annoyance and mild amusement.

"Aren't you missing the main ingredient to belly dancing, angel?" Rhys called over to Lis as she adjusted Molly's feet and stood. "Maybe add a few more pounds and try again in a month."

Lis's green eyes lifted to Rhys, a hint of warning flashing across her face. "Maybe I'll remove my tongue ring if you don't shut your yap, baby." She turned her attention back to her student. "You're doing great. Hip *up*! Hip *up*!"

Rhys fell into complete silence, making his way over to the doorway where Nichol was hiding out. "Add some of those protein mixes to the next grocery order," he whispered, his fingers digging into his tattoos. "She's still on the thin side since…" He trailed off and glanced at the women in the field. "But the order didn't come from me. Got it?"

Noting the request in his phone, he crossed his arms and leaned against the frame. "How's the strength coming along?"

"It's getting there," Rhys replied, stepping forward to interject into Lis's teaching before wisely pulling back. "Keeping Lis off my ass about the tats is a constant fucking battle, though."

They continued to watch the belly-dancing lesson in silence until Dominic appeared, his expression hungry as he took in the women's movements.

"Damn," he whistled, elbowing Rhys in the ribs. "Why didn't you tell me this is what they were heading outside to do? I mean, damn."

"Because I knew you'd be drooling like a teenage boy getting his first look at a nudie mag," Rhys explained, returning the jab with more force and sending Dominic against the wall.

Dom righted himself and grinned. "Why the hell do you two get to be here then?"

"I'm here to correct form. Nichol's here to keep the women from staking me."

When Dominic accepted the explanation without question, Nichol pushed himself off the wall and opened the door. "And now I'm heading back to the communication room to process the mail delivery. Good luck, dumbasses. Keep your mouths shut. I'm not in the mood to clean vamp sludge off the entry."

Scanning his emails while he walked through the haunt, he fired off quick requests for location updates to the vampires alerting him of their progress in fleeing the country.

In under two weeks, another seventy had touched base with the Kaius haunt.

The pile of boxes on the com room table sat undisturbed from Molly and Bianca's run into the city, the careful stacking indicated Bee had taken control of the unloading. Reaching for the smallest packages, he opened them and slid the glass vials neatly into his desk drawers.

"Are you able to lend a hand in the bloodslave

quarters?" Louis called into the com room, and he slammed the drawer shut. "Audra and I are trying to separate the remaining men, and Boy's busy in the tunnel."

He nodded tensely, his eyes flicking to the closed drawer before he followed Louis out of the room.

"I'd do it myself," Louis said, opening the door to the quarters, "but if anything happened to Audra—"

"Mick and I would behead you, yes," he finished for him, stopping in front of the cells where five men stood staring at him defiantly. "Have you considered handcuffing and blindfolding them?"

"Nichol! No!" Audra called out from the back room, her voice aghast. The rapid clicking of her heels echoed in the cement chamber. "We've decided to isolate them one at a time for intense therapy and re-integration prep." She looked up at him, hands on her hips to let him know his cooperation was non-negotiable. "We want to make use of the cells in the back."

"And you already have one set up, correct?" he asked, scanning the men carefully.

Audra stepped up beside him. "Of course. It lacks a proper bathroom, but I think we can make do with a camping toilet."

Wrinkling his nose, he gently nudged Audra further from the bars of the cell. "Which one do you want?"

Louis pointed to the largest of the humans. "We're pulling the ringleader first. By the time the others establish a new one, we should be ready to rotate another into the back."

"Move," he instructed Audra as he opened the cell, blocked the exit with his body, and addressed the feral-looking men in the enclosure. "Any of you so much as flinch toward me, and there's nothing Dr. Verdi can say or do to save your pathetic hides."

****

Nichol tossed a roll of wire over to Mickey before jumping to the ground. "Run that along the trench we opened and ease it under some of the loose bark on that tree," he instructed, using his foot to cover the wire he'd laid earlier. "And make sure to leave some slack."

Despite his height, Mick was amazingly agile as he shimmied up the old pine and secured the laser console amidst the branches. "That good there?"

"Duck down and let me check this run," he ordered, activating the motion detection system. "Wave your hand in front of the beam." When the alarm sounded, he turned off the system. "Only another forty-three to go."

The push to 'Fort Knox the hell out of the haunt' had consumed his nights and days for the past week. The tight timeline weighed heavily on his mind as Mickey grew closer and closer to securing a meeting between the Kaius haunt and the Denver mayor.

Infrared motion sensors.

Eleven new alarms.

Twenty-one additional cameras.

Ground-sweeping radar.

He waved Jagger over, passing him a handful of tiny cameras. "I need one on each of those trees before I test the area for blind spots," he commanded, keeping one eye on Mick who was disentangling his boot from a loose wire. "If you pull that one out of the ground, I'm going to rip your nuts off."

With a quick salute, Mick knelt down to ease the wire from his leg. "Those drones come in yet?"

Running a hand through his hair, he huffed in

frustration. "Nope. Until they do, all we can do in the event of a day breach is wait until the front door fucking opens."

Ignoring the buzzing phone in his back pocket, he continued to assess the functionality of the grounds-wide security systems until dawn threatened on the horizon. "Store all the uninstalled items in the com room and I'll get on it at dusk," he called to the others, waiting until his brethren were safely inside before following in and punching the lock code.

While his hauntmates headed to their quarters for the day, he logged into his computer and began dealing with the influx of emails that had arrived during the night.

Another young haunt looking for refuge.

Another Tender requiring a passport.

Another vampire sentenced to the Deepfryer.

One by one, he replied to the messages as more came in. His phone vibrated relentlessly with texts and questions, calls and alerts. As noon approached, he logged off, pocketed three vials, and made his way to his bunk, slamming his fist on Rhys and Lis's door as a reminder for them to quiet the hell down.

He turned the shower on to max heat and stared at his reflection while the steam began to rise.

He looked like shit.

Ovaled irises, filthy clothes, a chipped fang from a fallen laser console.

Hunger had paled his skin, accentuating his freckles and reddening his auburn hair.

With a quick shake of his head, he stripped down and stood motionless under the spray of the shower.

He needed to put in an order of cement mix for Boy.

Jagg's latest shipment of blades was being held at customs and needed addressing.

Louis and Audra needed an apartment and documentation set up for the last of the bloodslaves ready to be reintegrated into human society.

Wrapping his towel around his hips, he tossed his phone beside him on the bed and popped the cap off a vial.

Just enough to turn off my head.

As the blood worked through his system, he pulled up his messenger app and fired off a quick hello to Highsteaks before turning his phone to mute and falling back against his pillow.

****

Highsteaks1403: where the hell r u
Highsteaks1403: hey
Highsteaks1403: hey
Highsteaks1403: hey
Highsteaks1403: hey

Nichol sat up and glanced at his phone.

Midnight.

Tossing his blanket aside, he snatched his phone from the nightstand and tore over to his dresser. Ignoring Highsteaks for the time being, he responded to his brothers' texts quickly with one hand while pulling his cargos on with the other.

Fucking fuck.

Yanking his shirt over his head as he exited his bunk, he hurried through the haunt to the communication room to gather his security blueprints before heading topside to join his hauntmates.

"Where the fuck've you been?" Rhys called out, his bare chest covered in gashes from sparring with Jagger.

"Mick's been looking everywhere for you."

"Virtual meeting with a haunt in Europe," he lied, looking around the grounds for the others. "Are Audra and Louis in the bloodslave quarters?"

"Boy's standing guard for them," Jagg replied, stepping out of the makeshift sparring ring. "Molly and Dominic went with Bianca to the city to scope out a few potential buildings for vamp refugees."

He frowned and pulled out his phone to scan his texts. "I don't remember approving that."

A look of concern crossed Jagg's face briefly. "You okay'd it in last night's meeting."

"Right," he stated, shoving his phone back into his pocket. "I'm going to continue connecting the perimeter systems. Once you two finish practice, I'll need you and Lis to help twist wires and run cables."

He jogged to the opposite end of the property, out of Rhys and Jagger's line of sight.

Fucking Fuck.

Losing functional darkness during such a volatile time was not only unacceptable, it was dangerous. Every hour the haunt stood exposed was another hour they were vulnerable. Every delay in their own security meant a delay for the vampires needing refuge.

He worked quickly, his attention wholly on the task at hand to avoid careless errors and more setbacks. He passed the wire cutters and electrical tape to Lis when she arrived, eliminating one small task from the increasing list forming in the back of his mind. As Jagger and Rhys took over the camera blueprints, he made his way to the bloodslave quarters to check on Audra and Louis.

"We'll need to move him to a blank wall for his

identification photo," he said as he walked into the cell and saw the man sitting on a metal chair, his clothes and hair neat and clean. The man eyed him warily, glancing toward Audra. "No point looking to her for help," he growled, motioning for the others to follow him. "If you piss me off, no one can save you. And I'm not in a good mood right now."

Audra's hissed admonishments trailed him through the bloodslave quarters and into the hall where he could snap a few passable identification photos.

"How soon do you need these?" he asked Louis, flashing his fangs at the man when he took a step too close to Audra.

"Sometime in the next two nights would work," Louis said. "We have a place in Cheyenne prepped for him, as well as a job working construction" Louis dropped his voice to avoid the humans overhearing. "It's taking a lot to get his head in the right place for this. My hypnosis is getting in there and holding for the most part, but I'm experiencing a bit of subconscious pushback. If there's some way to monitor him, it would probably be a good idea."

He pulled out his phone and added the assembling of a basic surveillance package to his list. "Done. I'll bring the ID and monitor set-up down when it's ready."

With a quick text to check on Rhys's progress, he headed to the com room to make up for his lost hours.

****

587OriginalNK: Sorry. Work had me tied up.
Highsteaks1403: for 41 hours?
587OriginalNK: Pretty much

With only a few more hours of daylight to go before he jumped back into haunt business, he had finally holed up in his room to kick back with a vial and his phone.

587OriginalNK: call?

The strange ring of the app blared in the quiet room until he swiped his thumb across the screen. "How was work?"

"Hello to you, too," Highsteaks retorted. "Boring. A lot of sitting around on my ass."

He emptied the last drops from the glass vial and set it aside to wash out at nightfall. "Good. The more boring it is, the less likely you are to be injured again."

"And the more likely I am to become complacent," she retorted.

He frowned in the darkness. "Can't you get another job doing something less risky? Bookkeeping or something?"

She let loose a quick barking laugh that was hushed instantly. "I was taught that a while back, but I have zero interest in being a human calculator. So stalking the grounds it is." There was a pause, the rustling of fabric coming through the phone. "How are you holding up at work? You've been pretty non-stop for weeks now."

"It's fine," he replied on cue before stopping.

She had no clue who, or what, he was.

No way to connect him to his hauntmates.

As long as he kept the details vague…

"I'm actually pretty stressed right now," he said slowly, lowering his voice to avoid being overheard by Rhys. "If I fuck up any of the shit on my plate, a lot of people could get hurt."

Highsteaks went silent, her breathing the only indication she hadn't hung up on him.

He needlessly cleared his throat. "Nothing unmanageable, though. Did you find a dress for that event you were talking about last week?"

"Oh no you don't," she finally said. "No changing the subject. What sort of things are you doing? Banking or investments or something like that?"

"That's part of it," he replied, uncomfortable with the realization he wasn't all that uncomfortable telling her. "Security, resource acquisition, paperwork, strategizing, communication, legal mumbo-jumbo, and a ton of being nice about things I don't want to be nice about." He stopped for a moment. "There's more, but that's pretty much the bulk of it."

"Damn," she breathed. "Can't you delegate?"

"Already short-staffed as it is," he grunted, rolling onto his back and closing his eyes. "And most of the others have partners, so they can no longer be expected to pull the longer hours."

"What do you do to unwind?"

Unable to catch himself before his drug-fogged mind responded, he grinned into the darkness. "Talk to you."

Chapter Seven

Nichol scanned the list of names and rubbed his jaw. "This is a lot more than a mayor and a couple of security guards."

Mick's boots hit the table with a *thunk* before Audra subtly nudged them down. "I know it increases the risk of our location being leaked, but it was the best I could negotiate. Can we make it work?"

Re-reading the names of the mayor, thirteen council members, and fourteen registered security guards, he nodded slowly. "If this is what we have to work with, we'll make it work." He turned to Louis and leaned back in his chair. "What are the chances of hypnotizing our location out of the heads of this many?"

"Pretty much zero," Louis replied. "One by one, yeah, but I doubt we can orchestrate it so I'm alone with each human long enough to do it."

He looked around the room. "Then we vote. Yay or nay. Do we go ahead with the meeting despite the added potential for a security breach?"

Met with a resounding yay, he turned toward his computer. "Make it happen, Mick. Jagger, you and Bianca start preparing a media package we can release just prior to the meeting so we can alert the remaining North American vampires while simultaneously opening us up to the remote possibility of a positive media presence. Use Molly or Dominic for any video releases, though. No sense tying your image or Bianca's to this until we gain some ground."

Jagg's humming stopped as he rested his elbows on the table, the deaf vampire's eyes on Nichol's lips. "Will do. Are we releasing any statements about the Species Purifier and FANG wars?"

Shaking his head and doing his best not to roll his eyes at the reminder their most rabid supporters called themselves Friends and Advocates for the New Gods, he began pulling up blueprints on his monitor to re-examine holes in the haunt's security. "We'll deal with that later. One shitstorm at a time."

The room vacated quickly, with the exception of Boy.

"Tunnel's ready?" he asked, glancing back at the mute male.

Boy nodded.

"I have three extra SUVs on order. Once they arrive, we'll figure out a place to camouflage them near the exit," he said. "I want a smooth escape plan, and anything you can think of to assist in that, do."

He waited until the com room door closed before he pulled out his buzzing phone.

Kai.

His thumb hovered over the button until the call went to voicemail.

****

"There's nothing wrong with the system," Nichol said with a huff, running his fingers across the speaker wire of the common room's stereo system. "The settings are precisely where I put them."

Audra grinned as she toed off her heels. "Since you're here, you owe me a screening of that new Korean

War documentary."

He rose and glared at the smirking woman. "I'm busy."

"You can spare a hundred and fifty minutes to bond with your BFF," she stated, grabbing his arm and leading him to the large sofa. "It's all cued up and ready to go."

When the film opened and he pulled out his phone, Audra reached across him and snatched it out of his hand. "No."

He snapped his fangs at her. "Does Mickey know you've kidnapped me and are holding me against my will?"

"Mick was the one who suggested it," she said smugly. "He's handing out nightly assignments as we speak, and making the rounds for the next two and a half hours. That means you are MINE."

"No one can read Mikhail's writing," he grumbled, slouching into the sofa.

"They'll survive for the next two hours without you. I promise."

****

"What."

Highsteaks' laugh broke the silence of Nichol's bunker. "You have the worst phone manners," she chided. "How's it going?"

Pulling his boots off, he sank onto his sofa and lolled his head back. "It's going," he replied. "How was your night on the town?"

While video cables and monitoring stations had consumed most of his thoughts after his impromptu movie bonding, he'd been on edge knowing Highsteaks was heading into what she referred to as "the closest city" for a few hours. Not knowing her home base, he had been left in the dark as to her location and her safety.

It was unpleasant.

None of his business, but unpleasant, nonetheless.

"Tonight was wild," she drawled. "I see a lot of things online, but to be there in person again? I forgot how busy and loud and constant cities are."

"Is your boss a good driver?" he asked, still displeased with the knowledge Highsteaks' asshole boss had taken his employees to town for something he could have easily ordered online.

Or, more specifically, he was displeased Highsteaks had to go at all.

"You're still hung up on that, huh?" she teased. "Yeah, he was fine. We drove by a rally on the way to the supply store, though. Have you been following those?"

His muscles tensed. "What kind of rally?"

"It looked like an anti-vamp rally, but the pro-vamp people were on the fringes of it with signs." She cleared her throat. "It was kind of cool to be that close to one."

Leaning his elbows on his knees, he set his phone onto the coffee table. "So have you had a lot of problems with vampires where you work?"

"All the time."

He flexed his arms out and forced his jaw to relax before he cracked a molar. "You never mentioned that before."

"I work nighttime security, NK," she stated, her voice bordering on exasperation. "What the hell do you think I deal with?"

Thugs.

Criminals.

Drunk college students.

His lips drew into a thin line over his elongating fangs. "The guy who caught you in the ribs," he growled. "Human or vamp?"

"Vamp," she replied, apparently oblivious to his souring temper. "You probably don't see a lot of them if you're rural, but they move really freakin' fast."

"What did he look like?" he demanded, his mind focused solely on her attacker, primed to run down the list of vampires still known to be residing in North America.

"He looked like goo by the time I was done with him. I told you a million times, I'm good at what I do."

He sat back in his seat.

She was a fucking vamp killer.

Of course.

Chapter Eight

Rhys's brow lifted, his eyes on Nichol's back pocket. "You gonna answer that?"

"Nope."

He continued to scan the video surveillance of the haunt property, hunting for any blind spots.

"That's the ninth call in twenty minutes," Rhys continued, pointing at a small section of land in the far east quadrant that was exposed.

"Fuck 'em."

The incessant vibration of the past week had become part of the white noise of the haunt for him, alongside Molly's constant nattering, and the clicking of Audra's heels. Kaius, Highsteaks, another haunt begging for assistance after they failed to keep their members safe. None of it took priority over the meeting happening the next evening, a meeting that would voluntarily announce the location of the Kaius haunt to a handful of humans.

A handful of humans with political power, a police department, and the FBI Vamp Division on speed-dial.

Rhys stood up, his movements quicker than they'd been even the week prior. "I'll angle cameras fourteen and fifteen to cover that gap. Keep your phone on and maybe answer it when I check in."

Grunting in response, he tossed his buzzing phone face-down on the table and pulled up the camera feeds in question.

"I expect you standing beside my sewing machine in one hour," Bianca called into the com room as she passed. "If you're late, I'll shorten the hem on those pants just enough to annoy you."

"Fine." He glanced at the navy bag hanging in the corner of the room. "Can I keep my boots on?"

Bee's laughter echoed down the hall. "You're the fourth to ask. No."

Rhys's hand appeared on camera fourteen as his phone began to buzz. Ensuring it was Rhys, he swiped the screen. "Aim it an inch down and move your hand."

The camera jostled and stilled, the gap in the field closed.

"Let me check the other feeds to make sure we didn't open another hole," he instructed, bringing the affected quadrant into view. "Who the hell cut down all the flowers in the northern corner?"

"Who do you think?" Rhys retorted. "I'll give you a hint. I'm currently in her doghouse until I apologize for…fuck, I don't even know what, but it was probably bad."

Of course. Fucking Lis and her flower-wreath obsession.

"Double-check she didn't leave any exposed wires," he groused. "And tell her the perimeter flowers are off-limits."

"You tell her," Rhys said before hanging up.

Content with the visual ground coverage, he grabbed his suit from the hook and made his way to the former Tender training quarters where most of his hauntmates now resided. Audra was crouched at Bianca's side, discussing the cuff length of Mick's jacket.

"Use our room to change," Bee called over to him. "Boots off, Oxfords on."

His brows furrowed.

"She means those stupid shoes at the bottom of the bag," Mickey yelled from his room.

Easing his way past the women, he knocked on Mick's door. "Thanks for the clarification."

"No problem, man. Louis gave me a heads up, too." His voice dropped to avoid being heard by the women. "Don't fight it. Just do what they say, and don't argue. It's less painful that way. They have stick pins, and they wield them really close to your junk."

****

Nichol collapsed onto his sofa with a vial in his hand, the walls of his bunker providing a small respite from the non-stop decisions he'd been making for the past sixteen hours.

They were ready.

We could still call it off.

Staring at the pressed suit hanging on the back of his door, he pushed the thought from his head. They were ready. The haunt was more secured and monitored than it had ever been. Video monitoring stations were set up in the communication room, the former Tender quarters, the common room, the bloodslave quarters, and in his room. Live feeds fed to his phone. Alerts had been tied to every hauntmate's cell, with in-room warning bells secured in every bunk. Twenty-five thousand feet of wires and cables crisscrossed the property.

Weapons were sharpened, loaded, dispersed, and stashed.

Locks were reinforced, their codes changed.

Press packets were prepared and standing by to be

emailed out once an agreement was forged, courtesy of Jagger and Bianca.

Suits were hemmed.

They were ready.

His phone buzzed again in his hand.

Highsteaks.

He waited until the phone went still, wrinkling his nose as the ancient blood hit his tongue and revealed its staleness. He flicked open his email and fired off another coded order, his second that week. When the confirmation came in, he entered the banking app and transferred the payment to his supplier before deleting the email from the server and scanning his messenger app.

Fuck it.

She answered on the first ring, her voice hushed. "Jeez, NK. About time."

He stretched his senses, listening into the halls for movement as he put Highsteaks on speaker. "How's it going?"

There was a small laugh of relief. "It's going. I missed you."

"Yeah," he said with a huff as he walked into the bathroom. "It's been crazy around here." He started the shower, testing the heat level with his hand. "But I should let you go. I was just checking in so you knew I was still around."

"No, no!" Highsteaks called, her voice almost shrill against the rumble of the water. "Wait!"

His chin dropped to his chest. "What."

"Are you mad at me or something?"

Nope. Just figured out you're a vamp killer. Which goes directly against my own belief system of not being killed. By vamp killers.

"Just have a lot of deadlines to meet right now," he grumbled, dropping his cargos to the floor, and kicking them into the corner. "I'll be online more once shit settles down."

Highsteaks went quiet.

"Nothing personal," he added, stepping under the spray.

"Are you…in the shower?" she asked, the hint of amusement in her voice hitting him in the gut more than he cared to think about.

"I'm multi-tasking."

"Then talk to me until you're done and ready for bed," Highsteaks said. "You've ignored me for over a week. You owe me."

Scrubbing the shampoo into his hair, his mind flashed through rationalizations.

Not like we'll ever be in the same place.

Probably no more vamps in whatever area she's in anyways.

She tolerates your bitter ass.

"Fine," he relented. "How has work been?"

"Boring and uneventful. I'm on light rotation for a couple weeks." She yawned audibly. "Are you using that shampoo I told you about?"

He glanced at the oversized bottle of bulk shampoo on the ledge. "I'm not rinsing hundreds of dollars of soap down the drain, no."

"You probably don't want to know how much I spent on nail polish this week then," she laughed. "But it's totally worth it."

He grunted, frowning as his phone pinged. "Did you just send me something?"

"Take a look."

Drying his hand off, he leaned out of the shower and picked up his phone, opening the picture she had sent.

"Orange polish?" he asked, the forced disdain in his voice hiding the instant reaction his body had to the long, shapely legs in the photo.

"It matches my outfit. Not that I'm going anywhere. But it's cute. Admit it."

He set down his phone and resumed rinsing his cheap shampoo out. "It's loud. Why would you have clothes that color anyways? That's the color you'd find on an emergency vest."

His phone pinged again.

"I'm not looking at whatever that is," he warned as he turned his face into the water. "You can't convince me that shade of orange is 'cute' in any manner."

He turned off the shower and wrapped his towel around his hips.

"Tell me I'm cute," she sang. "Come on, NK. Tell me orange is super cute!"

Rolling his eyes, he picked up the phone and opened the photo, expecting to see some shapeless fabric on a hanger.

Fuck.

He closed out the picture, pulling her off speaker. "Well, it matches." He turned off the lights and frowned when the image of the plunging neckline of a bright orange shirt didn't disappear from his head at the same time.

"It matches and it's cute," she coached, enunciating each word slowly.

"It matches and it's bright," he stated, refusing to back down.

Or use the term 'cute'.

The carefully taken photo had no identifiable features in it, no glimpse of her face or hair. It had been cropped to eliminate as much background as possible while still displaying the bright nail polish, the khaki skirt, and the tight shirt revealing more cleavage than he wanted to think about.

It wasn't 'cute'.

It was hot.

Very fucking hot.

"Not exactly an effective vamp-killing outfit," he mused aloud, wincing as he brought up the one topic he didn't want to think about.

She laughed. "My job and my spare time are two totally different things."

He lay back on his mattress. "So you're a traffic cone by day, vamp-killer by night?"

"I. Look. Cute," she huffed, pointedly ignoring his prodding. "That was a quick shower."

"Efficient," he corrected. "I better get some rest. I'll ping you when things settle down here."

Highsteaks sighed. "All right. Have a good night, NK."

"You, too."

He set his phone on the bedside table.

Once the meeting was over, he could establish a plan to distance himself from Highsteaks. Research the easiest way to step back and eliminate contact without repercussions. Or guilt.

Maybe discuss it with Audra. Hypothetically, of course.

Flipping his phone over one last time, he opened the pictures Highsteaks had sent him and saved them to his phone's camera roll.

Chapter Nine

Nichol's arm muscles twitched under the constraining cut of his suit while he looked over the camera feeds. "What is it, Mick?"

"Are you…" Mick paused. "Are you humming?"

"Fuck off," he growled, flipping rapidly between two screens until he was satisfied the movement he saw was a squirrel. He looked over. "Ready to go?"

"Yeah," Mick replied, adjusting the cuffs of his jacket. "Audra and I are taking one of the SUVs in and Louis is following with Dominic in another." He pocketed the keys and grinned. "Didn't know you were a Rod Stewart fan, man."

Dodging the pen Nichol flung his way, Mick tore from the com room, leaving him alone.

He glanced over at his phone.

Nope.

He had better things to do than reopen a photo already burned into his head.

"Nichol!"

He snarled, spinning his chair toward Bianca. "What."

The petite woman marched over to him, hands on her hips. "Those aren't the Oxfords on your feet."

Jagger appeared in the doorway, his trademark hoodie covering the tattoos on his temples. "Just don't fight it," he hissed under his breath, too quiet for Bianca to hear. "Seriously, man. I don't want to hear about this for the next two nights."

His lips drawn tight across his fangs, he kicked off his combat boots and accepted the uncomfortable dress shoes from Bee. "You two are all set up in here," he said, wiggling his toes in the tight leather. "These tabs access the exterior cameras, these ones access the interior." He turned his laptop toward the pair. "The main computer is recording all video and audio. If you need to switch views, do it on here so nothing is closed out. Got it?"

Smiling at his appearance, Bianca nodded and reached up to adjust the lay of his collar.

Jagg pulled up a chair to the com room table. "I'm sending out a group text," he said, looking at his phone. "All communication for tonight should be limited to that chat so no one's in the dark."

Nichol's phone buzzed in his hand.

Jagg: why don't you ever sing for me, nicky-baby

He shoved his phone in the pocket of his dress pants. "If we survive tonight, I'm coming for you," he snarled. "Mick, too. You're lucky I need your eyes on those cams tonight."

Storming into the common room, he ignored the buzzing of his cell and scanned the ceiling for wires.

"Oh!" Lis exclaimed as he strode in, her hands filled with freshly cut flowers. "I was just finishing up in here."

He crossed his arms and watched as Lis scampered around the room, filling vases, and arranging the stems. She kept her eyes averted, her discomfort in his presence as strong as it had been since she first returned to the Kaius haunt.

Good.

Trusting Lis meant trusting Rhys's judgement, and

he wasn't quite there yet no matter how frail and harmless she appeared in her wispy skirts and bare feet. The woman was a known vamp-killer, a turned Tender who'd staked her master, gone to the media about the Tender trade, and then managed to become the less annoying half of 'Rhys and Lis'.

Vamp-killer.

He glared at Lis until she exited, giving him a wide berth. Skulking through the room, he ensured all cable connections were secure and out of sight.

"It's all good," Rhys called over from the doorway. "We're ready."

Grunting in response, he continued his assessment.

"What's the worst that could happen?" Rhys asked, sauntering into the room. "A species war? Angry mobs? Bounty hunters? A Deepfryer in every county?" He stopped at Nichol's side and tucked a small wire out of sight. "We're there already, Nicky."

"What's Mick's ETA?" he inquired, yanking at the cuffs of his jacket.

"Twenty-eight minutes," Rhys stated, checking his phone. "Seven vehicles. Mick and Audra are leading the pack, Louis and Dominic are bringing up the rear at a distance to avoid detection." He swatted at Nichol's hands. "For fuck's sake, let me fix that. You unsophisticated assholes are like a group of toddlers in these suits."

He stilled while Rhys straightened his cuffs.

"And lay off Lis," Rhys said, a slight growl of possessiveness in his voice. "If she's going to stake anyone, it'll be me and for good fucking reason." He adjusted Nichol's shirt collar and patted it down. "There. Now get those hot legs over to the back wall and wait for our guests."

****

Mayor Densbridge rested his elbows on his knees, his chin on his fist. "This could be political suicide."

Nichol watched as Audra crossed her legs and leaned forward. "This could be the catalyst for other counties to join the equality movement," she countered. "All it takes is one mayor to stand up and defy the federal government, and others will follow."

One of the female councilors rose to her feet and began pacing, her movements carefully monitored by him and Mick. "We would need to reassure our constituents the money donated by vampires was legally obtained, or we could run into issues."

He crossed the room and handed the woman a folder. "This is the account the funds would be directed through," he stated. "As you can see, it's tied to a legitimate investment firm with a reputation for transparency and little tolerance for unethical practices."

"Where are the others?" one of the men asked, looking around the room. "Is Rhys Kaius not one of you?"

He didn't miss the slight increase in the heart rates of two of the female councilors at the mention of Rhys's name. Firing off a quick text into the group chat, he resumed his place against the back wall and motioned for Audra to reply.

"The rest of the group are on their way," she said slowly, looking to him for confirmation. "While we wait for them, I'd like to pose a very possible scenario Denver may face in the near future."

The mayor leaned back in his chair and took a sip of coffee.

"I'm sure you closely followed the events that unfolded in St. Louis when the undead were crawling out of the sewers," Audra continued, pausing until she received confirmation the mayor and his underlings remembered the Deviant invasion. "While the United States faces a divide between its pro-vampire and anti-vampire factions, vampires themselves are facing a divide in their own ranks."

His back twitched at the sharing of such closely-guarded information, despite his approval of the tactic the night before.

"The vampires responsible for the bloodshed in St. Louis are still on the loose and are gaining support from some of the fringe element in the vampire community," Audra stated, making eye contact with every human in the room. "This haunt, this group, has been tracking both the vampires responsible and the followers. We were the ones who passed information to the Federal Vamp Agency on the most effective methods of eliminating the threat in St. Louis."

She paused again, ensuring she had the full attention of the mayor. "If we cut bait and leave, we take the last of the good guys with us. Because the good guys WILL follow us, and you will be left to your own defenses against some very bad vamps."

Audra sat back in her seat and smiled sweetly at the mayor, whose lips had gone tight.

"You're saying we need to align with you, or potentially face a more hostile threat alone," Mayor Densbridge finally stated.

"What she's saying," Rhys interjected as he sauntered into the room, Lis on his arm, "is none of you have the financial, political, or intellectual resources to go up against a pair of vampires hellbent on establishing their own violent coup. A refusal to side with us places your constituents at the risk of being turned or outright slaughtered if that duo makes its way here." He smirked at one of the younger female councilors and took her hand in his, bowing as he ran his thumb over her palm. "Rhys Kaius, m'lady."

He caught the roll of Lis's eyes as Rhys winked at the woman.

Lis's going to stake him. For good reason.

Jagger and Bianca arrived next, their hands locked together. The murmurings began as one by one the councilors looked from Jagg to Bianca to Audra then back to Rhys and Lis, and he knew they were thinking of all the press the five of them generated in recent years.

"That's…" one of the elderly men opened, motioning to the group. "This is a problem."

Nichol pushed off the wall. "This is no problem. Lis and Rhys have a fan following larger than most boy bands thanks to their star-crossed lovers schtick. And this, ladies and gentlemen, is Jagger Kaius and Bianca Schumann. We're well aware Jagg is easily recognized among humans from the media attention surrounding his escape from the Vansburg county jail with the help of Ms. Audra Verdi. He'll be working out of the public eye."

When the councilors looked skeptical, he took another step forward. "Jagger and Bianca run the coordinated responses to anti-vampire rhetoric and violence around the country, an extension of the work you probably remember seeing on the front page from their time in Nebraska. They are responsible for organizing every public retaliation on behalf of vampires and have contact with every influential vampire from coast to coast."

"In short, don't fuck with them," Rhys chimed in, squeezing Lis tighter to him as she attempted to elbow him.

Molly snorted, earning a glare from Nichol.

Mayor Densbridge looked around the room slowly as Bianca took a step forward. "Why don't we bring in some refreshments and we can answer questions in a less formal setting," she suggested. "Maybe get to know one another, give you all a chance to think about anything that might be on your mind."

****

Audra stood beside Nichol, her arms crossed as she assessed the room. "Bianca is absolutely brilliant," she murmured quietly. "Humanizing us."

He lifted a brow. "Humanizing?"

Audra rolled her eyes. "You know what I mean."

"Us?"

She grinned up at him. "Yes. Us."

While Audra rejoined the impromptu soiree, he kept his position in the corner. Few of the humans approached him, which was just fine by his standards. Dominic and Molly were surrounded by a small contingent of people around the stereo, admiring the vintage records in the haunt collection. Jagger was fielding questions about the court-ordered tattooing visible on his temples while Bianca stood with two other women and quietly discussed patriarchy in both human and vampire politics.

He listened in as Audra joined Mick and Louis in an intense explanation of the Kaius haunt's leadership role in the elimination of Tender trading and blood trafficking. The mayor appeared fascinated by the evolution and subsequent dissolution of the systems, interrupting frequently to better comprehend how the trades had come to be.

Then there was Rhys and Lis.

The intense media coverage the pair had received as the first vampire and woman sentenced to the Deepfryer in the USA made them minor celebrities among the councilors. Several humans approached the pair with questions about their relationship, questions Rhys slithered out of with ease while Lis countered with ambiguous replies and noncommittal smiles.

He was certain one woman asked for Rhys's autograph.

"Mikhail is your communications director, isn't he?" a man asked as he walked toward Nichol. "Councilor Ted Ashbury."

Glancing down at the offered hand before shaking it, he narrowed his eyes slightly and remained silent.

"The brains behind the idea are rarely the ones selling it," Ashbury mused. "They all look to you before answering any questions. Deferring to you." The man pushed his hands into his pockets and appraised him.

"What I want to know is what do you stand to gain by this? It's an expensive proposition for you. The organization and vamp-power you'll require to maintain a functioning perimeter security is a nightmare on its own. The tracking of threats, vetting of newcomers, training and mobilization of a force...it's a lot of work for a group your size."

He continued to monitor the conversations around him, listening in to ensure details were kept vague. "I dislike relocating," he replied off-the-cuff. "It's inconvenient."

Ashbury chuckled. "That's worth the hassle and expense? Come, now."

His nose wrinkled slightly as he caught the scent of Bianca's chemical-laden pink pastries. "We need a base," he relented. "One where we can focus on the vampire threat instead of the human threat. As you said, there are few of us. For the past three years, we've been stretched thin fighting on both fronts. Eliminating one benefits us as much as it benefits you."

He scanned the room, counting the humans to ensure none had slipped out of the room. "I'm acting head of the group right now. Their lives are my responsibility. If I can make it so they and their partners can leave the property with a modicum of safety, it's worth the time and expense on my behalf."

Chapter Ten

Boy slipped into the com room, his phone held awkwardly in his large hand as he extended it out to Nichol.

"You sure?" he asked, flipping between the bright security camera feeds on his computer he'd been staring at for almost a day and a half. "All right. I'll get a few hours, but if anything, and I mean anything, looks suspicious, get me immediately."

He vacated his seat at the computer and watched as Boy sat, his fingers resting uneasily on the mouse.

"If you accidentally close any screens, get me. If you see anything, get me. If…you know what? If anything looks different in any way from how it is at this moment, get me."

Boy nodded, a hint of amusement flashing across his blue eyes before they returned to their deadened stare.

The humans had vacated the premises an hour before dawn the previous morning, with Mickey and Louis following them to the city limits and tearing back before the sun breached the horizon. Since then, he had sat at his computer and waited. Waited for any sign of infiltration, any hint of attack, any movement on the grounds.

Waited. For thirty-one hours and counting.

He dragged his feet down the hall, his combat boots thumping against the hardwood as he made his way to his room. His suit long abandoned in the corner of his bunk, he shed his cargos and T-shirt and took a quick rinse in the shower. Half expecting Highsteaks to call, he kept his phone on the sink counter where he could keep an eye on it. When he found himself lying in the dark with a silent phone, he opened his message app and fired off a quick note.

587OriginalNK: survived the meeting. all looks on the up

He waited a few minutes, flipping back and forth between the two photos he had stored. When no reply came in, he turned the volume up on his phone and rolled over.

****

"Nichol! You in there?"

He growled, his eyes flipping open in the darkness as Audra's voice penetrated his head. "Yes, I'm fucking in here," he snarled as he jumped out of bed and pulled on his boxers. "What."

The knob turned and Audra strode in, completely oblivious to his mood.

Or completely aware and refusing to care.

"Mickey just got off the phone with Mayor Densbridge. Sanctuary is a go and he wants to discuss announcements and implementation schedules with you," she announced, walking over to his closet. "They want a video conference, so Bianca sent me into make sure you're presentable."

She swung his closet open, peered in, and turned. "Really, Nichol? Fifteen pairs of the exact same cargo pants and nothing else?" Her heels clicked as she crossed the floor and opened his dresser. "And fifteen black shirts. This is…well, expected, I suppose." With a heavy sigh, she tossed one of the newer shirts his way.

"Get out," he grumbled, pulling the tee over his head.

"Nothing I haven't seen before," she responded flippantly, returning to the closet. "I suppose the pants don't matter. We'll just toss that suit jacket on and… Nichol. Where's the suit?"

His eyes flicked to the corner of his bunk.

"You're kidding me."

Picking the wrinkled jacket up with two fingers, she held it out to him. "This is not how you treat a three-thousand-dollar suit."

Eat her. Mick would understand.

He glared at her as he tugged his cargos on. "I agreed to play dress up for one night. No more. Tell Bee I'm going in as is and I'll meet you in the communication room in fifteen."

"You tell her," Audra laughed, pulling his door closed as she left.

He grabbed his phone and sunk onto his sofa.

Highsteaks1403: I knew you'd nail it

Highsteaks1403: prefer the blue?

Glancing at the time stamp of the messages, he opened the photo Highsteaks sent of her blue toenail polish. Saving it with the others, he fired off a quick message.

587OriginalNK: You have abnormally short toes
****

Nichol ran his hands through his hair and slid his chair toward the printer. "Audra!" he barked into the hall. "The final documents for your bloodslaves are ready. Don't touch the ink for ten minutes." He eased the paper up slowly. "The ink doesn't adhere to this paper as quickly as the last batch."

Her heels clicked into the room, Louis and Mick behind her. "Looks good, Nic." She squinted to examine the details of the documents. "The birth dates on this one doesn't match the rest."

"Motherf…gimme that."

Skidding back to his computer, he fixed the typo and hit print. "So this time tomorrow, the Bloodslave Release Program will be officially over, right?"

"Aside from monitoring, yes," she replied. "Looks good. We'll head out right at dusk tomorrow." She smiled over at him. "Good work with the council tonight."

Mick grabbed the keys to an SUV. "If you have time, maybe tweak a security app so we can easily check in with this last batch on our phones."

Scrawling the request onto a list, he nodded and resumed shuffling money through the haunt's various accounts, reaching into his desk drawer and feeling around for any stray vials.

Nothing.

Linking through the haunt's servers, he fired off another order and transferred the payment when confirmation arrived.

"I'm going to need a favor," Rhys opened, frowning when Nichol instinctively moved to cover his computer screen. "What're you doing?"

"Banking." He closed out the email and reopened the haunt's stock holdings. "What."

"Boy agreed to spar me tomorrow evening," Rhys said, straddling a chair and looking over his shoulder. "If you could maybe sit in on the session, I'd owe you."

Jotting the request down, he grunted in agreement.

It wasn't easy for Rhys to ask, and Nichol sure as hell wasn't going to draw out his second's discomfort. "I'll be there. Now fuck off," he said, adjusting the angle of his laptop to better see the perimeter security footage.

"Appreciate it." Rhys shoved his chair into the table with a thud.

"Hey," he called out as Rhys walked out, "tell Boy Dominic is due for a few bags this week. The kid's looking a little pale." He frowned. "And three for yourself. That's an order."

Burying himself in paperwork, he burned through the morning hours without interruption while his hauntmates rested. It wasn't until Highsteaks began messaging him he finally noticed the time.

Highsteaks1403: haven't seen you play any games online in ages

587OriginalNK: no time

Highsteaks1403: but i miss you sending me all your extra inventory

He snorted, closing out his computer screens and wiping down his keyboard.

587OriginalNK: lot of guys online. get one of them to buff up your characters

Highsteaks1403: pfft no. too many perverts. i'll wait for you

Poking his head into the common room, he flicked off the lights and made his way to his bunker.

587OriginalNK: i can give you some of my logins and you can take what you need

He kicked his boots into the corner of his room and toed off his socks, making a mental note to remind Bianca and Jagger new email accounts were being diverted to their spam email.

Highsteaks1403: gimme gimme gimme gimme :)

Pursing his lips, he hesitated. Several of his passwords were combinations of those he used for haunt business.

But passwords could be changed. And gaming wasn't an option for him in the foreseeable future.

587OriginalNK: I'll make a list and send it to you

Highsteaks1403: can i call

He ground his molars as he looked between his phone, his bed, and his shower.

587OriginalNK: I really need to rinse off and get to bed

Highsteaks1403: nothing's slowed down yet has it

587OriginalNK: nope

His messaging app went silent as he showered off, texted a reminder to Molly to check all three mailboxes, and forwarded a weapon order confirmation to Jagg. He lay back in the dark, feeling around his nightstand for any unused vials and coming up empty.

The ring of his messaging app echoed in his bunk, earning a bark of annoyance from Rhys down the hall.

"What," Nichol greeted, his voice low.

Highsteaks laughed nervously. "Ummm, hi?"

"Hey." He rose up on one arm to listen for Rhys. "What do you need?"

"I…" She went quiet. "I, um, don't need anything. I thought maybe you might need something."

Satisfied Rhys wasn't barging down the hall anytime soon, he tucked his arm behind his head and closed his eyes. "Nope."

She breathed out loudly. "I thought maybe I could help you, uh…" She breathed deeply again. "You know, help you relax?"

His brows furrowed. "I am relaxed. I'm laying down."

Another nervous laugh. "Yeah, no. I was thinking...wow, this is kind of weird... I was thinking that I like you, NK. Like, like like you."

Pulling the phone away from his ear, he quickly searched up the terminology, his brows lifting. "Like like," he parroted.

"Yes, like like. And I thought since you don't have a girlfriend...at least I don't think you do...maybe I could, um, help?"

"Help," he echoed, confused by what she was getting at and still processing her earlier admission.

"You know what? Just, here." She let out a puff of air, muttering under her breath. "I was so not taught how to do this."

He could hear the rustling of fabric for a few moments before his phone pinged. He opened the image Highsteaks had sent, his jaw tensing as he took in the picture.

She'd once again been meticulous at hiding any identifying features.

Except the ones he already had burned into his head.

The blue nail polish.

The olive skin.

The long, shapely legs, completely bare.

The swell of her hip covered by black lace.

The fading knife scar partially hidden by a sheer black bra.

"Fuck," he muttered, closing out the photo only to reopen it seconds later.

"That's kind of the idea," she laughed, her nerves audible.

He shifted his hips and ground his teeth. "How do you know I'm not some old pervert?" he demanded as his mind flipped through the hundreds of assholes he'd come up against when he had time to game online.

"I'm really, really hoping you aren't."

Tossing his blanket off, he walked slowly to his bathroom, his ears alert for signs of his hauntmates in the halls. He held up his phone to the mirror, carefully angling it to avoid his face.

What the fuck are you doing?

Vamp. Killer.

With a quick crop to eliminate as much of the identifiable environment as he could, he fired it off to her.

"You're lucky I'm not a pervert," he said gruffly, flopping back into bed and propping the phone on the bedside table. "Those kind of pictures end up online all the time without women knowing. There's an insatiable market for images like that on the internet."

There was a moment of silence.

"You aren't actually lecturing me about online safety right now, are you?" she said slowly, the humor in her voice inexplicably easing some of his tension. When he refused to answer, her voice dropped a fraction. "It's too bad you aren't here right now."

He put his arms behind his head. "I don't know where 'here' is."

"If you were," she continued, apparently ignoring his comment, "I would be on my knees running my tongue across that incredible V-cut."

His eyes shot open. "What?"

"Nothing makes me hotter than a guy who lets me take control," she purred. "A guy who lays back and lets me explore every inch of him with my lips."

Glancing at his bunker door, he turned the volume down on his phone. "I…what?"

"I'd make my way up those abs, letting my nails trail along the inside of your thighs as I ran my tongue across your chest."

Images of blue-polished nails on his skin flashed through his head. "Highsteaks," he warned. "What are you doing?"

There was a soft rustling of fabric. "Right now, I'm touching myself and thinking about how you would look underneath me." She let out a soft moan. "Are you still in those boxers?"

"Yeah," he grunted, squeezing his eyes shut tight in a futile attempt to erase the visual she was creating.

"Will you take them off for me?"

His eyes strained to see the lock on his door. "I…yeah." He hooked his thumbs in the band.

"Slowly," she ordered, the slight breathlessness of her voice sending a jolt through his body.

He pushed his boxers off of his hips and kicked them to the foot of his bed, tucking his arms firmly behind his head again as she started to pant softly into the phone. "I'm so wet," she moaned. "I want you inside me so bad, NK. Are you hard for me?"

His muscles twitched as he fought to keep his hands locked. He looked over at the light of his phone, torn between hanging up or giving in to the game. "Yeah," he ground out, his back molars beginning to ache from the strain. He could hear every breath, every movement she made. His mind whipped through images of her spread out on her bed, her skin flushed while she pleasured herself.

She breathed out with a moan. "Touch yourself for me. Pretend it's my hand wrapped around you and go slow." When he didn't respond, Highsteaks purred. "Do you want me naked on top of you? Do you want to be inside me?"

"Holy fuck," he grunted, his hands linked tight behind him.

Her panting grew quicker. "I can feel you filling me and...oooh...I want it faster, NK. I want your hands on my ass while I'm riding you."

His hips bucked up instinctively, his lungs filling with unneeded air as he fought to regain control. "Highsteaks," he groaned, the warning tone bordering on pleading as his body reacted to the imagined sensation of her wetness sliding over him. His hands grasped at his pillow.

"I'm so close, NK," she whimpered, sending a jolt of lust straight through him. "I want you to come for me. Please, NK. I need you to come for me."

His heels dug into his mattress as his release barreled through him, his hands grabbing his headboard when his back arched off the bed. He bit back a growl while he exploded across his stomach to the sound of her moaning and cursing through her own moment.

The room went quiet, her soft panting ricocheting through the room and into his head.

"Wow," she finally gasped. "I really needed that."

He unhooked his fingers from his headboard and pushed himself up onto his elbows. "What the *fuck*, Highsteaks?" he snarled, his mind unnervingly warm and hazy.

"Feel better?"

He glowered at the phone.
"Yeah."

Chapter Eleven

"This is bullshit, Nicholai," Rhys growled, doubling back on Boy and finally landing a half-decent hit. "I'm fighting like a goddamn newbie."

Nichol walked over, his hand held up to stay Boy. "You were as close to true death as it gets," he stated, using his toe to push Rhys's stance out and shaking the image of Rhys's charred body from his thoughts. "It will likely take a full year before your strength and speed recover. So until that happens, we're going to focus on technique."

Rhys launched back at Boy and the males fell to the floor, fists and knees clashing. When Boy got the upper hand again, he ended the round.

"All right," he said, pulling two blades from his leg pockets. "Rhys, I trust Lis won't be making her way down here anytime soon?"

Rhys grunted. "Yeah. Like I need her to see this pathetic shitstorm. She'd leave me for a centurion. Just give me one of those."

He passed Boy and Rhys knives and stepped back. "First to draw blood wins the round, ten rounds. No fangs, stay within the arena. Go."

Barking corrections and warnings, he officiated the sparring match with his mind bouncing between the fight, his to-do list, and his unsettling call with Highsteaks hours earlier. "You can't afford to be sloppy," he called out, his eyes narrowing when Rhys paused long enough to flip him off. Boy took the opportunity presented and landed his seventh win.

"Rhys, out," he ordered. "Boy, you and I will square off. Rhys, watch his movements and look for his tells. Knives, fangs, full strength, open arena. Pause for instructions. Go."

Boy was first to move, the millisecond glance to his left giving Nichol all the warning he needed to deflect the blade and land a hit to the abs. "Pause. Rhys, how did I dodge this old bastard?"

Rhys scratched at his tattoos. "Fuck if I know."

He and Boy held position. "Watch his eyes. Boy, you look in the direction you're traveling. Use your peripheral to scan. Go."

They battled throughout the sparring room, bouncing each other off the concrete walls and floor. When Audra called down a ten-minute warning, Boy's distraction gave Nichol the upper hand and his fangs embedded deep into the male's throat.

The surge of energy accompanying the intake of fresh blood rocketed through him. He instinctively pulled at the wound, his high amplifying with every drop. When Boy finally tossed him onto the cement, the thinnest thread of reason anchored Nichol to the ground as his eyes locked on Boy's torn and bleeding neck.

"Go clean up," he barked, forcing his gaze to Rhys. "Grab a few bags for both of you. I'll get this place put back together."

Keeping his gaze averted from Boy's accusing glare, he waited until they vacated the room and closed his eyes to sink momentarily into the high.

****

Eleven a.m.

Nichol paced the com room floor, his back teeth grinding while Mayor Densbridge waffled back and forth, and the clock kept ticking.

"I just feel people would be more comfortable with a known force trained in policing," Densbridge stated. "It's an easier sell."

"Not if it creates an ineffective—and therefore dangerous—environment," he argued. "Highly trained military, be it Rangers or Marines, who have had sufficient experience in the field and on the lines will be less likely to over-react if a vamp moves quickly or a young one goes off the rails." He ran his hand through his hair. "I want a force that can handle the worst case scenarios from day one."

Densbridge paused. "I'll discuss it in council and get back to you."

The blood high had crashed an hour ago, leaving him agitated and twitchy. He slammed the communication room door shut behind him and stormed to his bunk. Yanking his nightstand drawer out, he dumped the contents onto his coffee table, tossing it against the sofa when it didn't produce a vial. He plugged his phone in, stripped down, and stood in the cold shower water for over an hour.

When the worst passed, he turned off the tap and fell into bed. His phone was alit with messages, but only one drew his attention.

Missed call: Highsteaks1403 12:21

Turning the volume down, he tapped her phone icon and waited for her to answer.

"Hey, Abs Man," she greeted.

He rolled his eyes. "Never call me that again."

"Buff Boy?" she suggested, her voice playful. "How about Guns o' Steel?"

"How about no," he countered. "How was work?"

As she launched into a detailed description of her boredom, he opened the photo she'd sent him the night before, his thumb hovering over the delete button while he debated the risk such a distraction was quickly becoming.

"So aside from pulling a few splinters from my ass, that was pretty much the highlight of my night," she laughed. "How did yours go?"

He thought back to his night. "Bit of training, broke up a few arguments, placed a dozen orders, fought with a city official. The usual."

"And all that on what, three hours' rest?"

"Two." He glanced at the time. "Did you get the list of logins?" When she squealed in response, he pulled his phone from his ear and growled. "For fuck's sake."

"You remember JerseyBoy863? I loaded up on your stuff and beat his ass into the ground. Completely obliterated him," she said, her voice giddy. "You should have seen it. He called me every name in the book. C-word this and bitch-that."

She sighed, completely oblivious to the fact he had sat up in bed and had opened his phone's browser to hunt down JerseyBoy863. "It was magnificent. I should've screen-shot the whole tirade for you."

Forwarding the quick info he found to his own email for further investigation that night, he snarled. "He wouldn't have started that shit back up if I'd been online."

Highsteaks laughed. "Of course not. That's why it

was so awesome. I got to knock him down myself without you standing in the wings to take him out." She paused. "He doesn't need to know it was your weapons stash I used."

He lay back, his previous agitation returning twofold. "You remember the agreement, right? Any time one of those assholes starts in on you in the chat, you send me his tag. Doesn't matter if I'm playing or not."

"With your accounts feeding mine, I can take care of myself now," she argued back. "I liked playing this morning. I was super tough."

She growled into the phone, and his body reacted instantly.

"Don't do that," he snarled. "Just send me the tags, okay?"

"Promise," she relented. "You're in a bad mood, aren't you?"

He tossed one arm over his eyes. "What the fuck gave it away?"

She yawned audibly. "Your normally sunny demeanor's been replaced by a complete crank."

He felt the sides of his mouth turn up slightly. "Go to bed and I'll text you later. I'm computer-bound all night tomorrow, so I'll be somewhat around."

"Okay. Night, NK," she mumbled, unaware of how much those two words lifted his mood.

****

587OriginalNK: got some news for you

Nichol returned to his spreadsheet and continued to input numbers for a vampire-safe hostel prototype.

Highsteaks1403: lay it on me

587OriginalNK: JerseyBoy863 has been sent back to level one on every game he plays

587OriginalNK: on every platform

He flipped through the material pricing lists, scanning for the most cost-effective option.

Highsteaks1403: you're a god and i love you for it

He frowned at the message, his mind quickly recalling the definition of 'like like'.

587OriginalNK: any others I need to know about?

The subconscious double meaning behind his text stared back at him.

Highsteaks1403: take out Cocktaildog69

He smirked and pulled up his browser.

Highsteaks1403: i'm so freaking bored out here. i should take up squirrel hunting

Deciding on the foam insulation for both the efficiency and the sound-proofing qualities, he began calculating the required amount for a single unit and entered it into the document.

587OriginalNK: I'm putting together a building quote and crunching numbers. Good times

Highsteaks1403: yuuuuuuuuuck

In his head, he could hear the drawn-out 'u' in the unplaceable accent she sometimes had when she was tired.

Highsteaks1403: i'm sitting in a tree watching my boss hit on a new chick

Highsteaks1403: she's giggling and pretending she's all shy but she's wearing a see-thru shirt and her skirt's so short i can tell you she's wearing blue panties

Snorting, he looked over the furnishing catalogue he'd printed off earlier, scribbling a quick reminder to himself to order more printer ink.

587OriginalNK: so you're in Peeping Tom mode tonight

Highsteaks1403: now she's dropped something and whoops has to bend over

Highsteaks1403: my boss is very obviously liking the skirt and now i'm completely grossed out

Selecting a sturdy bed with enough room for two should the incoming vampires be traveling with a companion, he entered the price and moved on to sofas.

587OriginalNK: look away and stop being such a lech

Highsteaks1403: now i'm looking at YOUR pic and being a lech

He adjusted himself in his chair and focused on the paper in front of him. A good sturdy sofa in a dark patterned fabric would be most forgiving, if not aesthetically pleasing.

587OriginalNK: pretty sure hunting squirrels would be more exciting

Highsteaks1403: squirrels aren't on my kill list

Highsteaks1403: are you in the mood for a little distraction?

Sliding his chair to the com room door, he popped the lock and rolled back to his computer.

587OriginalNK: yeah
****

Nichol lay awake, his mind reviewing what he needed to get done once dusk hit. He kept one ear open to the bunker hall, listening for Molly or Bianca's movements in the wing.

Mail day.

Delivery day.

He glanced at the time again and wondered briefly if Highsteaks was still awake. He considered heading back to the com room to log into his game tags online to make sure she wasn't staying up to play, scrapping the idea quickly.

It was none of his business what she was up to.

And it wasn't his concern if she was overtired. Even if it was dangerous.

Vamp killer.

He shook the thought from his head and picked up his phone, intending to reply to the emails he'd neglected all night.

Good intentions and all.

His thumb swiped his messaging app and he flipped leisurely through the texts Highsteaks had sent him in precise intervals well into the early morning hours.

—Are you alone?—

Nichol had fired off his reply, his mind adding up the costs of installing a fully functioning bathroom into each suite for the human companions.

Fifteen minutes passed before the second message came in.

—I'm gonna make you beg tonite—

He could feel himself harden as he read through the texts again, his body reacting exactly as it had when they first came in.

Another precise fifteen minutes.

—Tonites gonna start with me on my knees and end with you on yours—

Highsteaks had created an almost Pavlovian reaction with her explicit words and rigid timing. By the end of the first hour, he was intrigued.

By the end of the second hour, he was impatient.

By the end of the third hour, he was watching the clock like a hawk.

And by the end of the sixth, he had given up any

hope of work in exchange for staring at his phone.

—*Are you close?*—

The anticipation of her next message had him teetering on the edge as he replied.

—*Fuck yes.*—

Not a minute went by before Highsteaks responded.

—*Good. Stay there and I'll call you tomorrow morning. Night, NK :)*—

He groaned, dropped his phone on the pillow, and tried unsuccessfully to get some rest.

Chapter Twelve

Nichol strode across the yard, Audra's phone in hand. "All monitoring equipment in the last five bloodslave relocations now feeds directly into the app," he announced, pushing Molly's rifle to the side as he passed. "Louis and Mick have the same thing on their phones. The audio is fed and stored in the haunt servers, so you'll need to be connected if you're going back in time. Live feed's no longer glitching."

Audra handed her rifle to Jagg and opened the app. "How do I change their names? I'm not referring to those poor men as Jackass One, Two, Three, Four, and Five."

"Settings, change contact," he grumbled, pulling his own buzzing phone from his pocket. "What."

"Hello, Nicholai."

He spun on his heel and stalked toward the woods, away from the group before any of his hauntmates could overhear him. "Kaius."

The reception clicked on and off briefly until it settled into a low static hum. "I saw an announcement in the news tonight regarding Denver's establishment as a sanctuary city," Kai opened. "This is your doing?"

Pacing the tree line, his grip tightened on the phone. "It is."

"I want all hauntmates in the communication room in ten minutes when I call in again."

****

Nichol occupied himself with the computer wires while his hauntmates filtered in, their faces a mixture of wariness and excitement. While the others pulled their seats around the table, Rhys stood in the doorway, his arm blocking Lis from entering.

"Sit," he ordered, tightening the video cable.

"Fuck that," Rhys stated, his tone disturbingly light. "None of us should sit. Kai gave up the right to call meetings months ago." He looked straight at Nichol. "I answer to you."

"And I say sit," he growled, logging into the video conferencing app and watching the gray icon of Kaius's phone. When it lit up green, he clicked it and took his position at the back of the group.

Kaius's face flashed onto the screen, his brow furrowed, and mouth drawn tight over his extended fangs. The hard blue of his eyes softened slightly as he scanned the room, landing on Rhys who had taken up position behind Lis's chair. "Welcome home, Rhys." He looked to Lis. "You as well."

Rhys's jaw tensed. "Nichol already gave us the welcome basket, but thanks."

Kaius's eyes flicked to something offscreen before he needlessly shifted in his seat. "The women can leave," he stated, his voice flat. "Nothing I have to say concerns them."

"The women," Mick interjected, "are a part of this haunt. They leave, we leave." He glanced at Nichol, receiving a curt nod of approval that did not go unnoticed by Kaius.

Kai's face hardened for a moment before his shoulders slumped slightly. "Nichol informed me the sanctuary city plan was his."

"It was mine," Mick replied, crossing his arms.

"I seconded it," Jagger added.

"I voted for it," Dom called out. "We all did."

Kaius kept his eyes locked on Nichol. "Put an end to it."

Rhys snorted. "No one's putting an end to anything, let alone on the orders of a fucking deserter." He leaned onto the table, his face filling the camera. "Nicholai's word is the law here now. You want a say, you vote with the rest of us."

Nichol placed his hand on Rhys's back. "We weighed the benefits against the potential issues and felt it was a move that would best serve the long-term interests of the haunt while providing our species with a safe base to regroup and re-esta—"

"What you've done," Kaius snarled, "is painted a bullseye on yourselves."

"What the fuck do you care?" Rhys sneered, rearing up and booting the table. "Where have you been, Kai? Because it sure as fuck isn't here."

Nichol stepped back as Rhys stormed out, Lis hot on his heels. "I have a compilation of the pros and cons we discu—"

"Don't explain yourself," Mickey interrupted, rising to his feet and holding his hand out to Audra. He looked straight into the camera. "If you wanted a say, you should have come back, Kai. You walked out on us. Nichol's top dog now."

Nichol watched Mickey stomp from the room before he turned to the others, eying Kaius's reactions. "The rest of you can go," he said quietly.

The hauntmates stared at Kaius for a moment before obeying. Dominic hesitated in front of the computer screen, opening his mouth to speak before reconsidering and turning his back.

He straddled a chair as Boy closed the door behind him, running his hands through his hair before he crossed his arms and locked eyes with his creator.

Kaius leaned back in his chair. "Are they out of earshot?"

"Yes."

Kai looked offscreen again. "Dovidas is making his way to Stojanovski's," he said quietly. "He and Chen are backed by an ancient who makes Chen look like a newborn, and they intend to regroup and recruit on the Stojanovski compound."

"Jagger assures me Stojanovski is in our pocket," he countered. "We've orchestrated several hits on Dovidas's supporters on the grounds already."

"Stojanovski is a child. He's in the pocket of the strongest force in his sphere. Today, that's you. And in two weeks 'time, that will be Dovidas." Kai rubbed his jaw. "Declaring Denver a sanctuary city backed by the Kaius haunt is a shot across Dovidas's bow. And across that of his backer."

He leaned onto the table. "Then we're on the offensive. We have a network of solid support globally, and with a reinforced base city, we can focus our efforts on eliminating Dovidas, Chen, and any backer they have."

"What you'll be," Kaius hollered back, "is trapped like rats in a storm drain. Surrounded. You need to get out. *now*."

The video disconnected, leaving him staring at a black screen.

****

"Nichol, honey? Want to see the latest YouTube video?"

Nichol grunted at Bianca, setting the pile of mail aside for later. "Did you convince Dom to brush his hair before recording?"

The tiny woman's hands flew to her hips. "Do I look like someone who hears 'no' very often? Of course I did. I got you into a suit, I can get that mangy boy to untangle his mop. Now, come."

He followed Bee to the weapons room, firing off a quick text to Highsteaks as they walked.

587OriginalNK: Still swamped. Will text later

His phone buzzed back instantly.

Highsteaks1403: 3 days straight of excuses? go fuck yourself

"Bianca?" He turned back down the hall. "I have a quick call to make. I'll be there in ten."

He ducked into the common room, closing the double doors and retreating to the far corner. His thumb swiped across Highsteaks' phone icon.

"Don't," she hissed when she answered.

He ground his teeth, his head dropping. "Can I call you at ten?"

"You can lose my fucking contact for all I care."

The line went dead.

He flipped to the text app.

—I'm sorry.—

****

Nichol read over his notes from his discussion with Councilor Ted Ashbury and emailed them out to the rest of the haunt for them to read come dusk. The Councilor was adamant he be the human contact point for the vamp security, the face of assurance the force would be capable, armed, and prepared. Ashbury was already forwarding lists of names for him to check out, an impressive collection of retired marines and combat veterans.

Adding Molly's requests to the grocery order, he sent it off, shut down the com room, and headed to the former bloodslave quarters to check on Boy.

"How many cells do we have outfitted?" he asked, perusing the construction with mild interest.

Boy held up three fingers and resumed welding the reinforced steel bars together.

The vamp holding cells, designed under the knowledgeable eye of Rhys, were a last-minute negotiation with Mayor Densbridge. While the vamp force would eventually take over imprisonment for minor infractions, it would be months before selection and training was complete. And since the official announcement the week prior, his phone had been ringing nonstop. Densbridge wanted assurances the Kaius haunt could handle the heavy offenders.

Rhys had taken it as a personal challenge and had brought it upon himself to enlist Boy in the project.

And Nichol had no problem letting them.

"Text me any supplies you need," he called out as he ascended the stairs and headed to his bunker.

He sent off a message to Highsteaks, as he'd done for eight mornings straight.

—*I'm sorry.*—

Knowing it would go unanswered, he popped a vial from his latest order, downed the bottle, and crashed.

Chapter Thirteen

Nichol's phone buzzed on his bedside table, yanking him out of his drugged stupor. Squinting at the brightness, he looked at the time.

8:17pm.

Pushing himself up, he shook his head in an attempt to clear the last of the haze before reading the incoming texts.

Highsteaks1403: NK

Highsteaks1403: please be awake

Highsteaks1403: nk

He clenched his fists, forcing the numbness in his fingers to ease.

587OriginalNK: what's up

His limbs still felt weighed from overloading on the potent blood the night before. Dropping his feet to the floor, he trudged to the bathroom and started the shower.

Highsteaks1403: dropped my crossbow into the bushes

Highsteaks1403: hes looking for me

He snatched his phone off of the counter.

587OriginalNK: who

Highsteaks1403: vamp

Highsteaks1403: im unarmed

He yanked the shower tap off and stormed toward his closet, snatching a pair of cargos off of a hanger with one hand as he fired off a text with the other.

587OriginalNK: where r u

Highsteaks1403: tree

Pulling his cargos on, he grabbed a shirt from his dresser and took off toward the communication room.

587OriginalNK: where r u? city? state?

Highsteaks1403: can't say

Highsteaks1403: what do i do

Slamming the com room door closed, he swung his chair around and fired up his computer.

587OriginalNK: how far away is he

Highsteaks1403: 30 yards

Plugging his phone into his computer tower, he opened the haunt's customized location application.

587OriginalNK: phone light

Highsteaks1403: under my sweater

He began tweaking the settings in the program, breaking through his own firewall.

587OriginalNK: weapons?

Highsteaks1403: none

Highsteak1403: going to go higher

"Fuck!" he snarled as he entered a code and crashed the app.

587OriginalNK: he'll hear you move. stay still

587OriginalNK: know vamp's name?

He reopened the program, his molars cracking as the page loaded.

Highsteaks1403: no

Highsteaks1403: under me now

Highsteaks1403: what do i do

He tweaked the code and re-entered it, willing his program to move well past its capabilities and dropping his head in defeat when it was unable to pull Highsteaks' location from the incoming messages.

587OriginalNK: when this is over we're going to talk about the dangers of using a scrambler on your phone

Highsteaks1403: promise

Highsteaks1403: im scared nk

Highsteaks1403: hes sniffing the air

He booted his desk in helpless frustration.

587OriginalNK: how far up are u

Highsteaks1403: 15-16ft

587OriginalNK: he's scenting the air. Tracking you. Wind must be on your side if he hasn't locked on

Highsteaks1403: i fucking hate vamps

587OriginalNK: I know

He ran his hand through his hair and began pacing the floor.

587OriginalNK: how good a shot are u

Highsteaks1403: very

A vamp killer.

He stared at his phone.

587OriginalNK: on go you're going to black the phone screen. when vamp turns his back to you, toss phone as far as you can AWAY from the bushes.

587OriginalNK: you'll have 5-8 seconds to drop, find, and aim

587OriginalNK: one shot is all you'll get off before he doubles back

Highsteaks1403: just passed me

Highsteaks1403: im downwind

Highsteaks1403: he knows

Highsteaks1403: knows im here

587OriginalNK: go

****

Highsteaks closed her messaging app and turned off

the screen, her hands damp and shaking. Lifting her head back out of her sweater's neck opening, she slipped her phone from under the hem and scanned the terrain, a chill traveling through her limbs as she watched the vampire turn his head from side to side.

Tracking you.

Her phone flew through the air, the obnoxious ring of an incoming call filling the night and masking her drop to the ground as it landed in the dirt. She dove for the bushes, fingers wrapping around the barrel of her crossbow. Her foot hooked in the stirrup as she scooped an arrow from the grass and cocked the bow, lifting and firing when the vampire lunged at her, phone in hand.

She bent to load a second arrow as her target fell toward her, disintegrating into a sludge which drenched her skin and hair. She dropped to her knees, her hands scrambling through the vampire remains to find her cell phone as her boss closed in on her. NK's voice called for her as she powered the bloody phone down and slipped it into her cargos.

"Nice work," her boss grinned, lifting his foot to check the filth on his sole. "A little messier than I like to see, but impressive nonetheless." He rocked back on his heels, his hands in his suit jacket pockets as he watched her rise slowly to her feet, his eyes scanning her from head to toe. "Worth every dime. Hit the shower and take the rest of the night off."

She limped across the field toward her room, her right ankle protesting with every step. Her hands left bloody imprints on the railings while she made her way to her small apartment, leaning against the door as she turned the heavy lock and entered her security code. She stripped down, easing the sludge-covered phone from her pocket, and setting it on her boots before she trudged to the shower to wash the stench of vampire from her body.

****

Nichol frowned, grabbing the stack of papers from Louis' hands. "Did I what?"

"The contractor estimates," Louis repeated, his gray-green eyes narrowing slightly. "Did you look them over?"

"Yeah. Of course." He scanned the bottom lines of each one for the first time. "I'll leave the decision to you and Mikhail."

Louis nodded, backing out of the com room. "We'll forward you the payment conditions once we decide."

Turning his phone over, he tapped the screen to life and pursed his lips.

Twenty-seven hours and counting.

The seconds between the unknown vampire answering Highsteaks' phone and the moment it went dead replayed in a loop in his mind.

The phone line connected, the rustling of fabric and the muted mutterings of a male voice crackling through the earpiece. He strained to identify the voice before it was replaced by the sounds of footsteps and wind.

He could yell.

Get the attention of the male.

Warn him of the vamp killer gunning for him.

But he stayed silent until the unmistakable sound of dead vampire echoed through the phone. He heard Highsteaks' shaking breath and the line cut out.

He ran his hand over his face.

He'd called out to her in a pathetic need to hear her voice, to know she was okay.

Chosen to align himself with a vamp killer.

His phone vibrated, another incoming call from the east coast. He answered, grabbing a pen and noting the name of the haunt leader as he reassured him the Kaius haunt was indeed backing the sanctuary city.

"We're ready to aid in whatever way necessary, provided our young vampires can venture into the streets safely," the haunt leader stated. "It will take us a few weeks to travel along the bolt holes."

He knelt at his computer and pulled up his list of incoming haunts. "Pack lightly. The mayor's announcement was premature, and light-tight spaces are few and far between." He scanned the list of temporary apartments available until the permanent intake residence was built. "How many hauntmates are we looking at?"

The leader's voice tightened. "We are down to three," he replied.

He sat back on his haunches. Though a young haunt, its members had been prolific creators and quickly gaining political clout along the eastern seaboard. "Alert me when you hit Colorado, and we'll arrange for someone to guide you into the city. Safe travels."

He ran his fingers down the computer screen, matching the incoming haunt names to the numbers the leaders provided.

Two.

Five.

Three.

"We moved too late," he whispered to himself. "Too fucking little, too fucking late."

Chapter Fourteen

Dominic's footsteps came up quickly behind Nichol before he fell into step. "Jagg needs you in the yard."

"Go get Boy," he groused, pushing past Dom to enter the com room. "I have blueprints to review."

"I dunno, man," Dominic pressed. "Jagg asked for you."

He fired off a text to Jagger, glaring when no response came. "Fine."

He followed Dominic topside, slamming the door closed behind him when he stepped into the unseasonably warm night. His speed slowed as he scanned his hauntmates. "What are you doing?"

All the haunt's vampires were standing together in the yard, the women milling around the outskirts of the group. Rhys and Boy were already shirtless, Mick and Louis pulling off their own and tossing them aside.

Jagger tugged his hoodie over his head. "Brawl practice," he stated as he began scuffing a large makeshift sparring ring into the dirt. "Get in there and I'll go over the parameters once the area is set." He looked Nichol up and down. "Shirt off."

He joined the others, folding his clothing and placing it on the grass before elbowing Rhys in the ribs. "What the hell is this about?"

"Don't know," Rhys replied, his eyes narrowing as Jagger approached the women, pellet guns in hand.

"What the fuck is that crazy bastard doing?"

Jagg stood between the two groups. "Rule one, stay within the boundaries. That's it." He looked over his hauntmates and grinned. "It's a free-for-all. Goal is to stay upright, so if you're held down for a five-count, you're sidelined. Fight at max strength and speed or don't. Fangs, fists, boots are fair game. Fight dirty or hang back. If you were smart enough to have weapons on you prior to entering the ring, good on you."

Louis, midway into his second century of existence, yanked a blade from his pocket victoriously. "You're going down, Boy!"

Boy's brows rose a fraction.

"What's their role?" Dominic asked, suspicious of the armed women encircling the ring.

"You're their moving target practice," Jagg stated nonchalantly. "Pellet guns with quick load." He smirked at Mickey. "If any of you have fucked up with your partners recently, now's the time to apologize."

Mick flipped him off and turned to Audra, waggling his tongue suggestively.

Dominic's eyes widened nervously.

Rhys smirked at Lis. "I fucking love that skirt."

Lis spun quickly, her filmy skirt fanning out. "As much as you love me?"

"Subtle, baby."

Jagger began walking the perimeter. "Ladies. Rule one is stay outside the line. Two is no hits to the eye or your new targets will be the forest. And that's not nearly as entertaining." He entered the ring. "If you go down, exit immediately. Last one standing in the ring wins. Go."

Nichol stepped out of the fray immediately,

assessing the few weapons pulled in the first moments of the brawl. Mick launched onto Rhys, a ball point pen in hand. Louis' knife was confiscated by Dominic who immediately found himself face down in the dirt, Jagger's weight holding him still while Molly blasted his legs with pellets. Boy, with a screwdriver in hand, stood motionless inches from the boundary until Audra's gun unleashed a spray of bright red pellets into his calves.

Louis' boot made contact with Nichol's stomach, sending him back a step before he regained his footing and took down his honorary hauntmate with ease.

"Damn, Nichol," Louis grunted from the ground. "You play computer geek so fucking well I forget you can destroy me." He offered a hand and brought Louis to his feet as Molly zeroed in on her new target.

He turned his attention to Jagg who had teamed up with Mick to bring Rhys to his knees, succeeding only when Lis began pummeling her mate with pellets.

"Lay off my ass, baby," Rhys yelled over his shoulder, bucking Mick off of his back.

"Not what you said last night," Lis countered, meticulously hitting the same site time and time again until Rhys and Jagg rolled into the dirt, fists and taunts flying.

Boy hit Nichol from behind, his fangs burying into his shoulder and piercing the muscle. Flipping Boy up and over, he ignored the annoying peppering of pellets coming from the perimeter, his attention on keeping Boy at arm's length. The vampires circled each other as Rhys succeeded in bringing down Jagger, earning an admonishment from Bianca.

"Full strength," he stated, flexing his hands as Boy nodded. "Let's see it."

His mind barely processed his hauntmate's movements as Rhys and Mick were eliminated from the brawl, Boy holding both males down by their throats while Jagg called out the count. The dead blue eyes turned to Nichol, who launched at Boy only to find himself met mid-air and flattened to the dirt.

The women were frozen in spot, brows shot high. The hauntmates instinctively crouched in defensive positions, their eyes moving between him and Boy.

"You're an extremely old bastard, aren't you?" he finally said, comparing Boy's speed and strength with ancients he'd encountered throughout his existence and realizing none could compare.

Boy held out his hand and pulled him to his feet.
****

Highsteaks1403: NK?

Nichol shoved his phone into his pocket and knelt down to watch Bianca scroll through the thousands of comments on The Rising's YouTube channel she and Jagg established and filled with pro-vamp videos. "Have Jagger note repeat offenders on both extremes," he said, pointing at one name he'd seen flash by three times. "I don't care if they want us fried or want us knighted, if they're on here more than five times, I want names and links to their profiles."

Bianca nodded, rubbing him on the shoulder carefully to avoid the bite Boy had left earlier. "We'll look into them," she assured him. "No need for you to have that on your plate as well, honey."

Bristling at the touch, he backed up and stood. "Then make sure you forward the list complete with any information you dig up."

With a sigh, Bee sat back in her chair. "Will do,

boss."

Ignoring Highsteaks' message until he was alone, he texted Jagg the same instructions he gave Bee, receiving a 'k' in response.

He passed by the common room on his way to bed, banging on the walls as he stomped by. "There better not be food in there, Molly," he yelled, continuing on his way and listening while Dominic and Molly scrambled to hide the pizza he could smell down the hall.

Rounding the corner to the bunkers, he stopped and glared at Rhys and Lis. "Your room's right there," he barked, motioning to the door three feet away from the half-naked couple against the wall. "Holy fuck, Rhys. No one needs to see your ass as much as I have."

When Rhys flipped him off without missing a beat, he flung his door open and slammed it behind him, mildly amused when Lis launched into a tirade about Rhys's superior hearing and his inability to stop being a such a horn-dog.

587OriginalNK: She lives

Highsteaks1403: she does

Highsteaks1403: thank you

He sat on his sofa and kicked off his boots.

587OriginalNK: don't mention it

587OriginalNK: any injuries?

Highsteaks1403: twisted ankle, nothing major

He sat back, stared at the coffee table, and pulled a vial from his pocket. What the hell else was he going to say? Good work eliminating another member of my hunted species, glad I could help? How's work, where you kill off my kind without a second thought? Could you forward me the name of the vamp you sludged so I can cross him off my list?

He dropped his head back and closed his eyes, letting a few drops of the blood hit his tongue and one of her last texts swirled through his head, reminding him why he needed to end this.

I fucking hate vampires.

He knew she did. Probably for good reason. But he couldn't deny how hard it hit him when he saw the words on his phone screen.

He hovered his thumb over the messaging app. He could delete it. Delete Highsteaks completely. Abandon the game accounts he'd given her, maybe set up under different tags once he had time again.

And risk running into her every time you log on.

"Fuck," he sighed, dropping his head forward in defeat and typing out a message.

587OriginalNK: I was worried about you

Highsteaks1403: Can I call?

587OriginalNK: yeah

He cranked the volume down as his phone lit up. "How bad is the ankle?"

Highsteaks' laugh sounded relieved. "Worst phone etiquette ever," she sighed. "Ankle's sore, but not broken. I landed on a root."

She sounded winded, earning a frown from him. "You aren't working again yet, are you?"

"Off for an undetermined amount of time," she replied. "So I'm going to practice playing your accounts and mine simultaneously to set up anyone who annoys me. I'll lure them in with my weak-ass characters and obliterate them with yours."

"An effective technique," he commented, reclining back as he relaxed a fraction. "I got my ass kicked in a sparring match tonight."

She snorted inelegantly. "I know how big you are. Were you fighting a Sasquatch?"

"Pretty much," he grinned.

"Are you hurt?"

Just fang marks.

"Just a scratch," he said, tugging at the neckline of his shirt to check the healing. "You should've texted me sooner."

She went silent for a moment. "Yeah, well, I almost didn't tonight, either." She sounded like she was moving around, the clunking of drawers closing in the background. "The hot and cold game you play is hard on me."

He frowned. "I—"

"You answered when it mattered," she interrupted. "And I'm grateful for that. I am. But it mattered before for me, too. Probably more than it should have. And you disappeared."

Glancing at the bunker door, he considered calling Audra up because he wasn't liking the tone or the words he was hearing, and he had no idea how to respond.

"I'm sorry," he said, repeating the only thing he could think to say and taking another taste from the vial.

"Don't be. I get what this is. I do. And it wasn't fair of me to push more onto you."

He sat up straighter. "You didn't push anything onto me."

"NK, the first person I thought of when that vamp had me cornered was you. A guy I don't know from Adam. I know nothing about you. Not your name, not your job, not even your age. Hell, I've never seen your face," she huffed. "You could be twenty-five and married with five kids for all I know."

"I'm definitely none of those," he argued. "What…" He ran his hand across his jaw in frustration. "What do you want from me?"

Chapter Fifteen

Nichol yanked a paper from the printer and tossed it onto the com room table. "Dovidas and Chen are expected to arrive at Stojanovski's within the month."

Rhys snatched up the email, scanning the document and passing it to Louis. "We lure him here and take him out on our turf."

"We meet him there," he stated, straddling his chair. He looked at his hauntmates. "Dovidas and Chen have a backer. An unknown."

Pushing his hood off, Jagg grabbed the email. "Then we take out all three here and end this once and for all."

"The unknown is an ancient," he said slowly before unloading the information Kaius had shared the week prior. He finished and leaned onto the table as his hauntmates processed the intel.

"All right," Rhys finally opened. "What's the plan?"

He looked to Boy. "I'll be needing you to join me at the Stojanovski compound. Louis, you as well. I'm willing to pay off Jackson to overlook your last interaction with him to have you lurking in the wings."

Louis put his arms behind his head, his pride over having successfully hypnotized Stojanovski still apparent. "Sure thing, boss."

"End the boss shit," he grunted. "Rhys, you'll be in charge around here until we return, with Jagg as acting second."

Rhys arched his neck to look at Lis. "I'm the boss now, baby."

"Sure you are."

He tossed a pen at Rhys, hitting him in the chest. "I'll make up a duties list for you to assign and oversee. I'll be available for questions, but I'll be leaving the bulk of the work for you."

Rhys nodded. "And that sucks. Thanks."

Audra stood up and leaned over Jagger's shoulder to read the email. "And you feel Stojanovski's intel is correct?"

"I feel Kaius's intel was correct, and this merely corroborates it and specifies a timeline," he replied.

Dominic shook his head. "So you, Boy, and Louis going up against Dovidas, Chen, and some other ancient? I dunno, man. Those odds don't sit well with me."

The other hauntmates murmured their agreement.

He ran his hand through his hair. "Compromise. Louis, Boy, and I are first in. When we get a definite ETA, we'll consider sending for the rest of you fuck-ups. Agreed?"

****

Audra folded Nichol's shirt neatly and added it to his bag.

"I can damn well do that myself," he grumbled.

"No, you can't," she laughed. "I've seen how you pack. And how you fold. And you are sorely lacking those skills."

He snatched another shirt from her hands, balled it up, and stuck it into the black duffle bag. "My way's more efficient." He repeated his technique with his cargos, socks, and boxers. "Done. You can go."

She sat on his sofa, crossed her legs, and looked at

him hard. "Mickey has some concerns."

"He'll snap out of it," he called over to her, slipping the last of his vials into his palm and sliding them into a side pocket of the bag.

"About you."

His jaw tensed.

Audra patted the couch cushion. "He has some valid worries about your emotional state, and I think we should address them before you leave." When he didn't move, her cat eyes narrowed into slits. "Now, Nichol."

He stomped over and sat as far from her as he could. "I'm fine."

"Of course you are. Mick's just noticed a marked difference in your overall affect during the last two weeks, and he wants to ensure there's nothing serious going on."

"Is he feeling how pissed I am right now?" he snarked.

"I hope he is. Because that would be more in line with your personality than the total calm he's been getting off you."

He felt his shoulders twitch slightly.

Audra shifted in her seat. "With everything that went down with Rhys, I'm sure you can understand why angry, hostile you becoming placid would be a concern for Mickey. He doesn't want to see another one of his brothers sink into apathy," she said. "We all know the amount of pressure you're facing right now. And, frankly, none of us are calm on the sidelines, so I can only imagine what you're experiencing."

His eyes flicked to his duffle bag. "I have a plan and I'm backed by a strong haunt."

"You've always had those."

"Yeah, well, they're mine now," he stated, the weight of the words sitting heavy in his mind.

Audra purses her lips. "Fair enough." She rose to her feet. "You'll tell me if something's amiss, right?"

"Whatever."

She bent down and hugged him, unfazed when he didn't return the embrace. "No risks, okay? We need you."

****

Nichol glared at Louis until the jangling of the keys stopped. "Follow me tight, keep your phone charged, and go tell Boy we leave in ten."

Louis slowly began rotating the SUV keys on his finger, increasing in speed as he left the com room. "Will do, boss."

Turning to Rhys, he clenched his jaw and scanned the lists he'd assembled. "Who started this 'boss' thing?" he grumbled, penning in another item he'd forgotten. "Any questions on this?"

Rhys flipped through the pages, his dark eyes widening. "What the fuck? How am I supposed to stay on top of this shit?"

"Designate," he stated, loading a bag with disposable phones, and carefully placing his laptop in. "I broke down the major projects into assignable tasks, eliminated anything non-essential for the time being, and created a single account for expenses until I return. I'll continue to monitor and tweak via internet, so I should be able to spot any problems before they hit."

Rhys tossed the papers onto the table. "This is bullshit. I'll do it, but when you get back, we're going to have a haunt meeting about the amount of stuff you've taken on." He pointed at one of the items. "Why can't

Molly or Bianca order the groceries?"

"Under you, they can. And once the order is compiled, they can email it to me, and I'll filter it through the household account. Questions?" he asked, swinging his bags onto his back and heading toward the garage stairs.

Rhys fell into step. "Text me the names of the vamps on site and I'll send you info on any Tenders accompanying them. And remember we have ears on the ground there. Use them."

He nodded, pushing the garage door open and shoving his duffle bags into the back of SUV. He turned the key in the ignition and pressed the button to lift the overhead door as the rest of the haunt trickled in.

Louis and Boy brought up the rear, the jangling keys finally going silent as Louis turned the engine and assisted Jagg with the weapons stashes before they joined the group. Nichol crossed his arms and met the expectant eyes of his hauntmates. "Don't fuck with the stereo settings, don't go into my bunk, don't touch my shit in the com room, and don't sludge each other. Louis, Boy, let's go."

****

Nichol pulled onto the winding roads leading to the Stojanovski compound, turned his headlights off, and eased up on the gas. Louis and Boy followed suit as they made their way to the perimeter gates and parked in an alcove far from the vehicles of the other guests.

"Once we scout the area, we'll determine the best way to smuggle these weapons in," he said, hoisting his bags onto his shoulders and bending down to set the custom security alarms on the vehicles. "If either of you needs to get into these without me, the code is five, eight, seven, fourteen, zero, three."

He fired off a text to Stojanovski and watched as the heavy iron gates swung open. The males crossed the grounds, their eyes and ears open to the sounds of the night's hunt. As one particularly shrill squeal pierced the air, Boy flinched.

"Dahlia?" Louis asked, grinning when Boy nodded, confirming the Tender's presence on Stojanovski's grounds. "Nice."

Smacking Louis' arm, he picked up speed. "It cost me a fleet of vehicles to secure your safety here. Don't make me regret it."

Louis saluted and glanced over at Boy. "A month of free-range hunting doesn't sound too bad, does it?"

Boy remained silent.

Stojanovski stood on his stoop as they walked up, his hands deep in his jacket pockets. "Nichol Kiaus," he greeted, his head tilting as another shout came from the marsh, the nightly hunt for humans in full swing. "I'll show you to your quarters myself."

Jackson led them across the back of the central building to a tiny house at the far reaches of the property. "Fully functioning facilities and a bedroom up here should any of you decide to bring your nightly conquests back. Though the humans themselves have similar quarters in the central hall if you prefer.

"The latch for the underground bunker is in the back corner of the room with a personalized security code you can change at will. Keep in mind I have the ability to override the system should there be an emergency, a contingency I guarantee to use only during Armageddon. I expect you'll join us in the hall tomorrow evening?"

He nodded, tossing his bags on the large bed that

took up most of the room. "Any word on Dovidas?"

"Nothing new," Stojanovski replied, scanning Boy with interest. "No Tenders with you this time?" Boy growled a low warning as Jackson smiled. "Your haunt really does have the best women. Next time you see Audra, tell her I say hello."

****

Nichol sat on the grass outside their accommodations, his arms draped over his knees as he listened for the final sounds of the nightly hunt coming to an end. Boy stood motionless beside him, his blue eyes obscured by the long shag of his hair.

"Are you hunting tomorrow?" he asked, scanning the darkness for signs of movement.

Boy nodded, his head tilting for a moment when a deer approached the perimeter fence.

"I want Louis tied to you while we're here," he ordered. "Until Dovidas arrives, it's nothing more than a waiting game, so you two have the freedom to do whatever you want in the evening hours provided you keep an ear open for intel. Agreed?"

Boy nodded again, pulling out his phone and typing out a message. He angled it toward him.

—*Hunt with us*—

He grunted in response, the prospect of fresh blood piquing his interest. "It's been a long time since you and I hunted together," he mused. "Why not?"

Chapter Sixteen

"Nichol Kaius," a booming voice called from the back of the hall.

Nichol scanned the room until his eyes fell on the ancient male calling his name. "Vanito," he greeted, motioning for Boy and Louis to follow. "I wasn't aware you'd come state-side."

The old vampire chuckled, sizing up Boy. "Just cutting through on my way north. I've heard many things about this compound and have yet to be disappointed." He looked over to the group of humans filtering down the stairs. "Stojanovski has some pleasant game on the premises."

"That he does," he replied, his eyes dropping toward the ancient's wrist. "A moment outside?"

Vanito smiled wide, his slightly misshapen fangs on full display. "I do love to barter. Follow me."

Boy and Louis moved to trail them.

"Just a quick discussion about the European political climate," he said as he pointed to the increasing group of human prey who would soon be filling the forest, plain, and swamp, their eagerness to be caught countered only by the gifts bestowed on those who hid the best and made the hunt an entertaining challenge. "Scent out your favorites and I'll be back."

Vanito led him around the side of the building. "Rhys is well?"

"Very," Nichol lied smoothly. "Your haunt continues to be quite prolific, I've heard."

"Unfortunately, yes," Vanito chuckled. "We've had to accumulate a vast amount of land to accommodate the bloodline." He held out his wrist. "Still indulging?"

"On rare occasions," he replied, his fangs lengthening at the offering. "The price?"

Vanito rolled his sleeve up, unaware it was his blood Nichol purchased through an untraceable network. "I have one of my line making his way from Houston. If you could put him on your list for accommodation until he is on his feet, I will consider that payment for several… withdrawals."

He pulled out his phone and fired off a text to Rhys. "Done."

His fangs sunk into Vanito's vein, the ancient blood hitting his tongue and working its way through his mind. He pulled four mouthfuls before pulling back and wiping his mouth. The high was intense and immediate, and he could feel his irises ovaling as his senses opened.

Vanito adjusted his sleeve to cover the bite and turned toward the hall. "Come, Nicholai. The bell will ring soon."

He rejoined Boy and Louis as Jackson took the center of the room.

"Gentlemen," Stojanovski called out, bringing the room to silence. "Tonight we will be releasing the humans all at once, ten minute head start. No kills, no damage to the product. Once you claim your prey, return here for a post-hunt celebration prior to indulging in your winnings."

A chuckle rumbled through the room as the countdown began and he stepped against the back wall to watch the excitement build. Boy and Louis paced the room, with Louis pointing out his favorites and elbowing Boy for a sign of agreement that never came.

The bell rang, the doors to the compound flinging open and the humans pouring into the darkness. Louis sauntered over to him. "We're heading out toward the forest," he said, glancing toward the exit. "Boy had his eye on a blonde."

He subtly braced himself on the wall as his balance faltered. "Stay away from Dahlia. No sense in poking Stojanovski's temper."

Louis nodded and returned to Boy, leaving him alone to try and refocus his mind. He pulled out his phone and scanned his emails, his fingers itching to pull up Highsteaks on his messenger app and reach out to her for the first time in two weeks.

"Fuck it," he growled, his thumb swiping the application to life.

587OriginalNK: hey

His eyes flicked between his phone and the crowd of vampires as the anticipation rose exponentially in the room.

Highsteaks1403: hey
587OriginalNK: busy?
Highsteaks1403: working

He ground his teeth, his eyes blurring the words on his phone when another warmth of the high washed through his veins.

587OriginalNK: I want to be whatever you need

Highsteaks' icon went gray as the ten-minute countdown ended, and he joined his hauntmates on the hunt.

****

Nichol unhooked his fangs from the petite brunette, cringing when she ran her hand across his chest. "Don't," he growled, backing away from her and averting his eyes from the bare thigh on display. "I'll walk you back to the hall."

The woman's smile morphed into annoyance. "Aren't you a Kaius?"

"Yeah." He opened the door of the small house and led her into the yard.

Her heels clicked behind him until she hit the soft ground and grasped his arm for support. "You know you can have me all night, right?"

"I'm good."

They walked in silence to the hall where a few humans and vampires were milling around chatting. He shrugged out of the woman's grip once they hit the hardwood, earning a huff of exasperation.

"So am I dismissed?" she asked, her arms crossing and eyes narrowing.

"Yeah," he replied, looking around the room for Louis and Boy.

The woman stormed off toward a group of humans, shaking her head in disgust as one of the females approached her. "So?"

"Nothing," the brunette spat. "Fed and pushed me out the goddamn door." She looked over to Nichol with daggers in her eyes. "I thought the Kaius vamps were supposed to be a good lay."

Ignoring the slight, he backed against a wall and watched the comings and goings of the vampires and their companions, his high too far gone to push any interaction outside of a brief nod toward the younger vampires brazen enough to approach him.

"Maybe he just didn't think you were hot," a heavy Boston accent commented from the fringes of the group.

He focused on the woman with the brown ringlets interspersed with thin rainbow stripes as she leaned against the wall and tapped away on her phone. She was dressed in jeans and a plain black shirt, the pristine cleanliness indicating she had not been one of the humans in the hunt that night.

One of Rhys's trainees.

Racking his brain for her name, he shifted his balance and continued to listen in.

The woman he fed off launched into a slew of insults that were met with a casual flip off.

"You know, I thought Rhys was full of bullshit when he said you can tell the difference between a Rhys-trained Tender and...not a Rhys-trained Tender," the curly-haired woman smiled, looking the woman up and down, a sneer crossing her face. "Aim lower than a Kaius male, Jess. Much, much lower."

He fired off a picture of the woman to Rhys and the response came in instantly.

—Simone. Stay away.—

Simone lowered her phone as the brunette, Jess, stormed over to her. Her scathing blue eyes looked Jess over from head to toe slowly and she leaned forward, pointing to a young vamp standing near the doors. "That's more your speed. Young, stupid, and horny. Save your gold-digging until you're actually worth the price."

Jess's hand flew up to slap the unfazed Simone. He stepped away from the wall as she made contact, pulling back when Stojanovski intervened.

"Room!" Jackson bellowed, towering over Jess and

pointing toward the stairs. "All of you."

The groups scattered immediately, their whispers carrying up the stairs as they made their way to their living quarters. He watched while Stojanovski looked over Simone's reddening cheek. "One of these days, that tongue will be gone," he warned, noticing Nichol briefly. He reached up to touch Simone's face, his eyes hardening when she flinched away. "Take the night."

Jackson sauntered over to him and mimicked his pose against the wall. "Your hauntmates are still perusing the grounds," he said, watching Simone slowly ascend the stairs. "I should have warned you your presence here has been quite the news for those humans in my hunt looking to be purchased."

He grunted, giving a quick head bob toward Dahlia as she walked in on the arm of a young vamp and waved to him. "I have no interest."

"They'll figure that out soon enough," Stojanovski mused. "Until then, you can expect to be stalked by the humans as enthusiastically as my clients stalk them." He grinned, flashing his fangs. "There hasn't been this much excitement around here since you graced our hunt with that stunning female. Audra, was it?"

Pushing off the wall, he walked toward the exit before he ripped his host's fangs out and shoved them up his ass. He yanked his phone out as he began wandering the grounds for Boy and Louis, stopping when Highsteaks pinged him.

Highsteaks1403: what r u up to
587OriginalNK: on vacation touring the grounds
Highsteaks1403: seriously? how long
587OriginalNK: few weeks
587OriginalNK: give me a chance

He stumbled on a low spot in the dirt, cursing under his breath as he righted himself and turned toward his temporary bunker.

587OriginalNK: Come on, HS. One chance

He entered the code into the hatch and descended the ladder as his phone ringer blared to life. "Hey."

"Give me one good reason why you deserve another chance," Highsteaks demanded, her voice hushed, the words strangely enunciated.

He closed the door to his room and lay back on the bed, another wash of warmth flowing through his limbs. "Because I'm an asshole, but I'm not a bad guy?"

"All guys are bad," she stated without apology. "I'll need something a little more than that."

"Because I like like you?" he offered, wincing with both the admission and the juvenile sound of the term. He closed his eyes and sank into the remnants of his high as it began to wane.

Highsteaks breathed out loudly. "Show me your face."

"You know I can't do that."

"Your name then," she countered.

He groaned in frustration. "Highsteaks. You know damn well we don't cross those lines."

"Yeah, I know," she sighed. "But I want to cross those lines with you. And you can't do it, can you?"

He tossed his arm over his forehead. "I can't."

"I know." She drew a deep breath. "You should take your accounts back. None of the passwords were altered, so you shouldn't have a problem logging in. I'll see you in the games, NK."

The phone line went dead. He lifted his arm and stared at the messenger app for a moment before holding the icon down and clicking the tiny x that appeared. He lay in the dark until Louis and Boy descended into the bunker and called out for him. His limbs felt weighted as he opened his door and faced the late arrivals.

"Good hunting?"

Louis rolled his eyes and looked at Boy. "Not exactly a hunt when the prey is jumping out at you, is it?"

Boy's nose wrinkled slightly.

He smirked. "Welcome to a drawback of being a part of the Kaius haunt. Apparently there are several humans gunning to land one of us."

Louis snorted. "Hear that, Boy? You're a hot commodity." He ran his hands through his bright red hair, spiking it higher. "I'm stuffed. See you at dusk."

Boy grabbed a cushion off the small sofa in the living area and propped it beside the ladder as Nichol dragged himself to his room and collapsed onto his bed.

Chapter Seventeen

Nichol lounged in the leather sofa, spinning a pen between his fingers as another young haunt leader approached him.

"Nichol Kaius?" the vampire inquired, his hands slightly open at his sides and head bowed a fraction in a show of deference.

"What."

The male sat down in the chair opposite him, his knee bouncing as he spoke. "I was told you're the contact for those of us hoping to relocate to Denver. Is it true you're establishing a sanctuary city there?"

He nodded without glancing over at the male. "Name of your leader, how many are in your haunt, and when you anticipate making the trek."

"Christopher Wyatt, age one-hundred fifty-seven. We have…" Nichol looked over as the vamp paused. "We're down to four. My sire is Wyatt Angelo. He'll be traveling with us from Wisconsin once we get him free."

Sitting up straighter, he pulled out his phone. "How many of you were there two years ago?"

"Eleven. Most were young ones."

He fired off a text to Rhys to book the accommodation, then another to Jagger for information about the safest route out of Wisconsin. "Hand me your phone," he demanded. "I'm going to enter Jagger Kaius's contact info in here. When you're ready to make the trip, get a hold of him and he'll provide you with a list of safe houses, bolt holes, and sympathizers who will assist you."

He fiddled with the phone for a moment and handed it back. "If you need a strategy to release your sire, Jagg's your contact for that as well. We won't plan or assist on the ground, but we'll get every scrap of intel you'll need to prepare an extraction yourselves."

Christopher Wyatt gripped his phone tightly and rose to his feet. "Thank you."

Thank you.

Seven hauntmates down in two years.

Pushing the guilt aside, he waved the vampire off and returned to his pen until Louis flopped down at his feet. "This place is like a smorgasbord. It looks like such an awesome deal, but once you glut yourself once, it loses its shine."

"I take it you won't be hunting tonight?" he smirked as the wiry male patted his stomach.

"Six nights is enough for me," Louis proclaimed, leaning his head back. "How much longer are we here?"

"A few weeks. Where's Boy?"

Louis grinned. "Go outside and see."

He swung his legs over the couch and stood, shaking his head when a willowy redhead began walking his way. He exited into the yard and scanned the moonlit terrain until his gaze fell onto Boy.

The tall male was unmistakable against the trees, his prowling walk and the slight crouch he held giving him away despite the numerous vampires still indulging in the evening's hunt. Against Stojanovski's rules, the women employed by the compound to provide a solid challenge for the vampire clients were anything but well-hidden. Every few yards Boy traveled, an arm or leg would drop from a tree branch or slip from the bushes. The women had figured out his preference for the woods and had placed themselves accordingly, their heavy perfumes and scented lotions filling the air and burning Nichol's nose.

"Boy!" he called out, motioning for the male to join him. Boy broke into a loping jog until he arrived at his side. "Having fun?"

There was a flash of ennui in Boy's eyes.

"Yeah, I get it," he muttered, stepping aside when a woman walked by on the arm of an older vampire, her fingers trailing his thigh as she passed. "I've heard all I'm going to hear tonight if you and Louis want to go underground with me for the night. Stojanovski has something planned for tomorrow night, so we might as well avoid this shit as much as we can now."

****

Vanito sidled up to Nichol as he, Boy, and Louis entered the hall at dusk. "My youngest informed me Jagger made contact with him yesterday," he opened, scouring the increasing crowd of vampires. "Care to go outside where we can discuss his situation in private?"

He turned to his hauntmates. "I'll be right back. If Stojanovski calls us to order, text me."

They sauntered through the exit and headed toward the secluded back wall of the building.

"Jagger has provided a list of numbers and locations for his trip," Vanito said, rolling up his sleeve. "I'm grateful for the assistance."

He could feel his fangs elongate and puncture his lower lip as he caught sight of the ancient's vein. "The fewer we lose, the more strength we gain in the long run," he said, forcing his attention to remain on Vanito's face and not on the exposed wrist. "And having the offspring of powerful vampires overseas benefits us greatly."

Vanito chuckled. "I would never deign to claim the Kaius haunt acted with pure altruism. But I am grateful nonetheless. My youngest is a wanderer, and knowing he will be close to your haunt reduces my anxiety tenfold." He held up his arm. "This could be an interesting evening. Might as well enjoy it to the fullest."

He hesitated, his ears tuning in to the sounds around them to ensure no one was within hearing distance before he sunk his fangs into Vanito's wrist and pulled in eight mouthfuls.

"You're going to be flying tonight," Vanito laughed when he finally unhooked his fangs.

He licked the last traces of blood from his lips, a burst of unease ricocheting through him as the high began to build. "I fucking hate crowds," he said with a huff, one hand on the wall as they headed back inside.

Vanito smacked him on the back, testing his balance. "You won't this evening, compadre."

Boy side-eyed him as he approached and stood alongside his hauntmates while Stojanovski made his way to the center of the room.

"Gentlemen," he greeted his guests with a flourishing bow of his head. "Tonight I have a treat for you. One of my delicious little females will be joining the others on the grounds…as prey."

The room erupted in whispers, a few cheers from the younger males while the regulars began to hypothesize who the unlucky woman was. Nichol, Louis, and Boy shared a look of mild confusion and great disinterest.

"Come on, princess," Jackson called up the stairs, turning back to address the room. "To the winner go the spoils...until dusk, that is," he chuckled. "But be warned, she isn't taken down easily."

Hollers of approval echoed from the back of the room when the newer vampires caught sight of Simone descending the stairs. Boy adjusted his stance slightly, as though preparing for battle. Louis crossed his arms, his face locked down.

Nichol tilted his head and watched the woman walk through the crowd and stand beside Stojanovski. She was dressed for a fight, her black tank top fitted for sleekness and her combat fatigues heavily stocked. A black jacket was tied tight to her waist and her hands rested on her hips, fingers wrapped around concealed knife handles.

"She's not fucking around," Louis whispered just loud enough for him and Boy to hear.

Jackson placed his hand on her lower back, fisting his fingers when Simone took a step forward. "I hope you all read over your liability waivers carefully before signing, because this one is armed and ready for a struggle," he joked, earning a polite laugh from the younger crowd.

"For those of you who don't know, Simone is a Rhys-trained Tender. She comes complete with every skill set a woman of her caliber is equipped with. Plus a few extras," he added, flicking Simone's hand aside and patting her blade. Several of the older males in the room murmured their appreciation, their interest piqued. Stojanovski met Nichol's eyes. "Simone, wave hello to the members of the Kaius haunt joining us this evening."

Louis leaned in to him as the crowd looked their way. "This is fucking sadistic, pretending she's actually going to have a chance going up against any of us and surviving."

Simone continued to stare straight ahead, her jaw twitching.

Unbothered by her lack of cooperation, Stojanovski began to pace the room. "Simone will be released first, with the remaining humans following as usual. We will adhere to the ten-minute head start from there." He looked across the crowd. "Who'll be gunning for my girl?"

Most of the vampires hollered their approval of the game, with several calling out to her.

His high was holding steady, the crest still a good while off. He turned to Boy and Louis. "Rhys needs to know this is happening to her, that Stojanovski is using her as some kind of sick bait."

Boy looked at the floor for a moment, then pulled out his phone.

—*Rhys knows. He created her.*—

Louis' mouth opened, then snapped shut. Nichol stepped into Boy's space, his chest an inch from his hauntmate's. "Created her? You mean trained her. She was at the haunt last year."

Boy lifted his phone, tapped at it, and turned it toward him.

—*Trained her to be both a Tender and a weapon, marketed her as a hybrid, a Tender-Assassin mix.*—

He ran his hand over his face and pursed his lips. "This is the boot on the ground he warned us about. I'm going to fucking kill him." He refocused on the woman standing stoically in the middle of the room, her eyes subtly flicking toward every sudden movement in her line of sight. "There are seventy vampires tracking one woman."

Jackson offered his arm to Simone, shrugging it off when she ignored him and walked slowly to the exit. "Out she goes," he called into the crowd as the doors shut and the rest of the humans filled the room.

Louis elbowed Boy. "Can you feel her?"

Boy shook his head.

"Of course not. Rhys wouldn't risk tethering her to you through a blood exchange. I'm going to fucking kill him. If she takes out one of these assholes, there's a straight line to Rhys's involvement. There isn't a single vamp in this room expecting the fucking prey to be vampire-trained and lethal." He lolled his head back against the wall. "How many Dovidas sympathizers has Jagger sent her way already? Fuck. Didn't we just deal with this shit?"

An obnoxious chime rang through the hall and the humans took off into the darkness. He stretched his arms over his head, the tingling in his veins temporarily pulling his thoughts from the potential political shit-storm Stojanovski was unwittingly unleashing. It was one thing to feed targets to a well-hidden assassin. It was something completely different to announce it in a room full of vampires teetering on the edge of savagery.

He closed his eyes and listened to the din around him as the clock ticked down.

"This isn't right," Louis hushed. "We need to get our hands on her. Some of these young ones are hitting full-on bloodlust."

He opened one eye and looked at the group of males to his right. "You and Boy take the mountains and swamp. I'll cover the plateau and forest." He zeroed in on an ancient rallying his bloodline into a frenzy. "If anyone else finds her first, offer a payout. A large one. This isn't a fair hunt."

Pushing off the wall, he began to lead the others through the crowd. Most of the groups parted as he walked, several vampires bowing their heads in deference. When they reached the exit, Stojanovski joined them.

"Watch your backs out there, gentlemen," he warned quietly before facing the crowd. "Ten, nine, eight…"

The doors flung open, and Nichol sprinted toward the plateau, the fresh night air countering the rising warmth of Vanito's blood. Boy and Louis tore across the yard toward the swamp, a dozen males following suit.

He ran through the plain, ignoring the few humans he noticed lying motionless in the tall grass. When he reached the middle, he turned around slowly to assess the terrain, searching for any signs of disturbance.

Not here.

He made his way to the edge of the forested land and stopped, listening to the dozens of males trekking quickly through the woods in search of the Rhys-trained Tender. The few victory shouts ringing out pierced the quiet of the hunt, drawing the attention of those vampires more interested in a fast snack than a trophy.

He walked leisurely through the forest, scanning the dirt, the brush, and the tree branches for Simone, using his fractured memory of her blood scent to assist him. As the first hour came to an end, the more impatient vampires had given up their search for the elusive woman, settling for the easier prey. The number of males stalking the woods waned significantly while he walked deeper into the trees. His phone buzzed intermittently with updates from Louis, keeping him grounded enough to forge ahead when his limbs began to grow heavier.

The deeper he walked, the taller the trees grew and the thicker the brush. His eyes dropped to the ground to scan for footprints in the dirt, his mind becoming hazier with every passing minute.

"Hey," a woman's voice whispered from above, sending his senses into overdrive.

His eyes traveled up the evergreen to a strange shape nestled in the thick upper branches. The ball unfurled slowly, one leg dropping down, then another. Pushing the hood of her jacket off, Simone began to descend the tree with inhuman grace.

"You caught me," she hushed from eight feet up. "Call it."

He took a step back, cursing himself for not being more aware of the weapons the woman was packing. "Show your hands," he growled.

Simone exposed her empty palms one by one, swirling them for his appraisal. "Call it before a vamp in full-out bloodlust does," she hissed, looking toward the edge of the forest. "I'll owe you."

"I could be one of them," he warned as he took another step back to give her room to jump down.

Simone landed smoothly on her feet and straightened, brushing herself off. "I'm hedging my bets tonight." She pulled her blades from her pockets and handing them to him, keeping her voice low. "I recognize you. I've fed you. The red-haired guy and the tall blond, too." She rose to her toes and looked behind his shoulder. "Call it. Now."

He pulled out his phone and fired off a text to Louis. "Got her," he yelled into the night, motioning for Simone to lead the way back the hall and smirking as shouts of anger and disappointment rang through the air.

Chapter Eighteen

Stojanovski greeted Nichol and Simone at the door as they arrived, his brows raised. "Not a single war wound?" he inquired, his eyes raking over them.

Simone pushed past him silently as he slowed his pace and addressed his host. "Are we expected to wait here until the last of the hunt is complete?"

Jackson rocked on his heels, his hands deep in his pockets. "It's customary on these bonus hunts, yes," he replied, tracking Simone through the hall. "Make yourself comfortable."

The dim lights of the room hit his eyes when he entered and made his way to the wall where Simone stood ready for attack. He crossed his arms and leaned back, flexing his hands rhythmically as Vanito's blood began to resurge through his system. His ovaled eyes scanned the incoming vampires and their human prey, watching for sore losers as they passed Simone and nodded begrudgingly at him.

Louis and Boy sauntered in, earning a small snort of amusement from him when they strode like kings through the crowd. They made their way to him and Simone, flanking them against the wall while the last of the hunters filtered in.

"Gentlemen," Stojanovski called from the exit. "Tonight's hunt has come to an end. Please take some time to allow your conquests to fuel up at the buffet before retreating to your quarters for the day. Humans are expected back on the premises twenty minutes after dusk." He motioned toward the Kaius males. "This evening's winner is Nichol Kaius, a vampire tough enough to go up against my Simone and come out unscathed. This time, at least," he added with a fanged grin.

He rolled his shoulders out and widened his stance as a handful of males looked at him in challenge before escorting their night's companions to the feast. Jackson wound through the room, touching base with his guests while he made his way to Nichol.

"You may retire to Simone's quarters at any time," he grinned, patting Simone on the thigh and chuckling when her nose wrinkled in disgust. "The security there rivals that of the compound systems, so you have my personal guarantee your time with her will not be interrupted." He feigned an apologetic tone. "Unfortunately, I can't allow her to join your haunt in your personal accommodations. It would be grossly irresponsible of me."

Simone's jaw tensed, her arms folding across her chest. Louis waited until Jackson was across the room and leaned over. "Hourly check-ins?" he asked Nichol, one eye on Simone.

"Hourly check-ins," he confirmed, pushing off the wall and swaying slightly until he regained his balance. He gestured for Simone to lead, the pressure in his head increasing as the evening's tension gave way and the euphoria of the peak washed in. Simone stormed past the humans milling around the banquet, snatching an unopened bottle of wine from the table.

Gripping the railing, he followed her up the winding

staircase to the top floor and looked down. "That's really high."

She continued to march ahead silently, her fingers flying over the keypad and flinging the door open. Without looking back, she disappeared into her bedroom. "Lock code's 148403."

He punched in the code to test it before closing the door and slumping against the corner.

Way too fucking high for this shit.

He glared at the closed bedroom door and pulled out his phone to text Rhys.

—Why am I locked in the Stojanovski hall babysitting a goddamn assassin Tender—

His phone buzzed back instantly.

—Fuck. Don't turn your back on that one—

He scanned the living room, noting the numerous weapons casually laying around. "Didn't Rhys teach you to keep your stash accessible only to you?" he called out, crossing the floor slowly and lifting a switchblade from the kitchen table.

The bedroom door opened, and she stepped back into the living room, bottle in hand. "Rhys taught me a lot of things," she sneered, taking a long drink of her wine. "I prefer to forget most of them." She flopped onto the sofa, her eyes narrowing. "What's the price for your cooperation tonight?"

He started flipping through numbers in his head instinctively until his fried brain caught up with her insinuation. "Rhys will be covering it with his fangs," he growled, leaning on the counter when his balance began to fail.

She lifted a remote, turned on the television, and took another drink from the bottle. "Might as well sit," she said, her Boston accent becoming more pronounced. "We have eleven hours to go."

Making his way to the couch, he sank into it and lolled his head back. "You gave yourself up. Why?"

She tilted her bottle and swished it around. "Because I remember you from the haunt. And as much of a complete dick as you are, my veins are intact and I'm not being fucked across that table right now, so I made the right call."

Staring at the ceiling, he snorted. "Sad state when I'm the best choice you have."

"Agreed."

The pair sat in silence, Simone polishing off the bottle of wine she'd snagged from the banquet and Nichol counting imperfections in the room's paint lines to keep him from passing out. He tracked her movements in his peripheral, ensuring she remained unarmed and cursing Rhys's name.

"He really is an ass, isn't he?" he grumbled, spreading out more as his body grew heavier. "Rhys. Total ass."

She scanned him as he stretched across most of the sofa.

"You remind me of someone," he muttered, his eyes closing as another intense wave poured over him. "Audra. Tough as hell. She survived the night in Stojanovski's game, too. Unarmed." He could hear himself slurring as he spoke. "Mick tries to mess with her, but she keeps him in line. She's a smart fucking woman."

He felt her weight lift from the sofa and opened one eye in time to see her drop back down on her ass. "Shouldn't drink so much."

An incredulous murmuring was the last thing his mind registered as Vanito's blood took over.

****

Nichol rolled onto his stomach and pushed himself up onto his knees, his fogged head working overtime to make sense of his surroundings. Grasping the top of an unfamiliar coffee table, he rose to his feet and stumbled toward the light of a bathroom.

What the fuck.

He leaned into the mirror, blinking his eyes into focus.

What. The fuck.

He reached down and hiked the open zipper of his cargos up, staring into the mirror at his bare torso.

What. The. Fuck.

Supporting his weight on the door frame, he stumbled out of the bathroom and leaned against the wall to process what he was seeing.

A woman sprawled across the sofa.

Two black shirts dangling over the arms of the couch.

An empty bottle of wine.

"Fuck," he hissed, running his hands through his hair, and scanning the room for his phone. "Fuck, fuck, fuck, fuck."

The woman grumbled incoherently and tossed an arm over her eyes.

Simone.

Assassin.

He crept forward, his gaze flicking between the floor and the woman until he caught sight of his cell lying face down under the coffee table. He knelt down and snatched it, his head spinning when he rose back up and opened his home screen.

8:17pm.

He reached for his shirt and eased it off the couch, wincing when the hem brushed against Simone's arm and she shifted. He froze until she stilled, then swung his shirt over his shoulder and inched to the door. With one hand on the doorknob, he punched in the code, slipped out of the room, and pulled the door tight behind him.

Fuck.

Thumping his head against the wall, he rubbed his jaw with both hands.

What the hell did I do?

He closed his eyes, willing the events from the day to appear in his mind as his imagination began to play out all the possible scenarios.

And the longer he went without recalling, the worse his speculations became. And his guilt.

He yanked his shirt over his head and shoved his phone in his pocket as he walked a jagged line down the hallway. The humans were beginning to move through the upper floors, their doors opening and closing, their voices carrying down the staircase while he tightened his grip on the railing and took the steps two at a time.

"Nichol," Stojanovski greeted as he crossed the hall toward the exit. "A good day?"

With a grunt, he pushed the large doors open and stumbled across the field to his bunker.

Chapter Nineteen

Louis peered over Nichol's laptop, his eyed narrowed with suspicion. "I thought Rhys had a handle on all that shit."

"Rhys is handling the grunt work," he said, transferring another sum into the haunt's temporary singular account. "I'm on details."

Boy stood at the base of the ladder, one long arm draped over a rung as he waited.

"Three nights of details?" Louis pressed, standing to his full height, and pushing his hands into his back pockets. "Stojanovski was asking about you last night. I'm not sure how long I can put him off before he comes knocking here looking for you."

He entered the adjusted bank balance onto a spreadsheet. "I'll be topside tomorrow. Enjoy the hunt tonight and text me if there's an issue."

Waiting until his hauntmates dropped the hatch and engaged the lock, he flipped his phone over and connected it to his laptop. A few taps of the keyboard, and his messaging app icon appeared on his cell. He unplugged it and logged in, his knee bouncing as the sluggish internet connected him.

Highsteaks' icon loaded, the small green dot beside her name giving Nichol pause.

This is a mistake.

He reclined back on the sofa and kicked his legs

onto the armrest as he tapped her name and opened a new text window.

587OriginalNK: how are u

The minutes stretched out as his message went unanswered.

He needed a distraction. Badly.

Full vials called to him from his duffle bag, eager and willing to ease the edge of the withdrawal he was experiencing. His muscles twitched and flexed every few minutes as his mind wandered to his secret stash, and the simplicity with which he could put an end to the restlessness that had taken over his mind and body.

Highsteaks1403: heading out for work soon

Highsteaks1403: what doing

*Highsteaks1403: * r u*

He felt himself smile briefly before his discomfort took over again.

587OriginalNK: taking a break

Highsteaks1403: a break from vacation?

587OriginalNK: I get tense when I'm forced to relax

Highsteaks1403: that made me lol :)

587OriginalNK: can I call you

Highsteaks1403: gtg now but will call in the morning

Her icon went gray and he glanced at the time.

Ten hours.

He could last ten hours.

He turned his phone's volume to max and tossed his arm over his eyes to block out the minimal light in the bunker. His right leg kicked out involuntarily, earning a groan of frustration as images of three days prior flooded back into his head.

He'd been slowly piecing together the events at

Simone's, and those sporadic scenes played on an unyielding loop in his mind.

Flashes of her straddling his waist as he pushed her shirt over her head.

Flashes of his hands winding through her unruly curls while they kissed.

Flashes of her nimble fingers lifting his own shirt up as her tongue moved across his chest.

He grabbed a pillow off the floor and shoved it under his left knee to still the bouncing that had resumed.

No sex.

The only saving grace he could cling to was that he hadn't slept with Simone. He could lock the indiscretion away, far from the place in his head where Highsteaks resided.

Cheater.

The thought was ridiculous and unnerving. Highsteaks wasn't a consideration in his actions.

At least, she shouldn't be.

He could still feel the thump across his spine when he hit the floor with Simone, jolting both of them out of the moment and leaving him to pass out in peace. His right leg shot out again, and he stood, tossing the useless throw pillow aside and storming to the bathroom to steam the poison from his body. He stripped down and got under the spray, scrubbing every spot he could feel the remnants of Simone's hands.

He fucking hated being touched.

And he fucking hated the blood that made him want it.

When the water finally began to run cold, he dressed quickly, ran a comb through his hair, and ignored the reflection of his paling skin and darkened eyes.

He felt like hell. He sure as shit didn't need visual confirmation that he looked it.

He paced the enclosure, one eye on the time. His restless limbs needed more, needed an open field to push them to their limits and exhaust them until Vanito's blood worked its way out of him.

Two drops could end this.

Shaking the thought off, he continued to prowl the hall until his phone rang, echoing in the cement bunker.

"What."

"Stojanovski's put Simone back in the game," Louis whispered, the sound of the background din muffling his words. "She just went out, fully armed like a challenge. It's nuts in here, man. I think Boy and I are the only ones holding off the bloodlust."

He bristled at her name. "She hit the woods last time. Start there."

Louis went quiet for a moment. "Sure thing, boss."

Tossing his phone onto the sofa, he resumed pacing. He stretched his arms over his head, cracking his back and arching his neck to ease the building tension before snatching his phone up and climbing the ladder.

****

"I was never that stupid as a newbie," Louis grumbled as a chorus of howls rang through the air. "I know I wasn't. I had couth, man."

Boy nodded, ducking his head to avoid a branch.

Nichol pointed to the eastern side of the forest. "You two start on that side and meet me in the middle. Stick to the thicker areas and look high. She's a climber."

Louis and Boy jogged off, Louis giving a quick salute as he took off.

The woods were crawling with vamps anxious to get

their hands on Simone. The weaker ones snagged the nearest humans, desperate to indulge in the bloodlust overtaking most of the vampires on the premises.

Fucking Stojanovski.

Louis had been quick to report when they met up at the edge of the forest. Leading Simone through the hall, Jackson had scored a thin line across her throat to rile his guests as the scent of her blood was dispersed through the building. Even the ancients had begun to fall when they took in the visual of the red trails falling down her neck to her collarbone.

He picked up his speed as a large group threatened to overtake him, focusing on a lower cluster of pines and relieved when the vampires turned their attentions that way as well. Slipping away from the mob, he continued his path toward the tree he'd found her last. When there was no sign of life there, he fired off a text to Louis and walked deeper in.

The thickness became almost impassable as he neared the outer perimeter of the compound. His progress slowed significantly as he alternated his attention between the high branches and the cluster of overgrown shrubs at his feet.

"What the hell?" He knelt down and reached under a bush to pull out a perfectly smooth wooden rod. He turned the weapon over in his hands to examine the tip, dropping it as recognition set in.

He backed away from the bush, his back molars cracking under the strain of his clenched jaw. Scanning the area, he reached down to brush a light dusting of ash from a leaf.

No. Fucking. Way.

Scooping the arrow from the dirt, he shoved it into

the back pocket of his cargos and continued to push through the trees, his shoulders knotting as he pulled out his phone and fired off a quick message.

The faint buzz to his left dropped his stomach to his knees.

He stepped over a fallen log and leaned against his chosen tree. "I'm here," he said quietly. "You can come on down."

There was a rustling above, a few pine needles hitting his boots as Simone descended from the top branches. "Are you going to call it?" she asked, the Boston accent that had thrown him so easily returning.

He looked down at his phone and fired off another message, dropping his head back against the bark when her phone buzzed. "Got her," he called into the night as he began to make the long walk back to the hall. "Turn your fucking phone to silent, Highsteaks."

Chapter Twenty

Simone kept her eyes straight ahead while Stojanovski made his rounds, his slimy hands squeezing her shoulders when he passed behind her. Nichol Kaius was equally stoic beside her, his only movements the involuntary twitching of his muscles while he stood with her and waited for Jackson to finish his announcements.

"Again, the Kaius haunt emerges victorious and unscathed from the hunt," Stojanovski bellowed into the hall. "Nichol, we didn't see you at the start of the game."

He widened his stance, as though expecting an attack. "A lucky break during my evening stroll, I suppose," he replied, his flippant answer garnering a few chuckles from the older vamps.

Jackson's eyes darkened slightly. "Then congratulations to you and your luck," he said with a Cheshire smile, lifting his head back to the crowd. "Gentlemen, enjoy the rest of your night."

Louis and Boy flanked Simone and Nichol as they made their way to the staircase, Nichol pausing intermittently to arrange meetings with the compound's new arrivals. She listened carefully while Nichol took names and numbers, his rough demeanor taken in stride by the vampires seeking his help.

"Hourly texts," Louis stated when they reached the bottom of the steps. "Don't forget this time."

"Hourly texts," Nichol echoed. "Mingle until dawn

and we'll reconvene tomorrow at dusk."

The wiry red-haired vamp saluted and elbowed the tall mute blond in the ribs. "You find us a friendly bite, I'll find us a talker."

She gripped the railing and started the long walk up to her apartment on the top floor.

"That ankle's still bothering you," Nichol stated flatly behind her. "I didn't notice you favoring it earlier."

Closing her eyes for a moment and taking a deep breath, she continued the climb. "I got distracted and forgot to wrap it before I came down."

She could hear Nichol's heavy boots at her back, the steady rhythm pushing her to the top of the staircase and down the hall. She punched in her code, opening the door when the lock clicked open. "Same as before," she said, waiting in the doorway while Nichol tested the code for himself.

"You'd be wise to change the code tomorrow morning," he said, closing the door and standing against it with his arms crossed, his hazel eyes looking everywhere but at her.

She unloaded the weapons from her cargos, keeping one eye on Nichol as she lined them up on the kitchen counter. "You're the only biter who knows the code," she stated, cringing at her casual insult. "Vampire."

His lips tightened across his fangs and he went silent.

"I'll be back in a few minutes," she muttered, suddenly feeling exposed without her arsenal.

Her bedroom door slammed louder than she intended, the sound echoing in the small room. She knelt down and unlaced her boots, her mind whirring.

Turn your fucking phone to silent, Highsteaks.

Nichol fucking Kaius.

NK.

The snarky, intimidating vampire who would storm through the Kaius haunt during her time training there, his phone tight in hand while he barked orders.

The powerful vamp Stojanovski despised for his influence and admired for his control.

The biter the women on the compound fought to gain the attention of in hopes of being linked to one of the most prominent vampires in the country.

She placed her boots in the corner of her room, straightened her back, and opened her door.

Nichol remained in position, unblinking eyes slightly ovaled as he refused to acknowledge her return. She crossed the floor, staying tight to the countertop to avoid any accidental contact while she poured herself a glass of water and looked inside her small fridge.

"How did you know it was me?" she asked, pulling a plastic container of strawberries out and closing the fridge door.

He uncrossed his arms and reached behind him, pulling one of her crossbow bolts from his back pocket and setting it on the counter. "The ground was well-rinsed, but you may want to remind Stojanovski to wash down the surrounding bushes when he cleans up your kills."

She picked up the arrow and ran her fingers along its length. "I must have miscounted how many I brought with me that night."

Nichol was back in place, his gaze on the back wall and arms crossed over his chest again. Setting the bolt back down, she leaned against the counter and popped a strawberry into her mouth. "Why didn't you tell me what you are?"

"You never asked."

She pursed her lips and stared absently at the counter. "You knew damn well what I think about biters, and you didn't say a word."

Nichol's eyes blackened slightly, his locked expression remaining unchanged.

"It figures the one escape I had from your kind turns out to be…this," she laughed humorlessly, gesturing toward the motionless vampire. "Tell me this is a fucking joke."

She pushed past him and paced her small living room, her attention falling onto the gaming console Stojanovski had awarded her after her first kill. "So I guess I know what the NK stands for. What's the rest?"

"Birth year."

"I…" she paused, doing the math as she ran her hands through her hair, her fingers tangling in the curls. "You should have told me."

Nichol stretched his neck to the side for a moment before returning to his statuesque pose.

"Anything to screw with humans though, right?" she goaded, her anger rising when he refused to react. "You biters are so superior, playing with us little rats, aren't you? Making us do tricks to keep you entertained." Her lip curled in disgust. "How long did you intend to keep your experiment on me going? Another month or two? A year?" She shivered. "Oh god. You kissed me."

His jaw twitched, his eyes becoming blackened slits as a low growl filled the room.

Her gaze moved to her stash of weapons on the counter.

He could kill you in a heartbeat.

"You. Kissed. Me."

She looked over at the vampire blocking her door, his fangs extending past his lower lip. "What?"

He flexed his fingers. "I don't remember much about that night, but I know that. You kissed me," he snarled, locking his black irises on her. "So fucking repulsed by vampires you mounted me on the couch."

"I know how to stay alive around here, how to play the fucking game," she hissed.

"Game," he scoffed, shaking his head. "What game? I'd already pulled your ass out of the line of fire and was doing just fine crashing on your sofa for the day." He turned his back to her and punched in the pin code.

She took a step forward as he flung the door open. "What are you doing?"

"I don't need this. I have work to do."

****

Nichol's boots echoed rhythmically through the empty hall as he walked the length over and over, his fangs finally receding enough to stop the constant piercing of his lower lip. It would be another two hours before he could safely exit the building and make his way to the solitude of his bunker, and the clock was ticking down way too slow for his taste. His phone was tight in his fist, buzzing intermittently with incoming emails and hourly check-ins from Louis.

The only vampire he wanted to talk to was Rhys.

And 'talk' wasn't quite the word.

Mutilate. Pulverize. Those were more accurate.

He slumped onto one of the ornate sofas, his knees bouncing as he attempted to occupy his time with responding to the messages he'd ignored during the evening. Requests for help, requests for meetings, requests for money. He copied and pasted his answers from one to the next, changing identifying details and ensuring he addressed the senders by name.

Oh god. You kissed me.

Simone's voice intruded into his thoughts as he worked, the accusation and disgust as tangible in his head as it was when she spoke.

He'd missed so many signs. The hours she worked. The mystery of her location.

The vampire attacks.

With the rapidly declining population, Highsteaks' opportunities to encounter vampires while working a regular night security shift would have been almost non-existent.

He pulled up his email and opened the folder where he kept Jagger's intel messages. He scanned through them, searching for the names of the Dovidas supporters that had been forwarded to Stojanovski and his assassin until he came across the one he was looking for.

Marcus Cornelius.

The timing matched perfectly, his name sent to Jackson a week before Highsteaks texted Nichol for help.

Simone. Not Highsteaks.

He stared long and hard at the name of the vampire he'd assisted in staking. A young opportunist without a sire, a rogue following promises of power and wealth.

Your kind.

Nichol ran his tongue over his fangs.

He'd known.

He'd known Highsteaks would stop speaking to him once she knew what he was.

He'd known her playful tone would flip to utter

revulsion.

He'd known her concern would be replaced by contempt.

Without knowing her name, he knew her.

He sat back and flexed his restless fingers. "I don't need this."

Chapter Twenty-One

Simone sat at the top of the stairwell watching the festivities, largely ignored by the crowd. The compound's humans milled around the visiting vampires, their voices and chatter light while Stojanovski made his rounds. Networking evenings were frequently slotted into the monthly calendars, with esteemed guests such as the Kaius males drawing larger numbers of visitors than the hunting nights themselves drew.

And from her vantage point, Nichol didn't seem impressed with the lure of his presence.

Vampires were lined up to speak with the surly vampire, several holding files and papers that would be glanced at and tossed into a growing pile on the floor, the vamps summarily dismissed with a dead stare. The odd one received a small nod, with one earning a whispered aside.

He really is a pompous ass.

Nichol was noticeably absent during the prior night's hunt. She had been granted a reprieve from partaking, Stojanovski wanting her to remain unharmed and well-rested in anticipation of future compound guests who would be making their way onto her hit list. With the visiting vampires well-warned to keep their distance from her, she had been free to walk the grounds and observe the hunting techniques of the latest round of guests against their unarmed—and pathetically willing—prey.

She had noticed Boy standing in the shadows of the forest, always facing her yet never quite looking her way. Louis had been less subtle in his watchfulness, passing her frequently and commenting on the noisiness of the younger vampires participating in the nightly event.

But no Nichol.

She shifted to a higher step and examined the new faces of the evening. It was the largest crowd she'd seen since her first months on the compound, before the Deepfryers were legalized. Before her trainer made international headlines for his capture and subsequent escape. Before Stojanovski gained enough trust in her to allow her free rein on the premises.

Before she'd earned her first reward of a computer for a kill.

Before she logged in and saw 587OriginalNK obliterating every player he encountered online.

She watched the subconscious flexing of Nichol's hands while he listened impatiently to two vampires arguing loudly over a territory dispute. His stillness was artificial, his muscles tight to maintain the motionless old males were known for.

Jonesing.

She'd seen the behavior dozens of times during her pre-vamp life, long before she'd been pulled into the back of a semi-trailer while walking the backstreets of Boston: addicts fighting against the cravings driving their thoughts and their actions.

With movements too quick for her mind to register, the disagreeing males were on the floor, Nichol's hands wrapped around their throats. She jumped to her feet, fascinated by the control he exhibited as he restrained the thrashing vampires under him. Louis and Boy looked on with mild interest while the rest of the room stilled.

"Do *not* waste my fucking time again," Nichol snarled, kneeling between them as though he was flattening a rug and not holding down two sets of snapping fangs. "You come to me to solve your petty shit, make me listen to your inane arguments, then my word is law." He bounced their heads off the floor and rose to his feet, glaring at the onlookers. "Anyone else care to challenge my verdicts? No? Good. Leave me the fuck alone for the rest of the night."

Abandoning the pile of paperwork on the ground, Nichol stormed through the hall and out the door. All eyes turned to Boy and Louis, hers included.

"The boss has spoken," Louis grinned while Boy carefully picked up the stack of files. "Word of advice for those of you thinking of approaching him tomorrow for anything stupid: don't."

****

Nichol sat forward on the sofa, looking over the list Louis had compiled. "So we have two verified scouts and one potential?" he asked, firing off the names to Jagger and Bianca.

Louis kicked his feet up and crossed his arms behind his head. "The scouts are young. Probably in their seventies. They met at the far corner of the plains perimeter to discuss Dovidas's arrival next week."

"Any other intel?"

Louis smirked. "The pale one thinks getting tight with you would be a good cover. The short one thinks he's an idiot. And apparently Nichol Kaius doesn't leave the haunt much, so your extended presence here is throwing Dovidas and his partners."

"My extended presence here is throwing me," he grumbled, checking his emails. "So they didn't see you?"

"They saw me," Louis clarified, closing his eyes. "But they won't remember me."

"Nice work. Bianca's putting together a profile for each of these names, and we should have all the info we need by tomorrow night." He glanced over at Boy. "You two rest up, I'll be on watch. I'm in a pissy mood and gunning to answer some whiny texts."

He fiddled with his phone while the others retreated to their rooms for the day, disconnecting from his wifi booster and reconnecting under another VPN before responding to the messages he'd been ignoring all evening as his thoughts continued to loop.

Fucking vampires.

Fucking Tenders.

Fucking spam.

Fucking—

Nichol narrowed his eyes as a new email pinged in. He read the short message over a few times, contemplating the stupidity of responding but doing it anyways.

—How did you get this address?—

Forcing the distraction from his head, he continued to weed through his inbox until a reply came in.

—my boss. get back on messenger—

He rose to his feet and began pacing the short hall. There was absolutely no need for him to download the app again. No need to clutter his phone with another icon.

And he sure as shit wasn't in the mood to have another strip torn off him.

His phone pinged again.

—come on biter—

His ran his tongue over his fangs.

She was fucking baiting him.

He leaned against the wall and glared at the phone, his mind examining every scenario it could conjure as to her rationale.

He was on her list.

She figured out his economic value surpassed her hatred.

She needed his X-Box logins.

She was bored.

He downloaded the app and watched the icon load.

587OriginalNK: don't call here

Highsteaks1403: I won't

Highsteaks1403: you were pretty pissed tonight

He had seen Simone sitting at the top of the stairwell, her hunting gear exchanged for ripped jeans and an oversized green sweater. He'd noticed her watching the room like a predator, every quick movement catching her eye, her muscles tensing.

587OriginalNK: I'm pretty pissed most nights

Highsteaks1403: I noticed

Highsteaks1403: why do they all go to you for help when there are older vamps or their own sires

He paused for a moment before deciding Simone knew enough about vampire politics to make any information he provided little more than clarification.

587OriginalNK: The Kaius name is synonymous with power due to our creator, and due to Kaius's own sire. I was essentially born into a dynasty and as the eldest, my word is an extension of Kai's.

Highsteaks1403: so the biters you sired have the

same power?

587OriginalNK: I've created no vampires, but if I had, yes. Anything else?

Highsteaks1403: how did Kaius or his creator gain power

587OriginalNK: Through stories and rumors. And obliterating enemies who refused to see reason.

587OriginalNK: Shouldn't your screen name be Highstakes1403?

Highsteaks1403: I'm a crappy speller and you know it. Back off.

Highsteaks1403: what's your poison?

587OriginalNK: ?

Highsteaks1403: your addiction. i thoughts biters couldn't take drugs or drink

His hand grazed the small flask Vanito had passed him in the hall.

587OriginalNK: Not your business. Who's next on your hit list?

Highsteaks1403: not your business. see you tomorrow

****

Simone set her phone down and hunched over her knives, wiping each down with a dish towel. Stojanovski was being unusually silent about her next target, merely hinting it would be a tough one and it would be soon. She leaned over a large unopened box from the day's delivery and sliced the packing tape carefully.

A new crossbow. Complete with a supply of bolts.

She eased it out of the box and examined it, running her fingers along the barrel.

Nice.

Dropping to her knees, she flipped the box over for

the delivery label. The high quality of the weapon was counter to Stojanovski's relative cheapness when it came to outfitting her with an arsenal.

The weaponry Rhys had used to train her had been infinitely better than the supply Jackson had ordered up for her. She had been forced to tweak her aim to adapt to the slight curve of her old crossbow's flight track, a lesson learned after almost being taken out by an ornery biter early in her hunting. Her blades were no better, the longer knives warping and snapping during practice, leaving her unwilling to use them for anything more than a backup weapon.

The sender shipped out of a PO box based out of Nevada, labeled as a gaming system from a Mr. Cam Pewter.

She narrowed her eyes and stared at the name for a moment before picking up her phone.

Highsteaks1403: why did you send this to me

Repackaging the weapon, she carried the box to her bedroom closet, slid it into the back, and placed her long, useless ballgowns in front of it.

587OriginalNK: your bow is shit

Highsteaks1403: why

There was a long pause. She sat on the edge of her bed and waited.

587OriginalNK: Stojanovski's assassin has taken out every target our haunt established as a traitor to the species. And she's done so with inferior weaponry and inferior camouflage. The least we can do is ensure she's adequately armed, as it's apparent Stojanovski didn't see fit to do it himself. More packages will be arriving within the next 48 hours.

Highsteaks1403: i'm killing off biters

587OriginalNK: Through my indirect orders. I cannot fault you for that.

Chapter Twenty-Two

Highsteaks1403: southern quad of the swamp
Nichol glanced at the message before closing it out, pocketing his phone, and continuing with the video conference.

"Prepare for a departure time of dusk tomorrow," he said while Louis nodded in confirmation. "We can expect Dov—"

"Have you booked our accommodations with Stojanovski?" Audra inquired, waving Mick's hand off her neck as she leaned forward.

He frowned. "Women will not be included on the ground for this mission," he stated, sitting back until the din of protest lulled. "The bunker we're currently occupying is large enough to accommodate others. However, we anticipate a full house. Dovidas and Chen are confirmed, with a luxury bunker booked under a pseudonym we can only assume is the unknown backer."

"So you need all the help you can get," Bianca stated, crossing her arms and looking mildly intimidating, even over a computer monitor.

"What we need," he continued, "is no distractions or complications we can actively avoid. Stojanovski has been catering to bloodlust during our time here. Women on the premises will be hunted, regardless of their tie to any vampire on site." He leaned forward onto his elbows. "Molly, you're a good shot. But this is unfamiliar territory and any strategic placement of you would require me to assign Dominic AND another to guard you."

He turned his attention to the cat eyes narrowed in his direction. "Audra, you've survived this place. We all know it. But if you take one step on this property, Stojanovski will be gunning for you. On his land. With his rules. Your presence would pull Mick and likely Boy off the mission."

Mickey growled quietly until Audra's elbow met his ribs.

"Bee, you're too well-known. While your reputation would likely keep you untouched, you would be inundated with requests for help and favors. And although you would pull some of that networking bullshit off of me, Jagger would need to remain at your side and would be no help on the ground," he explained, relieved when her arms uncrossed and she nodded slowly. "Lis?"

Lis sat up straighter, her fingers twisting nervously around a pen as Rhys moved closer to her. "Yes?"

"You know why you can't come here," he stated. "A Master-killer on site wouldn't be well-received, which would keep Rhys distracted with ensuring your safety. And since there's already one assassin undercover here, we can't risk it."

Rhys met his eyes. "How's she doing?"

"She's well-trained," he replied, keeping his voice level. "Very good. Ill-equipped, but I'm taking care of that." He sat back and tilted his head. "You didn't include a minimum weapon quality addendum in the contract."

All eyes turned to Rhys. Boy and Louis exchanged

a quick look.

Rhys ignored the attention, his jaw twitching slightly. "An oversight you're rectifying through backchannels, I assume?"

"A careless oversight," he corrected. "But yes, your assassin-Tender hybrid is being properly outfitted in anticipation of Dovidas's arrival. However, I've been unable to determine if Stojanovski will be adding Dovidas or Chen to her list."

Audra cleared her throat. "While I know we all have some questions for Rhys regarding this 'assassin', I'd like to know who you want traveling tomorrow, who will be staying behind, and what our roles will be during this mission."

He pursed his lips. "Louis will be driving back to the haunt tomorrow. His work here is done and yielded a lot of information I've forwarded to Jagger."

Jagg nodded, lifting a stack of papers from the table. "I'll be reviewing the intel with the others once we're done here."

"I've run every scenario I could think of to best address the Dovidas front and the ongoing sanctuary establishment effectively." Running a hand through his hair, he dropped his gaze for a moment. "This mission requires age, skill, and speed. The other requires organization, visibility, and communication. Boy and myself will remain at the compound. Rhys, you'll be joining us tomorrow. Jagg, you're in charge of the haunt in our absence. All decisions will be finalized with your word, no need to pass anything through me until our return."

The hauntmates were silent, Jagg giving a single nod of acceptance.

"Mick, you're acting second. Dominic and Louis will answer to you to free up Jagger for the amount of work he'll be facing while we coordinate housing, security, vetting, and public relations with the mayor and his council," he listed off, his stress beginning to rise as his mind rolled through the enormous number of tasks each of those areas required. "Rhys, arm yourself well. Jagger will outfit you with as many small weapons as he can, anything we can smuggle in without notice." He scanned the women. "I expect each of the you to work alongside your partners. You answer to Jagger and will be taking orders from Bianca."

Lis's eyes flicked to Rhys.

"Lis," he called, bringing her attention back to him. "Rhys's absence places you in a unique position, given my previous rules about your level of freedom and movement within the haunt." Ignoring Rhys's low snarl, he pressed on.

"You'll be partnering with Louis until our return. His assignment includes nightly tours of Denver's perimeter for early arrivals or vampires we've yet to approve. I trust you understand the level of freedom you're being granted and will ensure I don't regret this decision."

Louis flopped onto the sofa beside him and grinned into the camera. "Just don't ash me, and we'll be all good."

****

Simone rose from the mucky water of the swamp land, flinging her filthy ringlets back and spraying Nichol down in the process. The look of disgust on his face was mildly amusing.

"That was a bitch move," he stated, taking a step

back and gingerly shaking off what mud he could from his bare arms.

Hoisting herself onto the slippery bank, she began squeezing the water from her hair and clothes, running her hands over her face to remove some of the more stubborn residue on her skin. "Coming from the king of bitch moves, I'll take it as a compliment."

She knelt down to unlace her boots, dumping the water out before sloshing her feet back in. "Jackson handed me new targets. No names. Estimated arrival date of Tuesday, but I'm under orders not to attack until I'm given explicit instructions."

The biter—Nichol—remained motionless, his eyes slightly blackened. "Sensitive intel to be imparting on the enemy, don't you think?"

She strode past him and pulled her new bow from under a bushel of cattails. "Just figured you'd want to see this baby in action," she replied casually, glancing toward the main building for signs of movement.

He slipped his hands into his pockets and rocked back slightly on his heels. "You want backup."

"Will I need it?"

Nichol's jaw tensed, the sound of his grinding teeth at odds with the stillness of the night. "Knowing what I know about your potential targets, *I* need it."

She felt a small chill rumble through her bones. "They're that dangerous?" she asked, trying unsuccessfully to keep the nerves from her voice.

He tilted his head. "If Stojanovski is gunning for the same vamps I am, yes. But I'm not stupid enough to believe your boss holds any loyalty to me." He looked her in the eye, his lips tight across his fangs. "And in that case, I suspect Rhys's little hybrid experiment may be on the hunt for me before the month runs out."

Frowning, she hiked her bow into her shoulder and crossed her arms. "You seriously think I'd hunt you?" she demanded, almost insulted.

Nichol's low chuckle rumbled deep in his chest. "Yeah, Highsteaks, I seriously think you'd hunt me." He crouched down beside her, lifting the hidden bolts from the bushes, and passing them to her. "Would being taken out by the very weapons I supplied a hunter be considered irony or just poor decision-making?"

He lost his balance a fraction as he rose.

Barely noticeable to the untrained eye.

But Simone was trained.

Well trained.

"You're high," she stated, accepting the arrows and shoving them deep into her back pockets.

Nichol rolled out his shoulders and straightened his spine. "I'm done here." He turned to walk away, stopping mid-step. "Several small packages will be arriving in your name over the next few days. The stiletto blades are yours, as are the retracting wood stakes. If you happen to leave the others in this spot for me, it would be much appreciated." With a smirk, he shrugged. "Think of it as giving me a sporting chance on the field."

"Wow," she said with a humorless laugh, breaking into a slow jog to catch up to the retreating vamp. "The switch was kind of subtle online, but in person? It's so obvious."

He continued to walk ahead of her, his long legs allowing him to gain more ground despite her increased speed.

"Stojanovski will have you booted in broad daylight if he finds out you're using me to smuggle weapons onto the premises," she panted as she finally aligned herself with him.

Nichol stopped, swaying on his feet. "Calculated risk," he replied with a grin, his fangs long. "You need me and Boy to pull you out of whatever games Stojanovski wants to play in the foreseeable future. You're good, but you're not good enough to sludge a dozen vampires in full bloodlust." His blackened eyes flickered hazel for a moment. "I need those weapons. By the time I'm of no use to you, I'll be well on my way to completing my mission and getting the hell out of here."

She grabbed his arm. "You'll be looking over your shoulder the whole time."

He glared down at her hand, shaking himself free. "I'm always looking over my fucking shoulder," he snarled. "How many vamps are still hunting?"

Scanning the landscape, she pursed her lips. "Seven."

"Eleven, including me," Nichol corrected. "Sixteen humans. And one hunter who's really testing my fucking patience." He turned his back to her and resumed walking. "Go to bed, Highsteaks."

She watched him as he crossed the fields to his bunker and disappeared through the door. A young biter sauntered past her, wrinkling his nose at her muddied appearance and the stench of swamp water that clung to her skin before he beelined into the forest.

Breaking into a run, she made her way to the main hall, taking the stairs two at a time until she was secured in her room, her lock engaged. Stripping her soiled clothes and boots off, she dumped them into a plastic bag and set them beside the door to be dealt with later. Dollops of expensive shampoo and soaps erased the swamp from her body and hair, the water finally running clear as the shower turned tepid.

Fucking biters.

He was right.

She needed him alive.

Nichol and his hauntmates were pulling the heat of Stojanovski's games off of her, a reprieve which hadn't gone unnoticed by the humans and vampires roaming the grounds. Even in Nichol's absence, the silent claim he'd inadvertently placed on her echoed across the compound, a clear warning to the others she was not to be touched as long as he was on site.

He won't always be on site.

Collapsing onto her bed, she pulled out her phone.

Highsteaks1403: I want to make a deal

She rolled over and grabbed the TV remote, flipping on a cooking show and muting the volume.

587OriginalNK: I don't deal with terrorists

Highsteaks1403: whatever, biter

587OriginalNK: suck it, curly

Her brows shot up. She tapped the phone icon and waited impatiently for Nichol to answer.

"What."

"Suck it, curly?" she said flatly, vaguely unimpressed but mildly intrigued with the flippant comeback so at-odds with Nichol's sullen demeanor.

She could hear him opening and closing a door. "Call me biter again," he snarled. When she didn't respond, Nichol grunted. "What deal?"

She lowered her voice. "If Jackson hands me your name, or any Kaius, I'll stand down in exchange for my freedom." She sat up and looked out into her dark living room. "I want out."

"I'm not turning a vamp killer loose into the general population."

She groaned in frustration and fell back onto her pillow. The silence on Nichol's end drew out as she lay there, the light of the TV bouncing off her walls.

A weary sigh suddenly broke the quiet. "I'll see what I can do. Go to bed, Highsteaks."

Chapter Twenty-Three

Boy's nostrils flared as Nichol joined him at the gates of the compound. Ignoring the dead blue eyes while they scanned him, he released the tension in his jaw and stared down the road. "We'll have to test Rhys's strength in the bunker before we hit the main hall," he stated, his fingers stretching out at his sides. "Better to underestimate his current status than be caught unprepared."

Boy nodded and refocused his attention down the dark path.

He knew he'd pushed his luck, taking Vanito's vein before he could hide the scent under the cover of the masses of vampires in the gathering room. As his fangs had unhooked from the ancient's wrist, a blast of guilt had shot through him, dulled only when the warming dissociation the blood provided crept into his head and through his body.

Rhys's unmistakable saunter appeared on the dirt road, his backpack slung over his shoulder. He alerted Stojanovski of his brother's arrival and pushed the heavy gate open when the lock disengaged.

"Holy fuck, Nicky," Rhys grinned, switching his bag to his other shoulder and rolling his neck out. "Lis must've called me eight times on the way up. Is there any way you can cap her phone use? Cuz I'm about two calls away from putting myself in the doghouse again."

"I'm well aware," he said, nodding to Boy to flank the younger hauntmate. "She's called me twice asking for the key to her room lock which was somehow reversed while she slept." He smacked Rhys's arm. "I need all hands on deck, dumbass. Locking her in your suite is a waste of resources."

Rhys's navy eyes glinted with a mischievousness he hadn't seen in close to two years. "I'll lead her to the key before dawn," he grinned, his fangs lengthening while he smoothed his shirt over his chest. "Am I presentable?"

He veered off the path toward the main building and led the group to the bunker. "We're strength-testing before we head in there tomorrow night," he stated, keeping one eye on the swamp as they moved farther away. "Dovidas and his crew are expected Tuesday. That gives us two nights to run scenarios and prep our combined weaponry."

"Combined?" Rhys inquired, cocking a brow. "How much have you managed to smuggle in and how?"

"I have my ways."

****

Nichol dug his boot into Boy's ribs, alerting his hauntmate to the end of the round. "That's it," he announced, offering a hand to Rhys and helping the snarling male from the floor. "Your speed's peaked at a five hundred, strength inching toward six. It's not ideal, but better than it was." He passed a bag of blood over. "We can work with this."

"You should've called in Jagger," Rhys spat, running his tongue over his cracked fang. "Abso-fucking-lutely pathetic. Even that pussy Stojanovski could take me down right now. I usually clock in at nine hundred, minimum. Fucking bullshit."

Boy crossed the room quietly, his phone extended toward Rhys.

"*I know your tells,*" Rhys read off the phone while he sucked back the last of the A-negative and turned his glare on Boy. "What do I care?"

Nichol began righting the furniture in the living room, pulling it back from the perimeter. "Placing you between five and six hundred is a conservative estimate," he explained. "Boy and I know your style and the few tells you have alerting us to your attacks and responses. Tells only those of us who trained you in combat would know." He yanked the sofa into place. "Your time in the Deepfryer was well-documented and has likely been viewed by every vampire on the premises. They'll be expecting you to be weak. Far weaker than this. And for the time being, we'll play it up."

"The hell we will," Rhys snarled, tugging his shirt over his head and examining the bite marks on his shoulders. "I'm not walking into that hall as a weak-ass newbie."

He ran a hand through his hair, his high finally stabilizing. "All I'm asking is for you not to play up your recovery. Leave them guessing. Dovidas holds the element of surprise, so any aces we can keep to ourselves right now will only help to level the playing field."

Rhys sat down, scratching at his tattoos absently. "Fine," he relented, leaning back. "What's my role tomorrow night?"

"Easy," Nichol replied. "You're playing the role of Rhys Kaius."

****

The rise of the sun sent a tremor through Nichol's limbs as he scanned through the revised blueprints of the vampire-safe housing. Rhys's bare feet dropped from the coffee table with a *thunk*, his sour mood from earlier lifting while he dialed Lis, his smirk returning when she answered in a huff.

"Calm down, baby," Rhys called out over her tongue-lashing, rising to his feet. "We're going to play a little game to find that key." He covered the mouthpiece with his hand. "I'm heading to bed." Sauntering down the hall, Rhys's voice dropped. "Get into that blue number I like and call me back on video."

Boy's brows lifted a fraction.

Logging out of the haunt's investment accounts, Nichol opened the maintenance ones and looked over to Boy. "Rest up. I want top form tomorrow."

Boy nodded and pushed off the wall, tilting his head to Rhys's door for a moment before wrinkling his nose and disappearing into his room. Tuning out Rhys's low murmuring to Lis, he refocused on the financial accounts, shuffling money between them to maintain a healthy balance. When the numbers began to run into one another, he closed out his laptop and reclined back on the sofa, opening his messenger app.

587OriginalNK: Up?

Highsteaks1403: unfortunately

587OriginalNK: any new info?

Highsteaks1403: no hunt tomorrow. social instead

He rubbed his jaw, the tingling of his muscles almost hypnotic.

587OriginalNK: you going?

Highsteaks1403: like i have a choice

Highsteaks1403: packages dropped

587OriginalNK: you like the blades?

Highsteaks1403: all the better to stake you with my

dear

He sat up, his head heavy. He forced himself to his feet and stumbled to his bedroom, listening for any movement from his hauntmates before he flopped onto his bed and hit the phone icon. "You aren't funny."

Simone snorted. "You used to think I was."

"I was being tolerant," he retorted, putting one arm behind his head. "I have a few questions for you."

The line went quiet for a moment. "Okay..."

"Your accent," he opened, curiosity trumping necessity. "You had a heavy, unmistakable Boston accent during your time at our haunt. Same on site when you're around Stojanovski or the other humans. But when we talk, it's an unrecognizable disaster. Why."

"Jackson and I came to an agreement about speech training last year," Simone stated, her tone hard. "Now when I'm less guarded, the training mixes with my natural accent and here it is. Next question."

Frowning, he rifled through the litany of information he wanted, narrowing in to only the intel he needed. "Your feeding schedule since you arrived at the compound. Has it been steady and adequate?"

"Better than I had in the bloodslave quarters," she replied flatly. "Though I'd prefer pizza more often."

"Your quarters," he pressed, ignoring the bite in Simone's voice. "Are they adequate and secure?"

She laughed drily. "You've been in them. They're fine. What's this about?"

His head flashed across the snippets he could recall from his first day in her small apartment, his fingers flexing involuntarily as they relived the feel of her skin under his hands. "The easiest form of extraction for you is a contract breach," he grunted, forcefully pushing all memories of her lips from his mind. "I'm starting from the most common master failures and working my way through the list."

"Master failures," Simone parroted. "How about I don't want to be here? Does that fit into a fucking contract breach?"

"No." He closed his eyes and fought through the fog in his head to bring up every tiny infraction he could use. "I know that's not the answer you want," he said quietly when Simone didn't respond. "I'll work on it."

Silence.

He shook out his restless legs. "Highsteaks?"

"I'm here," she sighed. "I'm going to bed. Night, NK."

The phone line went dead.

He lay in bed and stared into the darkness.

Rhys's standard contract ensured a higher level of treatment than most other trainers wrote into their agreements, but aside from blatant neglect, Tenders had few options for release as long as their masters lived.

He tapped the phone icon beside Highsteaks' name. "What."

His brows knotted at the harsh greeting. "I have a proposition."

****

Simone descended the stairs into the main hall, subtly tapping the new stiletto blades tucked into the cargo pockets running the length of her thighs. Stojanovski stood in the more secluded seating area, his hands deep in the pockets of his blazer as he spoke to the vampires lounging on the ornate sofas. He glanced up at her, looking over her outfit as he motioned for her to join him.

"Here she is," Jackson announced, running his fingers along Simone's neck, his jaw tensing when she jerked away from his touch. "Princess, you remember Rhys, don't you?"

Ignoring Nichol's sullen stare, she gave her former trainer a tight smile. "You're looking well."

Rhys rose to his feet, his slinking movements bringing on an unwanted deluge of memories. He stalked around her, navy eyes appraising her. "Walk for me."

She looked to Stojanovski for confirmation.

"Go ahead," he ordered.

She crossed the floor, pivoted, and returned.

Rhys's lips tightened. "Why is she limping, Jackson?"

"Hunting injury," Stojanovski replied tersely. "Old one."

Kneeling in front of her, Rhys lifted her right foot to his knee and began unlacing her boot. "Old injuries in healthy specimens shouldn't continue to flare if they were treated correctly." He ran his thumb over the slight swelling still present under her ankle bone. "Boy?"

Boy joined Rhys on the floor as she kept her eyes locked on the wall ahead of her. She could sense Stojanovski's angry glare at her back as a peculiar low growl rumbled, barely audible to her, but enough for Rhys and Boy to exchange a wary glance before their eyes flicked to Nichol.

"Proper medical care is listed under section 5," Rhys stated, rolling her sock back up and lacing her boot. He rubbed her calf gently and placed her foot back on the ground as he stood. "I'm noting this injury on her file, Stojanovski," he warned, sitting back on the sofa and sprawling out. "Before the place gets too crowded, how's she been handling for you?"

She clenched her teeth, forcing herself to remain still and silent while Rhys spoke to her master as though she were nothing more than a second-hand car.

"She delivers as promised," Jackson replied as he placed his hand on her hip, squeezing it slightly to remind Rhys of his ownership. And her of her place. "Perhaps you'll get to see your work in action during your time here."

He released her, giving the Kaius males a quick bow of his head. "I'll leave you to hold court for the evening. Many of my clients are anxious to speak with you, and I would hate to tie up more of your time than necessary."

As Stojanovski retreated, she moved to follow.

"Hold."

Rhys's hand brushed her thigh as she stepped past him, his lips unmoving with his command. She halted and waited.

"I want to hear it from you. That you're well," he finally said, his head lolling back as he grinned up at her. "I'm in a lot of shit for creating you, you know."

She brushed a stubborn purple ringlet from her eye and crouched down, refusing to be swayed by the roguish biter's innate charm. "I hate it here."

"I know, angel," Rhys said, glancing over at Stojanovski. "It was the best I could do." He tilted his head and narrowed his eyes. "You should go back to the blue eyeliner. The black is too harsh for your features."

Fixing him with a dead stare, she stood.

Rhys smirked and resettled into the sofa. "I never did manage to break that look of utter contempt," he mused, elbowing Nichol in the ribs and earning a snarl from the surly vamp. "You've done well, honey. We'll talk soon."

Dismissed, she marched over to the buffet and loaded a plate, one eye on Nichol. His hardened profile showed little emotion while younger vamps began approaching the group, their hands open and heads bowed. Periodically, Nichol would tap something into his phone and give clipped responses, his elongated fangs a good indication he was in no mood to hold court that evening.

Rhys, however, was the complete opposite. He took up as much room on the large sofa as he could, his movements smooth and relaxed while he flashed his fangs and grinned at those addressing him. His booted feet were resting on the expensive table, hands locked behind his head in a pose so familiar, she had to forcibly block the images of her early training sessions from her mind.

Shaking her head, she focused her attention to her meal and the gossiping humans surrounding her.

****

Nichol tapped open his banking app. "I'm transferring twenty grand to you now, scheduling twenty more once you make Denver," he said quietly to the sire-less vampire sitting beside him. "We will discuss your position alongside Jagger once you're settled."

The vampire nodded, his irises elongating with hunger.

"Boy will get you fed before you depart," he offered, rising to his feet and stepping aside as Boy moved closer. "I'm truly sorry for your loss."

He vacated the area quickly, unwilling to dwell any longer on the young vampire's hardships.

Too little, too late.

Heading out the heavy doors, he walked toward the swampland, easing the small flask of Vanito's blood to his mouth and draining it dry. The potency was lacking its usual punch, but the small rush was enough to take the edge off his twitchy muscles and spinning head.

Another young haunt gone.

Another new vampire alone.

Another reminder he had waited too long.

"You alone?"

Pausing to locate the direction of Simone's voice in the thick cattails, he nodded. "Sorry to disappoint."

Simone snorted inelegantly and sat up, twigs and moss tangled in her colorful curls. "I only packed one stake, so if you'd had company, I would've been screwed."

Extending his hand to help her to her feet, he looked around the swamp. "So where are the packages?"

She began leading him through the muck to the perimeter fence, getting five steps in before she released his hand with a snap. "You would never know Rhys had been fried," she said, tucking her hands into her back pockets. "He looks completely healed. And is as cocky as ever."

He rolled his shoulders and flexed his arms out for a moment. He'd been displeased with Rhys's manhandling of Simone's foot and his ingrained flirting with the hybrid Tender.

Displeased enough to contemplate using the stake Simone had tucked into her cargos while memories of Rhys's comments about her back at the haunt slammed into his head.

Five-foot-five of leggy perfection.

He glowered at the woman stomping ahead of him.

"Didn't you say you were five-foot-six?"

Fuck you, Rhys.

Simone glanced back at him. "I almost am. Stojanovski was anticipating Rhys would be weakened for a long time. I think seeing him so Rhys-ish threw him."

He refused to respond. Whether she was fishing for intel or for her own curiosity, Rhys's condition was none of her fucking business.

"It's weird having him here," she continued, oblivious to his souring mood as she knelt down and began rummaging under a bushel of greenery. "I mean, training experience aside, I know I answer to Jackson, but I answer to Jackson under Rhys's orders." She passed over a small box and reached down for another. "Always answering to someone though, I guess. So does it really matter who's issuing the orders?"

He took the second and third packages from her hands and tucked them into the larger pockets of his cargos.

Simone rose and faced him, wiping her hands on her pants. "You answer to a lot. Don't you ever get sick of it?"

"Vampires don't get sick."

"Don't be obtuse," she snarked back, grinning when he lifted a brow. "I overheard you use that word last week. I liked it, so I looked it up."

As the pair began their trek back to the center grounds, she kept in close step with him. "Are you worried about tomorrow night?"

"Nope."

Her steps slowed slightly. "Is that a nope because you're ready or a nope because you're too damn high to know?" She smacked at his thigh, making contact with the flask concealed against his leg. "Your eyes are completely fucked-up right now, you know. All blackened and angry."

"Perhaps it's because I'm pissed off," he replied, flashing his fangs at her.

She stopped cold and crossed her arms, her scathing blue eyes narrowed. "What the hell is your problem, NK?"

"I don't know, *Highsteaks*," he sneered, the high of the stale ancient blood less euphoric and more agitated than usual. "Why is a woman who despises vamps so fucking much interrogating me every goddamn chance she has? Why is she so interested in the *biter* who sold her?" He patted the smuggled packages to reassure himself they were still there. "How about you back the hell off of me? I've armed you, I've ensured your relative safety until I vacate the compound, and I've given you a potential out. What the hell else do you want from me?"

Without waiting for a response, he broke into a jog and took off toward his bunker.

****

Simone tossed the X-Box controller onto the sofa and powered down the unit. She picked up her phone and opened her messaging app.

Highsteaks1403: up?
587OriginalNK: what
Highsteaks1403: i really do apreciate it
Highsteaks1403: apprecciate*
587OriginalNK: APPRECIATE

She bit her lip and smiled at his response, one she'd received from him dozens of times over the past year and a half.

It was normal.

A throwback to pre-vampire NK.

It's been over a thousand years since he was pre-vampire, dumbass.

She flopped back and turned the brightness down on her screen.

Highsteaks1403: i APPRECIATE what you've done. i just worry about you

The moment she hit send, she flinched. It wasn't Nichol she worried about. It was NK, her online friend-turned-crush-turned—

Turned what?

587 OriginalNK: you have your own ass to worry about. Focus on that.

Chapter Twenty-Four

Nichol and Boy casually flanked Rhys as they entered the main hall, Nichol's shoulders twitching under the constraint of his suit jacket and Boy tugging at the collar of his shirt.

"Cut it out," Rhys said with a sigh of exasperation while they ascended the steps. "It's like you two were raised in a fucking barn."

"Barns weren't invented where I was raised," he grumbled, stilling his arms when the sharp tear of stitching hit his ears.

"Fair enough, Neanderthal," Rhys grinned. "But Bianca told me to tell you that if either of you destroys these suits, she's outfitting you in cheap ones from here on out, and trust me when I say there is nothing more uncomfortable than a cheap, ill-fitting suit. Boy, have you picked up Dovidas's scent yet?"

Boy shook his head, unhooking his fingers from his collar and letting his arms dangle awkwardly at his sides.

The males pulled open the doors and strode in, their arrival garnering the rapt attention of the compound humans as they made their way to the center of the room to greet Stojanovski.

Jackson smiled wide, his fangs on full display. "I have it on good authority my other esteemed guests will be arriving shortly. It's a full house tonight, so I expect everyone to keep it civil."

Rhys caught Dahlia's eye and winked at her before addressing their host. "Is there a hunt planned this evening?"

"Of course," Stojanovski chuckled, gesturing toward the buffet table where dozens of men and women were conversing. "Black tie hunts are a favorite among my guests and their prey."

Nichol scanned the room for Simone, his last clipped message to her still hanging around his neck. He nudged his hauntmates toward the back wall where they would have an unimpeded view of the entrances and the room while he continued to look for unruly brown and rainbow ringlets in the crowd.

"Jagg was right," Rhys hissed, elbowing him in the ribs. "Chen looks like fucking hell."

Boy's posture morphed instantly, his instinctive predator side taking over when Dovidas and Chen entered the hall. Nichol widened his own stance, stepping slightly in front of Rhys as the ancient vampire's head swung in their direction.

"Manners," he muttered just loud enough for Boy and Rhys's ears to pick up. They remained still while Dovidas and Chen cut through the throngs vying for a look at one of the oldest known vampires.

"Rhys Kaius," Dovidas called out as he approached, his gray eyes traveling over Rhys's healed form. "I'm surprised to see you looking so whole." He feigned a confused look over the group. "You didn't happen to bring my Tender back to me, did you?"

Nichol refused to acknowledge the sadistic vampire's statement, Dovidas's treatment of Molly while she was under his roof as a Tender still a source of fury within the haunt.

Rhys smirked, rising to his full height and towering over Dovidas by a good five inches. "Violations of clauses seven and nine, Kaspars. Should've read your contract before signing."

Stojanovski stepped between the vampires, his host smile in full force. "Kaspars, Chen, would you care to join me for a few minutes prior to the start of the hunt? I have a delightful companion selected to keep you company this evening should you take a liking to her."

His jaw tensed.

Dovidas held Rhys's stare for several seconds before replying. "We'd be honored. Perhaps the Kaius haunt would like to join us."

****

Simone yanked at the boning of her dress bodice, readjusting the constraining garment as she eased down the staircase in absurdly high stilettos.

Fucking Stojanovski.

Her outfit had been waiting for her when she awoke, her instructions clear.

Get dressed.

Get downstairs.

Smile.

Her eyes raked the room, locking on the Kaius vampires sprawled across three sofas, their attention on Jackson and the two vamps sitting alongside him. Nichol was taking up as much space as possible, his arms stretched across the back of the couch and his feet planted firmly apart on the floor. He caught her eye, his fangs elongating and his lips drawing tight across them.

"There she is," Jackson called out, drawing the attention of every vampire in the room. "Come, princess. We have guests."

Her focus was torn between Nichol's blackening eyes and her balance, her ankles protesting the height of her heels. As she reached the group, she stopped beside her master and locked down her expression.

"Gentlemen, my Simone is one of Rhys's specimens. I'm sure you'll find her to be an adequate companion for the evening if you prefer a more relaxed night over a hunt," Stojanovski announced, his hand settling on her hip. "Darling, this is Chen and Kaspars Dovidas."

The handsome gray-eyed male stood, smoothing out his jacket. "Always a pleasure to indulge in the company of a Rhys-trained Tender," he purred, cupping her chin as his gaze flicked to Rhys. "I believe I answer for Chen and myself when I say your presence would be a welcomed treat."

A low snarl erupted in the room, dying off instantly when the heads of several vampires turned to locate the sound. She forced a smile when Jackson's fingers dug into her hip, and he nudged her toward Dovidas. "The pleasure's all mine," she enunciated, stepping between the two biters and sitting. "Have you traveled far?"

****

Nichol ignored the incessant buzzing of his phone, his attention wholly fixated on feigning disinterest in Dovidas's hand creeping up Simone's inner thigh.

And in her apparent lack of concern over the intrusion.

Stojanovski remained over his shoulder, monitoring the situation closely and periodically chiming in while Simone engaged them in casual conversation, her unruly curls bobbing as she laughed at the poorly-spun tale Dovidas was weaving. Boy sat mutely on an adjoining sofa, a petite redhead curled up under his arm and trying desperately to gain the interest of the silent male.

A shrill giggle drew his eye to the two women flanking Rhys, the high slits of their dresses tossed open and the plunging necklines leaving little to the imagination. Rhys's tattooed arms were draped over the back of the couch, his hands tucked behind the cushions while he ran his tongue over one fang.

Jackson's voice cut through his head. "Will any of you gentlemen be participating in the hunt this evening? We're about the get the games underway."

Chen shook his head slightly, rising unsteadily to his feet and turning from the group. "I must go."

Dovidas brushed Simone's curls from her neck, oblivious to his partner's departure. "I'm up for little cat-and-mouse." His eyes locked onto Simone's throat. "What are the rules tonight?"

Stojanovski kept Chen in his sights as he spoke, glancing at him intermittently. "Black-tie hunts are contained within the main building. The humans will be lining up shortly for appraisal. Once every vampire has had the opportunity to scent out his favorites, the humans will spread throughout the upper floors." He flashed a fangy smile at Simone. "Compound favorites tend to be won by the most determined and the most skilled."

Nichol wrinkled his nose in disgust when the women sitting with Rhys squealed and jumped to their feet, coquettishly waving their wrists before they sashayed off to join the other prey. Boy's couch-mate rose slowly, as though waiting for him to acknowledge her.

Not happening.

Dovidas nuzzled Simone's neck, inhaling deeply. "I

think we all know who I'll be after." He stood and offered his hand to assist her to her feet. "Rhys, any favorites?"

"I believe I'm spoken for," Rhys smirked, thumbing through his phone.

"Ah yes," Dovidas mused. "The Master Killer. What's it they say? Tenders are a reflection of their trainer?"

"Must be why mine are always so badass," Rhys replied, waggling his tongue at Simone and receiving a dead stare back.

Kaspars' irises elongated a fraction before he turned his attention back to his companion. "Any hints on where you'll be, pumpkin?"

Slipping past him, Simone brushed against Nichol's knee. "Now where would the fun be in that?" she laughed as her blue eyes locked onto him for a moment, flashing with rage and revulsion.

"I would make up for it with better games," Kaspars purred while she stepped away from the group.

He kept his arms slack on the back of the sofa as images of Molly's confinement under Dovidas barreled through his head.

Chains.

Collars.

Tracks.

He glanced over at Rhys. The narrowing navy eyes of his hauntmate indicated they were on the same wavelength.

Dovidas strode off without acknowledgement, joining a pair of young vampires on the fringes of the room.

"Who's going after Simone?" Rhys asked quietly,

his lips still.

He scanned for Stojanovski. "You and Boy beat it out of here when the hunt begins. I'll track down the hybrid and secure her until dusk."

"Don't turn your back on her," Rhys warned, rising to his feet.

"Yeah. I know."

****

Nichol checked the clock.

Two more minutes.

He flicked open his texts, frowning at Mick's most recent message.

Mick: can't feel you or rhys. is dovidas on site?

Nichol: yes. Rhys available for briefing in twenty.

Dovidas's subduer abilities had slipped his mind, explaining the sixteen texts Mick had sent over the past hour. All vamps developed an extra ability upon their turning. Louis could hypnotize, Dominic was a Soother who emitted a calming pheromone akin to a mind-numbing drug, Mick was an empath. The innate talent to mute ties between bloodlines was yet another edge Dovidas had, along with his unknown backer. Mick's ability to monitor the Kaius vamps was now hindered, leaving all of them with one less tool in their arsenal. The fact Mickey didn't add in a joke about him and Rhys being sludged was a stark reminder of how precarious their situation was, and he fired off a quick apology for forgetting the impact Dovidas's presence would have on Mick's ability to feel him and Rhys.

"Ten! Nine!"

He fixed his attention on Dovidas while the younger vampires began counting down the clock. The vampire had made his way to the bottom of the grand staircase, casually leaning against the rail, and watching the Kaius hauntmates.

"When can we end him?" Rhys asked with a grin, winking at Dovidas. "I may not be at full strength, but I can take his three-century-year-old ass out."

"After we find out who his backer is," he replied, taking a small step forward. "Boy, make sure Chen isn't sniffing around while you two make your way to the bunker. I'm not in the mood to wash away any sludge tonight."

Boy nodded as the countdown ended and the vampires poured onto the stairs, Dovidas in the lead. Ensuring Rhys and Boy were on their way out the side doors, he took his time ascending the steps. Dovidas was already approaching the third floor, veering right as Simone had done ten minutes prior.

You better be as smart as I think you are, Highsteaks.

Chapter Twenty-Five

Simone kicked her dress into the back corner of her bedroom and pulled a shirt over her head. Several of the gown's hooks lay strewn across the carpet, casualties of her desire to unbind her movements as quick as possible.

She hiked her cargos over her hips and began filling the pockets, listening carefully to the ruckus in the halls as humans and vampires played their twisted game of hide-and-seek. The din died down fast, the few rooms occupying her side of the floor holding little more than towels and bins of unused clothing.

The click of a lock.

Not even her own room was out of bounds tonight.

But only one vampire knew the code.

She gripped a blade in her hand as her door opened and closed quietly, the lock re-engaged.

"I'm on guard," Nichol stated into the darkness. "Perhaps keeping the same code was wise."

Breathing out, she made her way through the unlit apartment. "I'm smarter than I look," she whispered. "Follow me."

Nichol's boots thumped behind her as she led him to her bedroom and closed the door.

"There's a decent level of soundproofing in here," she said softly, turning on a lamp and tucking her blade back into her pocket. "That asshole shouldn't be able to detect us."

Nichol made his way to her bedroom window and shimmied it open. He leaned out, looking down before craning his neck up toward the roof and inhaling. "Impressive. Sloppy, but impressive."

She crossed her arms. "Dahlia's room has attic access," she stated. "It's not something I like to do, but it works in a pinch."

Her hands were still shaking from her descent from the building's roof onto the narrow ledge of her bedroom window. One of her high heels lay on the ground below, fumbled when her precarious balance nearly toppled.

Nichol closed the window tight. "I'll text Boy to retrieve the shoe."

He backed into the corner of the room, pushing her discarded dress aside with his toe and locking his gaze onto his cell, his biceps periodically flexing and his nose wrinkling while he thumbed through his phone.

"So that's Dovidas," she opened, mimicking Nichol's position and scanning the game alerts on her phone. "Seems nice."

Nichol kept his attention down. "Very."

"Chen didn't seem as powerful as I expected," she mused, deleting several updates and shoving her phone into her back pocket. "I'd anticipated more oomph from an ancient."

He glanced up at her, his hazel eyes worn. "An incapacitated ancient ranks high on my worst-case-scenario list," he stated. "It means his strength has been drained for other purposes."

She frowned. "But you can easily take him out."

"Chen isn't the ancient I'm concerned about."

When it became clear Nichol wouldn't be expanding on his thoughts, she began to pace the floor, listening at the bedroom door periodically for signs of Stojanovski or Dovidas.

"Does he have the code?" Nichol suddenly inquired, joining her at the door, his head tilted.

"Jackson? No. Apparently it's in the contract he had with Rhys that I have a secured apartment separate from my compound duties. I'm just paranoid he'll override the system if Dovidas pays him enough." She rolled her eyes and took a step back as Nichol pushed his way past her. "Go ahead. I wasn't standing there first or anything."

He grunted and continued to listen to the faint sounds in the hall.

"Do you think there'll be repercussions for me hiding in here?" she asked, wedging herself back into her spot and elbowing Nichol in the ribs. "Or for you?"

His shoulders tensed, his teeth grinding slowly. "For me, no. I'm older than most on site for now, and my prior tenuous claim on you remains in place. For you? Dovidas will be displeased you purposely evaded him, but I don't believe he'll do anything to you that would risk him being ejected from the compound." He lifted one hand to the door frame and turned to face her. "But know that Dovidas has sadistic tendencies our haunt is more familiar with than we care to be. You know Molly. You've seen her jump when metal clangs. You would be wise to avoid any contact with him in the foreseeable future."

She huffed and copied Nichol's pose. "Like I have a choice. I'm owned, remember?"

He rubbed his chin and stared at the floor. "I may be able to pay off Stojanovski in the short term," he muttered, his brows knotting. "Jagger might know where his starting price would sit."

"Why?"

Nichol's contemplation came to a screeching halt, his expression locking down into an annoyed disinterest. "Protection of assets on the ground is a responsibility I don't take lightly."

"Right," she nodded. "An asset." She swayed slightly closer to him, pursing her lips when he drew back a fraction. "We used to be friends."

"Under false pretenses," he snarked, the faint silver hue of his viper fangs visible in the lamp light. "We were game-mates."

"Game-mates," she echoed, flashing back to the countless late mornings and early evenings spent online chatting with NK. "If I'd known what you are, we would never have talked."

His eyes ovaled and he focused on the wall behind her.

She cocked her head.

Nichol had been a constant in her life for eighteen months. His sour mood and rare bursts of wry humor had drawn her to him, pushing her to counter his constant negativity with what little cheer and hope she had left. He became a respite for her, a safe haven from the fear and stress of her surroundings.

He was a miserable bastard.

An arrogant, miserable bastard.

An arrogant, miserable bastard who was still NK despite the lengthening fangs and blackening irises.

Vampire and male.

Physically, he represented everything she despised. By birth and by transformation, Nichol was the prototype of her enemy, a perfect representation of all she raged against inside her head.

He was also NK.

And she'd been drawn to NK like a moth to a flame since she'd first watched his avatar demolish every player in his path without hesitation, apology, or a single taunting word. She'd been fascinated by the guy who entered the games on and off in the early morning hours, ignoring the online chatter while he obliterated the strongest gamers and defended the weaker ones.

The few losses she'd witnessed had been intriguing, 587OriginalNK disappearing from the screen for precisely thirty minutes before he'd return better equipped, running a completely different tactical offense, and annihilating everyone in his way.

A hunter.

A strategist.

She'd respected it right out the gate.

"Stop staring at me like I'm on display in a traveling freak show," Nichol grumbled, shoving his hands into his back pockets. "It's pissing me off."

"Everything pisses you off," she replied, stepping tight into his space and continuing to appraise his features. "Did you know your eye color shifts between green and brown?"

He glared at her.

"And it's not good for you to grind your teeth," she chastised, reaching up to still the slight movement of his jaw. When he tried to flinch away, she gripped him tighter. "It can cause enamel erosion and tension headaches." Narrowing her eyes, she tilted her head and tried to envision him without the canines laying across his lower lip. "How old were you when you became a vampire?"

"Into my twenty-fifth summer," he answered,

arching his chin from her hands. "Don't touch me."

"Okay, okay," she sighed, dropping her arms to her sides. "Is it weird to be so old but look so young? I mean, your freckles make you look even younger than that. Like, barely twenty."

He grunted, his head dropping a fraction in defense while he stared at the floor. "Back off."

She rose onto her toes, her hands clasped behind her as she brushed her lips against his. His eyes remained locked onto the ground, his brows knotted and shoulders flattening against the door.

She kissed him again, lifting one hand to the back of his neck to steady her balance.

"Playing the game again, are you?" he murmured against her lips, his eyes blackening as his muscles tightened. "I already told you Rhys's hide would be paying for your security detail."

The well-deserved dig shot through her and settled heavily in her stomach. "No game," she replied, nuzzling the faint scruff of his jawline and stepping flush against him. "No game, no payment, no anything."

He wrapped his fingers around her wrists and lowered them to her sides. "I'm going to need to see that in writing," he snarked, stepping away from her and prowling to the opposite side of the room.

She glared at him and walked to her bedside table, yanking the drawer open and grabbing a worn pencil and list of game codes. She scrawled a quick message on the back of the paper and approached him, mashing it into his chest. "There."

He lifted the crumbled note, his nose wrinkling. "You spelled 'encumbrances' with an extra 'e'," he stated, folding the paper, and slipping it into his pocket.

"You're such an ass," she hissed as she wrapped her arms around his neck and kissed him with everything she had.

****

Nichol's fingers flexed at his side as he fought to keep his hands from locking onto the woman pressed against him. Her tongue traveled along his lips until he finally relented, unclenching his teeth and relaxing against the wall when she deepened the kiss, completely unaffected by his reluctance.

Huge fucking mistake.

Logically, he knew every moment he didn't extricate himself from the warm body pressing against his was a moment he would come to regret. Despite her misspelled note and the fingers inching their way under his shirt, he knew Simone harbored too much hatred of vampires to hold any true investment in what she was doing.

Scratching an itch.

And scratching, she was. He shivered involuntarily as her nails trailed down his stomach and looped back up his chest.

"Like that?" she whispered into his ear, her tongue flicking against the shell and sending another tremor through him.

"Yeah," he ground out, relenting to his hands demand to touch her. He dragged his fingers down her ribcage to her hips, gripping them when she wedged herself between his legs and rubbed against him. "Stop wiggling."

She ground into him defiantly. "Not with the reaction I'm getting." She grinned, dropping her head into the crook of his neck, her curls tickling his chin as her thumb hooked into the band of his cargos. "Are the rumors I heard back at the Kaius haunt true? That you haven't slept with anyone in, like, decades?"

He dropped his head back against the wall and closed his eyes while she popped the button of his pants. "I've been busy."

Burying her face into his shirt, her body heaved as she attempted to quiet her laughter. "Busy? Really." She gripped his waistband and began backing up toward her bed, tugging him along with her. "Lie down," she ordered, giving his shoulders a light shove.

Huge. Fucking. Mistake.

He complied, locking his hands behind his head and watching, enthralled, as she pulled her shirt over her head and tossed it aside.

"That is really orange," he commented, forcing his eyes off her bra and back to her face.

"You don't like orange, do you?" she teased, shimmying out of her pants and turning slowly to give Nichol a good view of the matching thong.

"I'm warning up to it." He frowned at the faint scar still visible across her ribs.

She crawled onto him, straddling his hips, and placing her hands on his biceps. "Shirt. Off."

He hesitated a moment, unsettled by the ease in which he wanted to comply. Ignoring the unusual feeling, he yanked his shirt off, dropped it over the edge of the bed, and locked his hands behind his head again.

She leaned back, her blue eyes narrowing as she ran her hands along his skin. He stilled while she explored him, every inch of his torso firing up where her fingers grazed over him methodically. "You sure I can't call you Abs Man? Because this is seriously impressive." She caught his bland look and smiled sweetly. "You should consider walking around shirtless all the time. Like a living art display."

"You should consider not talking," he grumbled, thrown by the hunger in her eyes as she scanned him.

Big. Big. *Mistake.*

She lowered herself onto him, reaching behind his head to lace her fingers in his while she ran her tongue across his throat and down his chest. He arched up, growling in approval when she nipped his skin with her blunt teeth.

"Like that?" She inhaled sharply, dropping one hand to his zipper and easing it down.

"Fuck. Yeah."

Her warm hand gripped him through his boxers, sending his hips bucking toward her. He laced his fingers through her hair, pulling her lips to his while he inched his other hand under the bright fabric of her bra and rolled her underneath him. The heat of her skin against his began to cloud his head, her scent overtaking any rational thought while her small hand ran along his length.

His dropped his head to her breasts, circling his tongue over one perfect nipple and running his thumb over the other, earning a soft moan. "Like that?" he murmured, trailing his hand under the orange thong.

"Fuck. Yes," she gasped, pressing against his hand as he slid one finger through her wetness and began to gently circle her nub. She tugged at his hair, bringing his mouth back to hers and kissing him hard, her tongue battling against his until it grazed his fang.

He felt the shift in her instantly as she recoiled, the move tossing ice water onto him and ripping him from his lust-infused haze.

Chapter Twenty-Six

Nichol reclined back on the sofa and flipped through his emails, ignoring the intermittent sniffling still coming from Simone's bedroom. He fired off responses to the easiest ones, flagging the others for later when he had the time and inclination to research the required information.

Big fucking mistake.

His spine still ached from slamming against the wall when he had launched himself off of her, putting as much distance between them as he could in that moment.

Two hours later, and she was still whimpering apologies.

Apologies he neither wanted nor needed.

He kept his attention on his phone as the soft shuffling of her feet grew louder, her bedroom door creeping open.

"Nichol, I'm s—"

He held up his hand and shook his head. "Done and forgotten," he stated, forcing his jaw to relax when he caught himself grinding his teeth again. "I've arranged for Boy to be on duty until we vacate the compound. He's a little strange, but he's good at what he does."

She wrapped her bathrobe tight around herself and knelt beside him, laying her head on his knee. "I didn't mean to."

His leg twitched at the contact and the memory of

her assuming the same pose at Rhys's side in his communication room another lifetime ago. "Can't fight instinct," he replied casually, thumbing over his texts. "I've messaged Stojanovski to apologize for over-indulging in his hybrid today. It should buy you one, maybe two nights of solitude."

She closed her eyes. "I don't have any bite marks."

He tossed one arm behind his head before he gave into the urge to run his fingers through those wild curls. "If he's bold enough to ask, which I doubt, tell him the femoral and leave it at that."

He felt his fangs lengthen as his traitorous mind brought up an image of Simone's thighs and her neon orange thong.

"How long until you go?" she asked, resting her hand on his stomach, her thumb drawing small circles on his shirt.

"One hour until sunset," he answered, torn between retreating to the safety of the hallway and indulging in the unexpected calmness her touch was bringing him.

"Will you come back tomorrow? Boy makes me nervous. I just…I don't want him in here."

He leaned back and closed his eyes. "I'm sure Rhys would be open to it."

Sitting back on her haunches, she scowled. "So we're back in business mode again."

"We never should have left it," he huffed, opening one eye to meet her fired gaze. "What?"

"I said I was sorry," she spat, crossing her arms. "It was one stupid little freeze-up. It meant absolutely nothing."

He swung his legs over the edge of the sofa and held his phone with both hands. "I don't have it in me to fight right now, Highsteaks." He ran his tongue over his fangs, grunting when she flinched a fraction away from him. "Yeah, that's pretty much it, isn't it?" He rose to his feet and listened for a moment at her door to ensure the night's less successful hunters were no longer stalking the halls in search of a rogue human. "I'll wait downstairs in the reception room until dusk, then send one of the others over to keep an eye on you tonight."

He exited the room, pulling the door shut quickly to drown out her protests.

****

"There's no need to go upstairs unless Dovidas moves that way," Nichol reminded Rhys over the phone as the sun finally set and he sauntered out of the main hall and into the night. "Any problems, call me."

He ended the call and made his way toward the forest where he could have a few minutes of solitude before the nightly hunt began. The grounds were still, few vampires making their way across the fields from their bunkers. Within hours, the place would be crawling with vamps and humans, and any chance at a quiet evening would be long forgotten in the mayhem.

And he needed a quiet evening. Badly.

He also needed a shower.

Simone's scent clung to his skin, every movement he made amplifying it until he forced himself to stop inhaling, to stop torturing himself.

It was harder than he cared to admit.

He reached into his side pocket and pulled out the small flask of staling blood. Uncapping it, he downed the remnants, tossing the container over the electrified fence when he was done.

He needed a fresh batch from Vanito. Soon.

Climbing one of the higher trees, he scanned the grounds for movement, the stale ancient blood sending a lethargic, unpleasant high through his mind and body as his phone buzzed incessantly in his back pocket.

"What," he barked into the cell, his temper eroding quickly.

"Where are you?"

Kaius.

He steadied himself on the branch and glanced down at the unrecognizable number. "At the Stojanovski compound," he replied. "Rhys and Boy have accompanied me here."

Kaius was silent for a moment. "You intend to take out Dovidas and Chen there, I assume?"

"That's the plan."

"They're accompanied by an ancient," Kaius warned. "You know this."

He ran his hand through his hair, an unpleasant heaviness settling in his limbs. "I believe it's wiser to face them here than wait for them to hit Denver." He paused. "There are a lot of lives on my head right now."

"What is the contingency plan if you fail?"

"A mass deportation into Canada," he said, tracking the movements of a human walking through the fields. "If we fail here, we lose three. If we wait for Dovidas, Chen, and the unknown to make their way to our doors, we could lose more. Jagger and Mikhail have established an escape route for the haunt, as well as for any asylum seekers who make it to Denver should they choose to use it."

He watched the human turn toward the main hall and relaxed back. "Rhys and Boy have been instructed to vacate the premises immediately should things turn from our favor. I'll be last out."

"And you feel prepared?"

"Not in the least."

Kaius chuckled drily. "I've never felt prepared, either." His voice became muffled. "I'm attempting to make my way to you."

He straightened up. "When?"

"As soon as possible." The line became grainy. "I'm proud of you, Nichol. Reluctant as you may be, you've proven yourself a strong leader. I chose my second in command well."

The call disconnected, leaving him alone in the silence of the night.

Proud of you.

He looked over at the bushes where his discarded flask lay empty.

****

Rhys's boots appeared on the bunker ladder. "I really should have included an addendum on hair dye quality before printing off the last few decades of contracts," he called over his shoulder. "Dahlia reeks of cheap chemicals and those blonde streaks she put in have a brassy tint to them that just don't do it for me or her complexion."

Nichol watched as Rhys pulled the hatch closed and hit the floor.

"Boy's monitoring Dovidas and Simone," he reported, scratching at his tattoos and scenting the air. "Who's here?"

"No one," he grumbled, frowning at Rhys's report. "Simone's not downstairs, is she?"

Rhys's navy eyes narrowed. "She came down for a moment. Stojanovski mentioned something about you over-indulging and sent her right back up." He cocked his head. "What the fuck is that smell?"

No amount of showering was able to rid him of the stench of stale ancient blood in his veins, the odor emanating from his skin.

"You've got to be fucking kidding me," Rhys growled, stalking toward him. "Tell me you aren't back on that shit."

He held his ground, easing his hands from his pockets and crossing his arms.

"Nicky," Rhys snarled, drawing up to his full height and towering over him. "I want you to tell me this isn't fucking happening right now."

"I can't."

The first blow caught him across the jaw, sending his head bouncing off the wall. Before he could regain his footing, Rhys sent a second hit to his gut. He took a step back, hunting for his balance while another shot landed on his cheek, cracking the bone and shattering his left fang.

"Fight back, you worthless fuckup!" Rhys growled, landing another two hits to his kidneys. "We're following you into this fucking shit and you're fucking *high*? Fight. Back!"

He dropped his arms to his sides as the next blow fell on his ribs.

Rhys's fist drew back again, his eyes black. "Do you have any idea what your highs have cost me over the centuries? Do you have any. Fucking. Idea?" He gripped the collar of Nichol's shirt, his fangs slicing into his chin as he spoke. "Goddamn it, Nichol. How long has this shit been going on?"

"Around a year," he stated, watching when the rage

in his younger brother's face morphed into disappointment.

Rhys released him, running a hand through his hair as he stared at the floor. "Does Kai know?"

He shook his head, the taste of his own blood on his tongue.

"Boy?"

"He suspects."

"Anyone else?"

He shoved his hands into his pockets, his mind whipping to Simone. "No."

Rhys dropped his head and stepped back. "I'm going topside for a bit."

****

Nichol read over Boy's text confirming his location. *Simone's room.*

He deleted the message and listened to Rhys descending into the bunker.

"No one else can know," Rhys stated as his feet hit the ground. "Not Mick, not Jagg. Especially not Dominic. This stays between you and me."

Running a hand through his damp hair, he sat forward in his seat and rested his elbows on his knees. He'd run dozens of scenarios through his head since Rhys left the bunk. Most ended in his final death. A well-deserved ending.

Rhys sat across from him and sprawled out on the chair. "Where are you getting it?"

"Online through a series of VPNs and untraceable emails," he answered, refusing to meet his brother's eyes. "But since we arrived here, directly from Vanito."

A flash of anger crossed Rhys's face. "Vanito. Of course. Fucking Vanito." He shook his head, strands of his black hair falling into his eyes. "How often?"

"I'm managing it," he muttered. When Rhys snorted, he leaned back. "Nightly."

"But you're managing it," Rhys sneered. He gripped the arm of the chair, his fangs lengthening. "Why? I mean…fuck, Nicky. Why?"

He leaned back and rubbed his jaw. "Fuck if I know." He risked a glance at Rhys, his stomach knotting when he took in the look of betrayal marring his brother's face. "Stress, I guess," he added with a huff, rising to his feet and pacing the floor. "Kaius leaving, you incapacitated, the Deepfryers, Jagger's imprisonment, you and Lis burning, sanctuary, knowing I moved too late, Dovidas, Chen…" He yanked his phone from his pocket and tossed it to Rhys. "Forty phone calls and over a hundred emails since you left three hours ago. And it's still going. Not including the texts. Or the news alerts."

Rhys swiped open Nichol's phone, his lips tightening across his fangs. "We can help you with this," he said, flipping from app to app, his brows knotting. "Fuck, Nic. This is what you have left *after* designating to Jagger and Mickey?"

He snatched the phone back as he remembered the messaging app he used for Simone. "It'll slow once things settle."

Rhys hung his head. "This is really fucking bad."

"I've managed so far," he replied tersely. "A blood high here and there isn't going to make or break any mission we have right now."

"Fuck," Rhys groaned, falling back into his seat. "Is the withdrawal still harsh?"

He nodded.

"Another lifetime," Rhys said with a humorless chuckle as he shook his head. "Lis knows, you know. That you used to use that shit. And I told her you were an addict in another lifetime." He chuckled humorlessly. "I took seventeen years in Vanito's pit for you, Nicky. Seventeen fucking years, a shit-ton of rats, and a few thousand cockroaches in my hair thanks to your little issue."

He froze in place, his mind flashing back to the blurred, flickering memories of his last visit to Vanito's estate.

"Yeah, Nicky, it was you who messed with his Tender," Rhys said quietly, his gaze locked on the floor as Nichol recalled with cruel clarity the off-limits woman he bedded, the only one he wasn't allowed to touch.

She was nothing special, one in a long line of warm bodies he sought out when under the spell of his drug of choice. Hell, he hadn't been able to remember the woman when Vanito confronted the Kaius haunt, their bloodline's scent all over the Tender tied to him and him alone.

His brother shook his head. "Whatever, though. We'll deal with this shit on my terms this time."

"I...I'm sorry," he stammered, guilt and shame pounding through his head.

"Done and forgotten," Rhys stated, his eyes hardening. "Okay. We'll secure what you need to make it through the next however long. But every major decision will pass through me before being executed. Once we're back at the haunt, you'll go on lockdown until the worst of the withdrawal passes, and we'll go from there." He lounged back casually. "You'll be on nightly scent-tests from me until we're through this."

He nodded, unable to respond.

"And no more Vanito," Rhys said. "I'll find another source on site. No way in fucking hell do I need that asshole's stench near me again." He stood up and approached Nichol. "We got this, okay?"

Chapter Twenty-Seven

Simone tossed her controller onto the floor and glared at her babysitter. "I thought you didn't play video games."

Boy bent down to retrieve the remote, passed it back to her without a word, and returned his attention to the bright graphics on the television. The dead blue eyes which left her unnerved back at the Kaius haunt held a glimpse of amusement as the game characters danced victoriously on the screen.

"This is such bullshit," she grumbled, pulling up another race she felt certain she could win against the mute vampire. "We'll see how cocky you are after I kick your ass at this one."

She glanced down at her phone while the game loaded.

Silent.

Since Boy's arrival, she had been anticipating a message from Nichol. A check-in. A call. A quick text to make sure all was well.

Nothing.

Boy leaned forward, his hulking form less intimidating when he was hunched over the tiny game steering wheel than when he was standing guard at her door, his long blond hair hanging in his empty eyes. As the race countdown began, he flexed his fingers quickly in preparation.

"You're going down, Boy," she taunted, elbowing her bodyguard in the ribs and chuckling when he veered off the road into the abyss. He side-eyed her briefly, shuffling away from her while his character reloaded.

And then he proceeded to kick her ass.

"I give," she huffed, tossing her hands up. "You play, I'm going to bed."

As she closed her bedroom door, the faint sounds of another race beginning followed her into her room. She plugged her phone in and stripped down. Pulling on a pair of sweatpants and a tank top, she placed her weapons around her room strategically to ensure she had easy access from any position before she crawled into bed.

Highsteaks1403: u up?

587OriginalNK: yeah

587OriginalNK: Boy behaving?

Highsteaks1403: kicked my ass at racing, but yeah, all good

587OriginalNK: I didn't know he played

Highsteaks1403: silent asshole's been holding out on you

Highsteaks1403: it'll be dark for another hour…

587OriginalNK: yeah

She rolled her eyes.

Highsteaks1403: your being obtuse again

587OriginalNK: *you're

Highsteaks1403: come over

587OriginalNK: dealing with some things here. you're safe with Boy

Highsteaks1403: but I'm happy with you

Her phone went silent, Nichol's icon greying out almost immediately. She tossed her arm over her eyes and tried to ignore the cheerful music coming from her television in the other room. Game after game played, Boy obviously enjoying himself as victory music erupted every few minutes.

Beginner's luck.

A soft knock from the hall caught her attention. She shot up in bed while Boy crossed the floor, keyed in the lock code, and opened the door. Tilting her head, she listened to the quiet voice in her living room and slipped from her bed. Gripping a blade in one hand and a small stake in the other, she tiptoed to her door and turned the knob slowly, cringing at the slight creak in the metal hinges as she opened it.

"Hey."

****

Nichol's hands were fisted in his pockets, his eyes locked on the stake in Simone's hand. "You want to put that away?"

I shouldn't be here.

Simone shook her head, her curls bouncing. "I...yeah. Yeah, I will." She set her weapons on her dresser and looked up at him. "You look terrible."

"Long night," he replied, second-guessing his decision to crawl to her door.

Second-guessing it for the hundredth time.

Her hand rose to his cheek and traced what was left of the bruise Rhys had given him. "What the hell happened?"

"Nothing I didn't have coming to me." he stated, arching away from her hand. "So Boy likes video games?"

She nodded as her blue eyes locked on his. "We already established that. What happened?" She squinted and leaned closer to him, her thumb tracing his lower lip. "Open."

He clenched his teeth and took a step back, glaring at her as she followed suit.

"I said open."

He parted his lips, turning his gaze to the door while she assessed his teeth.

Her disgust was the last thing he needed to see tonight.

"I'll kill him," she stated, her thumb running down the length of his broken fang. "Point me toward whoever did this, and I'll stake his pathetic ass while he sleeps."

"It was well-deserved," he replied, brushing her hand away. "I'm on guard-dog duty tonight, so go back to bed. I'll beat Boy's high score and send him a picture of it."

"That's not why you're here."

He backed up toward her sofa. "No, but it'll annoy the hell out of him, and that'll be worth a laugh."

She nodded slowly. "Okay. Have fun, NK."

He watched as she retreated to her bedroom, flicking the lights off. He slumped onto the sofa and picked up the controller, selecting an easy track to warm up. After a few unsuccessful attempts to beat Boy's scores, he tossed the remote down and crept into her room.

"I fucked up," he said into the darkness, closing her door behind him.

She sat up in bed, her form becoming clear as Nichol's eyes adjusted to the faint light. "What happened?"

He shook his head and shoved his hands back into his pockets. "I just…I fucked up bad, Highsteaks. And I don't know if I can undo it."

She stood and walked toward him, putting her arms around his neck and pulling him tight to her. "When someone hugs you, you should hug them back," she said, her voice muffled. He dropped his head into her hair and wrapped his arms around her, resisting the urge to crush her to him. "See?" she whispered. "That's better."

The tension he had carried since Rhys first recognized his fall back into his addiction dissipated slightly while Simone tightened her hold on him. "I'm sorry," he murmured, nuzzling her hair.

"For what?"

"For not telling you what I am." He ran his tongue along his broken fang. "For being what I am." Her arms clasped around him harder. He frowned as he picked up the scent of tears the air. "I really don't do well with crying women. Rhys can attest to that. So stop. Now."

She sniffed. Loudly.

"That was exceptionally unattractive," he stated, tilting her chin up and brushing his lips against hers. "Repulsive, actually."

When she didn't recoil from him, he ran his tongue across her lips, a knot in his stomach undoing when she opened her mouth to him and ran her hand through his hair. She moved her lips down his chin to his throat, her tongue tracing her path over his skin as his hands wormed under the waistband of her pants, making contact with her bare skin and sending his lust into overdrive.

Slow the fuck down, dumbass.

"Off."

The small corner of rational thought still remaining in his mind froze his progress. "What?"

"Shirt off," she commanded, lifting the hem of his

tee up and raising onto her toes to push it over his head. Catching up with her request, he yanked it off and tossed it aside as her lips found his again. Her fingers wrapped around his hands and pushed her sweatpants down her hips, the thin string of her thong hooking into his thumb.

This isn't slowing down, fuckup.

He dropped to his knees and eased her out of her pants, his tongue traveling along the inside of her thigh while she fisted his hair in her hand. Avoiding the one place he desperately wanted to go, he trailed his lips up her body, pushing impatiently at her shirt until she pulled it off for him. He rose up from the floor, gritting his teeth when she went for his cargos and shoved them and his boxers to his knees in a single smooth movement. He fumbled his way out of them, his attention torn between removing the clothing from his ankles and getting his hands on the incredible breasts in his line of sight.

"This is a big fucking mistake," he muttered, kicking off the last of his boxers and sliding his fingers through her wetness.

"Yeah, well, at least it'll be a fun one," she sighed into his ear, her hips grinding against his hand. "Right. There. Don't move."

He could hear himself panting needlessly as she rubbed herself against him, her nails digging into his shoulders while her breathing grew more ragged. "You don't even need me for this, do you?" he teased, his eyes rolling back in his head when her blunt teeth made contact with his throat.

And then she froze.

Nichol's stomach knotted instantly.

"Is that your phone or mine?"

"I…" Nichol listened as the phone buzzed. "Mine."

"Answer it."

He looked down at his hand wedged between her thighs. "You're joking."

She cupped his chin and kissed him. "Are you supposed to be here right now?"

He dropped his head to his chest in defeat, disengaging himself from her and storming across the room, swiping his thumb over his screen and snarling into the mic. "What."

"Hey man! I have a few things to run past you," Mick called out, completely oblivious to his sour mood.

A sour mood which morphed very fucking fast when Simone dropped to her knees in front of him and ran her tongue along the underside of his dick. He shook his head at her while Mickey reviewed some security concerns he had with several lone vampires who had arrived in Denver the night before. She smiled up at him, nodded, and wrapped her lips around him.

"I… what does Jagg think?" he asked, watching in lust-fueled fascination as his length disappeared down her throat. "Fuck."

"That's pretty much exactly what Jagger said," Mick huffed. "Without you or Boy to scent out the bloodline, I'm not—"

He grasped the dresser for balance and tried unsuccessfully to focus on Mick's words. Simone worked him leisurely, her tongue swirling the tip before she'd devour him again, curling his toes every time. "Toss them until we get back," he interrupted, glaring at her when she smirked up at him. "Or hold them in the cells. I—" He dropped his head back as she hollowed out her cheeks and sucked. Hard. "I'll call you back." He tossed his phone on the dresser and tangled his fingers in her hair. "Kiss me?"

She released him, bringing her lips to his and running her tongue across his damaged fang. He stilled, anticipating her reaction.

"I want you," she murmured against his mouth, guiding him toward her bed and pushing him onto it.

He knew his eyes had blackened with hunger as she crawled up his body, her breasts brushing against him and ratcheting his lust even higher. She straddled his hips, gripping him tightly and easing her body down onto him.

His back arched off the bed when her warmth enveloped him, a sensation he hadn't experienced in over thirty years. He grasped for her thighs, running his hands along the smooth skin to ground himself as she took him in completely and whimpered. She began to ride him slowly, circling her hips as she rose off him and sending his eyes rolling back into his head.

"Watch me, Nicky," she commanded, reaching behind herself to run her nails along his inner thigh.

He forced his eyes open, his chest heaving. "You've got to be kidding me," he groaned, his control almost snapping as she arched back to give him an even better view.

"You like?"

"Fuck, yeah," he replied, unable to look away while he pumped his hips into her. He inched his thumbs toward her center, frowning when she swatted them away.

"Lay back and enjoy," she ordered, her hips bucking involuntarily as she increased her speed. She grinned at him. "Can you feel that?"

He nodded, his molars cracking with the effort not

to come before she did. "I can feel everything right now," he ground out, tightening his hold on her thighs while he pounded up into her. He shifted his hips a fraction, hoping his rusty memory wouldn't fail him.

"Fuck, Nicky!"

Not that out of practice.

Holding her in place, he increased his speed and watched as she lolled her head back, cursing him over and over. He pushed himself onto his elbows, desperate to get closer to her as her body began to tighten around him. "Kiss me," he gasped when the first tremors of her orgasm fluttered around him. "Please."

She leaned forward, her lips pressing against his as the first waves hit her. He held her to him as her body shook, her moans muffled by his tongue. He reached between them, his thumb working her as her first orgasm began to fade, the second cresting while his own barreled through him. He arched his neck away from her lips, snapping his fangs into the darkness when the desire to bite began to take hold as he came inside her.

When his body finally went limp, he opened his eyes, his vision struggling to catch up. She lay on him, her ragged breathing and racing heart rate providing him with something to focus on while his brain slowly began firing on all cylinders again.

"You okay?" he asked, trailing his fingers down her spine.

"Hmmmm," she hummed, nuzzling into his chest and resting her weight on him. "I don't know why Rhys is the trainer. You're way better at this than he is."

He pursed his lips and glared down at her. "I'm still inside you. Maybe leave my brother's name out of it until I'm not."

"Just sayin'," she grinned, wiggling her hips and sending jolts of lust through him. "You should be flattered."

"Yeah, well, you should be flattered that I'm about thirty seconds away from wanting another round."

****

Nichol caught sight of the microwave's clock and groaned. "I need to go."

Simone pushed back against his hips and arched her back, looking over her shoulder at him. "And I'll let you. After this."

He pulled out of her and spun her around, lifting her onto the counter and sliding back into her warmth. "You're going to shower and use every ounce of those expensive shampoos and soaps after this." He dropped his head to her shoulder as her legs wrapped around his waist. "I don't want my scent on you when you go back down there."

She tilted her head and trailed her fingers down his neck, her thumb tracing the shell of his ear. "Maybe I want your scent on me."

"Not a joke, Simone," he growled, stilling inside her until she squirmed against him. "It's too risky right now."

"Fine," she huffed, laying back on the counter and arching her breasts toward him. Taking the hint, he grazed his fangs over one pert nipple, circling it with his tongue before drawing it into his mouth.

When her legs twitched at his hips, he turned his attention to the other one and increased the speed of his thrusts until she was a whimpering mess beneath him.

Stojanovski owns her.

He shoved the invasive thought from his head,

focusing instead on the way she said his name when she was close to coming, the way her blue eyes darkened, and her breathing grew more shallow.

The way she bit her lip in anticipation every time his hand dropped to her core.

"Harder," she groaned, her legs pulling his hips tighter to her.

"Demanding little thing, aren't you?" he panted while he complied, watching with satisfaction when she became undone, her nails digging deep enough into his skin to draw blood. He pulled out of her and dropped to his knees, running his tongue through her folds as his thumb worked her nub to bring on her second orgasm. As it hit, he slid back inside her and released, his arms shaking as he fought to keep his weight off her. "Okay," he grunted, pushing himself up. "I'm gone."

She locked her arms and legs around him. "Carry me to my room."

He rolled his eyes but obeyed, dropping her onto her bed and snatching his cargos off the floor. "If you can avoid the main hall for one more night, do it. The less Dovidas sees of you, the less chance he'll keep interest in you."

She wrapped herself in her blanket. "Will you be down there tonight?"

Pulling his shirt over his head, he nodded. "Every night until this is done."

She watched him as he pulled his boots on and laced them up. "Will you be here again?"

You don't belong to me.

"I'll try," he said, bending down to kiss her curls, inhaling her scent once more before he left. "Text me in a bit."

Ten minutes later he was descending the ladder into his bunker and activating the lock before he began to make his way to his room.

"You're fucking Stojanovski's hybrid?" Rhys's voice called from the sofa, the disdain clear. "We don't have enough shit on our plates?"

"I wasn't *fucking* the hybrid," he snarled, storming past Rhys toward his bunk.

"I know that scent," Rhys taunted, rising to his feet. "I know that scent very well, actually. Tell me, Nichol, how do you tune out that look of pure revulsion she has when she's on her knees? Do you look away or does it do something for you?"

He spun, flattening Rhys to the floor as Boy peered out of his room. "You know those things that are none of your fucking business?" he growled, his fangs elongated with rage. "This is one of those things. Stay out of who I fuck, and I'll let you keep your head attached to your useless body."

Rhys's eyes darkened for a moment before they reverted. "It's a thing, isn't it?" he barked out, rising to his elbows as Nichol released him. "Holy shit. Nichol. You have a thing for her, don't you?"

Ignoring Rhys's questions, he stormed into the bathroom and turned on the shower, letting the water run as hot as it could before he stepped in and began scrubbing Simone's scent from his skin.

That look of pure revulsion.

He rinsed the shampoo from his hair and scanned his memories of the past twelve hours.

Frustration.

Anticipation.

Lust.

Mischief.

He turned off the water and wrapped a towel around his hips.

Simone had a lot of looks over the day, but revulsion was one he knew he hadn't seen.

Hadn't wanted to see.

He exited the bathroom and ducked into his bunker to dress, knowing he'd be expected topside within the hour. As he flipped through his phone, Rhys knocked on his door.

"Fuck off."

"I'm coming in," Rhys replied, opening the door and crossing the room. He stood in front on him and narrowed his eyes. "You know she belongs to Stojanovski."

Nichol fired off a quick text to Mick.

"How long has this been going on?"

Checking his flagged emails, he began replying to the most crucial.

"I'll make you a deal."

He looked up from his phone.

Rhys lifted a brow. "If we get out of this with our asses and heads in their rightful places, and *if* you get clean, I'll find a loophole and get Simone released."

Released.

Once her choices were no longer bound to vampire society, he would be relegated to the bottom of the pile, lumped in with Jackson and Dovidas and all the vampires she despised. Free from the compound, free from the quarters. He would be nothing more than a forgotten romp during her confinement.

"Deal."

****

Simone clomped down the stairs in her heels, earning a look of annoyance from Stojanovski as he met her. "Finally well enough to join us," he mused, scanning her ornate dress over and humming his approval. "Good. Dovidas has been asking for you." He placed her hand on his arm and began to lead her across the room. "You aren't permitted to go anywhere with him alone, am I clear?"

Nodding, she glanced around the room. "Will I be in the hunt tonight?"

"It would appear you have a benefactor willing to shell over a lot of money to keep you off the grounds and out of the beds of any other males this evening." He chuckled. "One of these nights I'm going to need to sample this costly blood of yours." Jackson slowed his pace. "Entertain Dovidas and Chen. Keep the conversation light and the flirtation sweet." He pointed toward Dahlia. "Think blissful airhead. Channel that."

Setting a smile on her face, she approached the sofas where Dovidas and Chen sat, the ancient male looking closer to final death than he had before. Kaspars Dovidas rose, bowing as he took her hand in his and kissed it. "I was wondering if you'd bless me with your presence again," he drawled, gesturing toward the couch and sitting tight beside her. "You're better at playing cat-and-mouse than I anticipated."

She smiled at him, shyly wrapping her pinky finger around his. "The thrill of the hunt and the delay of gratification is a hard drug to fight," she said coyly, forcing her back to relax into the cushions. "I suspect you also thrive on the sweet torment of anticipation?"

Dovidas chuckled, his laughter drawing the attention of several vampires and humans in the vicinity.

"I do," he agreed. "Though I admit I can be a bit indulgent of immediate gratification when the mood strikes me."

"Probably not a big online shopper then, are you?" Rhys's voice called out behind them, his long arm draping over her shoulder. "Simone here was trained to lie in wait. To withhold from instant gratification in favor of a more satisfying payout in the end. Right, sweetheart?"

Keeping her eyes on Dovidas, she held the smile plastered on her face. "Patience is a virtue, after all."

Rhys circled around them, flopping down beside Chen. "Patience, and keeping those knees locked. Am I right, my virtuous little angel?" He grinned, flinching when a strong hand gripped him by the back of the neck. "Nichol. I was wondering when you'd make your way over here."

She refused to look up. Dovidas's hand rested on her thigh, his manicured nails inching their way toward the slit of her gown. "So Kaspars, will you be hunting this evening? Several of the humans have their eye on you."

Dovidas looked over at the huddle of women at the stairwell, their interest in the swarthy vampire obvious. "I very well may," he murmured, his eyes drawn to one woman as she hefted her ample bosom up. "Jackson informed me you've been unwell. I assume you won't be playing?"

Feigning disappointment, she gave an apologetic shrug. "Human frailties and all," she sighed. "You'll have to let me know how it goes out there. I'm always fascinated by the vampire experience of the hunt."

Nichol walked away from the group silently, approaching the crowd of humans and singling out

Dahlia. Simone tracked his movements, her lips pursing as he bent down to scent Dahlia's neck. Humming polite replies to Dovidas, she watched the way Nichol's hands flexed at his sides, the twitching of his arms, the restless shifting of his weight as he stood against the wall, phone in hand and grumbling brief answers to the young biter who joined him.

The young vampire.

"I'll be starting the countdown shortly," Stojanovski stared, giving Rhys a pointed look. "Will you be participating?"

Rhys lolled his head back dramatically. "Nope. Taken male, and all." He grinned at Dovidas. "When you're hooked to a Master Killer, you want to keep your fuck-ups to a minimum." He gestured toward Simone. "I'll babysit this fashion disaster while the rest of you have fun. She needs a few reminders on heel-pairing and skirt length."

Dovidas assisted Chen to his feet, lifting her hand to his lips and scoring his fangs across her skin. "Perhaps you'll be well enough tomorrow."

Smiling at him and ignoring the slight sting on her hand, she forced a light-hearted giggle. "I look forward to it."

As the vampires made their way toward the humans, Rhys casually moved over to sit beside her, stretched his arm across her shoulder, and leaned close to her ear.

"So Nichol's caught that spiteful eye of yours, has he?"

She kept her attention on the crowd forming at the base of the stairs, watching Nichol and Boy inch along the outskirts of the group.

He followed her gaze. "He's a miserable bastard,

isn't he? Moodier than Mickey. Angrier than me. Probably smarter than Kaius." He chuckled. "Not a good combo for a woman with a temper and the training to do something with it."

The humans poured out of the hall, the heavy doors slamming as the countdown for the vampires began. The pair sat in silence until Stojanovski began to rev his guests.

"He has enough on his mind right now," Rhys finally continued, nonplussed by her refusal to respond. "You would be wise to find a more suitable toy."

The vamps tore from the room, Nichol and Boy among the first out the doors, Dovidas slowed by the weakened ancient at his side.

Alone in the hall, she turned to Rhys. "Nichol has had enough on his mind for far longer than he's known me. Long before I was even in the training quarters. Perhaps if you or your hauntmates had been more attuned to it, he wouldn't be turning to me now for respite."

Rhys's navy irises elongated, his fangs extending. "You—"

"Who coordinated your release from the Deepfryer?" she pushed, straightening her back. "The buzz around here about sanctuary? Who's organizing that? You're a wealthy haunt. Who controls it? Who pays the bills? Who stepped up to fill every void your absentee leader left? Every void your absence left? The damage you sustained must have taken months to heal. Who stepped into your role?"

Rhys leaned back, his eyes narrowing. "He talks to you."

She tightened her lips and stared at the closed doors.

"We need him at his peak," Rhys stated. "If Nichol begins fucking up now, there's a good chance our haunt will be wiped out. Ours and a lot of others."

Her mind flashed to Nichol's hazel eyes when he walked into her room the previous dawn.

Tired.

Broken.

Scared.

I fucked up bad, Highsteaks. And I don't know if I can undo it.

She stood, smoothing out her skirt. "He knows that, Rhys. He knows, and it drives every moment of his existence. Don't shred him apart for doing what he needs to do to shoulder that weight."

"He doesn't need a pity-fuck from a vamp killer," he called as she made her way toward the stairs.

"Strange," she said with a chuckle, clomping her heels loudly up the steps in spite. "Isn't that how you ended up with your girlfriend?"

Chapter Twenty-Eight

Nichol dangled his legs over the eavestroughs, scanning the deserted hunting grounds for any remaining signs of life while the faintest hint of the morning sun peaked. Calculating the distance to Simone's window, he rolled onto his stomach and lowered himself to the narrow sill, using his toe to nudge the pane.

"Cutting it a little close, aren't you?" she asked as she pushed the window completely open and stepped aside to make room for his large form to contort through.

He slammed the glass shut, pulled down the shade, and closed the heavy light-tight curtains. "It took me a good hour of licking shingles to get the taste of Dahlia's blood off my tongue," he groused, unlacing his boots and kicking them aside.

She swatted his arm and glared at him. "Don't be ungrateful. Dahlia's a sweet girl."

"Dahlia," he stated, "is a ditz." He rolled his shoulders out, stretching his chin to the ceiling. "How long did Rhys keep you downstairs?"

Something changed in her eyes briefly, a hardness flickering across her face before she shrugged. "Fifteen minutes after you guys left, maybe? Where did Boy end up today?"

He opened his phone and glanced over the messages. "He was back at the bunker by four." He flipped through a few more texts. "Rhys was back shortly before five." He read through another brief text from Rhys, hovering his thumb over the message and deleting it, ignoring the buzzing alert of another incoming email. "How much of an ass was he?"

"Rhys?" she laughed, her curls bouncing as she shook her head. "As much as expected. No better, no worse." She walked over to her bed and pulled back the covers. "Get in. I'm exhausted."

He looked her over, his brows knotting as he took in the dark circles under her eyes and the slight paleness of her skin. "You shouldn't have waited up."

"I've waited up for you dozens of times," she yawned, flopping gracelessly onto the mattress. "What's once more?"

His fingers stretched and fisted at his sides, the disquieting restlessness of withdrawal settling into his muscles.

She patted the empty spot beside her, her eyes already closed. "Lie. Down."

He heaved his shoulders and obeyed, crossing his arms behind his head as she curled up at his side, one hand resting on his chest as her breathing became slower and deeper. He fought to keep his movements to a minimum, tightening one muscle at a time as the aches traveled through his limbs.

"Is it bad?" she whispered groggily, her hand reaching up to his cheek.

"Yeah. Get some rest."

He ran his hand through her hair, lifting one curl at a time and watching it bounce back. She sighed and mumbled something unintelligible, shifting against him while her breathing leveled out again and her heart rate slowed.

—Got you taken care of.—

Rhys's text ran through his head on a loop. He flipped through every vampire he'd seen at the evening's hunt, separating the eldest and trying to work out which one Rhys would have approached.

—Got you taken care of.—

He ran his tongue over his fangs as they lengthened, dropping one leg to the floor and flexing his calf muscles in a desperate attempt to stave off the restlessness overtaking his legs.

—Got you taken care of.—

Stretching one arm behind Simone, he contorted his shoulder to avoid jostling her while he curled his bicep in a slow, repetitive cycle.

—Got you taken care of.—

He lifted his hip and pulled his phone from his back pocket to check the time.

It was going to be a long fucking day.

****

Simone's eyes snapped open as the sound of rushing water hit her ears. She reached across the bed, patting the empty mattress for physical confirmation Nichol was no longer beside her before she padded to the bathroom door and knocked lightly.

"Nichol?"

"I'll be out in a minute," he called back, his voice gruff.

She wandered into the kitchen and turned on her coffee maker, listening as the shower turned off and Nichol muttered quietly to himself.

When he exited, she was momentarily stunned by how young he looked. Nichol's short auburn hair was wet, sticking out in all directions as he roughly dried it with a small towel. His cargos hung off his hips, undone and exposing the band of his boxers while his shirt rode up, clinging to his damp skin.

A frat boy late for class.

"I'm, like, ten years older than you," she laughed, shaking her head and pouring a cup of coffee from the half-percolated pot.

"I'm, like, a hundred and forty decades older than you," he grunted, hefting his pants up and yanking at the zipper. His irises were little more than blackened slits, his freckles standing out against his pale skin. He kept his head down, doubling back to the bathroom to retrieve his phone.

"Are you all right?" she asked, leaning on the kitchen counter, and setting her mug down. "You seem off."

"Fine." He paced the living room and typed rapidly on his cell. "Should you be up already?" He glanced up at her, his jaw grinding back and forth.

She narrowed her eyes and watched him walk a repetitive line on her floor, his biceps knotting and straining. "I have coffee. I'm good." She eased herself around the counter and stepped into his path. "How can I help?"

He stretched out his neck and gave her a tight smile, his fangs running long and slicing small lines into his chin. "You can let me walk it off," he said, looking pointedly at the other side of the room. When she didn't budge, a flash of frustration crossed his face. "I need to move, Simone. Just let me, okay?"

She sighed and returned to the counter to grab her drink. "Who are you texting?"

"Jagger," he answered, distracted. "Mick. Dominic.

I have a three-way with a Tender held up at the Newark airport and her master who's already hiding out in the Philippines. Another with an ancient offering a questionably large amount of money to hide out one of his offspring in Denver." He frowned. "The offspring wants to stay in New Jersey."

Scooting by him, she sat on the sofa and curled her legs up. "I guess it's dark on the East coast already, isn't it?"

He nodded, his thumb moving at lightning speed. "I have under an hour to get the coastal issues shored up before the Midwest comes online." His phone buzzed as he typed, and he growled in annoyance. "Fucking emails. Outdated communication source."

She laughed. "This, coming from a guy alive before the printing press? That's hilarious."

The faint grin appearing briefly almost broke her heart when his jaw twitched and it vanished. "Precisely. If I can identify texting is the most efficient method, these forty-year-old assholes should be able to," he huffed, rubbing his chin and smearing a small droplet of blood onto his fingers. "Fucking *fuck*!"

"It's not a big deal," she called after him as he stormed to the bathroom sink and rinsed off his hand. "Don't you have something to level you out a bit?"

His lips drew into a thin line as he arched his head back. "Not your business, Simone."

She snorted. "Well, I think anything in my apartment as snarly and spastic as you've been tonight is definitely my business. You're freaking me out."

Anything.

Anyone.

She cringed as he nodded slowly and made his way

into her bedroom, returning with his boots.

"Where're you going?"

He tugged them on, not bothering to tie the laces. "Sunset's in fifteen. I'm heading downstairs, and then I'm heading back to my bunk." With his phone still locked in his fist, he opened the door. "Text me once you know Stojanovski's plans for you tonight."

There was barely a pause between the slamming of her door and the clicking of her coded lock.

Dammit.

She grabbed her own phone off her bedside table.

Highsteaks1403: im sorry

She peeked out her curtains and watched as the sun disappeared.

587OriginalNK: So am I

****

Rhys held his position on the bunker sofa as Nichol descended into the room, his footing slipping on the final rung of the ladder. He'd heard his brother's heavy stumbling gait as he made his way across the hardwood floor overhead, the unsteady lumbering conjuring memories he neither wanted nor needed.

He lifted a wine bottle from the coffee table and held it out. "Take it easy on this," he cautioned when Nichol's feet hit the floor of the bunker. "I'm not sure I can get my hands on any more."

Nichol rested his forehead on the ladder, his arms draped over it to hold him upright. "Thanks."

He sat up and rested his bare feet onto the table. "Am I safe in assuming you were with Simone again?"

His eldest brother nodded, his nostrils flaring as the scent of the ancient blood hit him. "Is that—"

"Yeah." He pushed a stray strand of hair out of his

eyes. "I won't say Boy was willing, but he understood the rationale."

Nichol pushed off the ladder, his eyes on the floor as he made his way to him and the bottle. He sank into the sofa, his fingers twitching while he reached for the blood and brought the bottle to his lips. "I'd rather you not be in here."

He dropped his head to his chest for a moment. "Just take it," he muttered, no more anxious to witness his hauntmate indulge his addiction than Nichol was to have him witness it. He looked over and gave him a tight smile. "If we make it out of this compound alive, I might join you in a victory swig myself."

"Not fucking worth it," Nichol grumbled, raising the bottle and taking a long drink. He closed his eyes and lowered the blood to his lap. "So not fucking worth it."

Grunting in agreement, he watched as the tremors in Nichol's limbs stilled, the involuntary jerks ceasing as Boy's blood worked its way through his body. "So are you in the doghouse?"

Nichol's eyes snapped open, the hazel of his irises visible again. "What?"

"The doghouse," he repeated. "You know, when your woman decides she's had enough of your shit and needs a break from your innate stupidity? The place I live in almost constantly since Lis moved her lotions and those goddamn pink towels into my room?"

Nichol placed the bottle on the table and tapped at it gently. "Where's your strength sitting?"

Fucking work mode.

He ran his tongue over his fang. "I could probably take Chen in hand-to-hand."

"Where's Boy?"

"In his room." He glanced over at the closed door. "He's all good. No worries, right?"

Nichol nodded and leaned back into the sofa, closing his eye again and ignoring the incessant buzzing of his phone. "I owe you."

"I'll put together my list of demands once we're back on home turf, Nicky. I'm going to get suited up for the night and then we can head topside. I'm fucking sick of playing nice with Dovidas." He squeezed Nichol's shoulder as he passed. "The sooner Dovidas gives up the name of his backer, the sooner we know if we're all gonna die in this shit-hole."

****

Nichol waited until he heard Rhys's closet door open before he lifted the wine bottle up and took another long swig of the fresh blood. Boy's blood was potent. More so than Vanito's. Richer, too. His muscles relaxed as the familiar rush of warmth coursed through him, slowing his mind down enough to push all but the most pressing thoughts aside.

Simone, unfortunately, being one of the most pressing thoughts, and the one thought he sure as hell didn't need pulsing through his head.

He flicked open his emails and stared at them as they loaded. Fifteen unread. Twenty-three. Forty-one.

One more hit. Just one more.

As Boy's blood coated his throat and filled his gut, he knew he'd pushed it too far.

****

Simone crouched against the wall, her hoodie hiding her hair while she craned her neck to peer through the banisters at Stojanovski and the striking brunette prowling the hall while she spoke.

"A referee," the woman called over her shoulder, grazing her fingers over an ornate tapestry hanging on the wall. "An impartial referee to ensure an honest battle."

Jackson's face was locked down, his stance widening slightly when the woman turned to face him. "The cost to my reputation would be significant," he stated, his attention wholly focused on his leather-clad guest while she examined a vase displayed atop a column. "The prestige of the compound will be called into question."

Simone shifted, lowering her knee to steady her balance.

"Jackson, dear," the woman purred, crossing the floor in sky-high stiletto boots, "if I don't get my way, the compound, and you, will cease to exist." She pursed her red lips. "Your bank account has been adequately compensated, correct?" When Stojanovski nodded tersely, she reached up and cupped his chin. "Then let me play."

His fangs lengthened. "My grounds are open to you. But I see no reason my participation is required. Surely you know the rules you want enforced."

The woman squeezed his face quickly and patted his cheek, turning back toward the vase. "I want this," she murmured, lifting it for closer inspection. "I gave my word but I have a favorite, and I fear I won't be as objective as I should be to ensure a fair fight. Your job will be to balance me if I attempt to sway the match in favor of my baby." She cradled the vase in her arm. "May I?"

She inched back from the banisters as the woman faced her direction, her attention on the artifact in her hands as Jackson murmured his agreement.

"Wonderful!" the woman exclaimed, smiling brightly. "In an hour, then, my dear!" she called out while she strode through the heavy doors, vase in hand. "Oh, and Jackson? Get the party started in here soon. I do so love celebrations."

Crawling toward her door, she inched her phone from her back pocket and opened her messenger app. She keyed in her lock code to her room, tossing the door open as she hit the call icon.

"Come on, Nichol," she whispered, locking the door behind her and beelining to her bedroom. "Pick up."

The phone rang over and over while she armed herself, filling her weapon's pack with bolts and crossbows. When the line disconnected, she tapped open the text screen, the woman's cheerful smile burned into her mind.

Highsteaks1403: where does a female vampire rank on your worst-case scenario list

Chapter Twenty-Nine

Nichol bit his lip as he climbed out of the bunker, his depth-perception off just enough to force him to focus heavily on his movements. He stepped aside to allow Rhys and Boy to exit the hatch, kneeling down to slam it shut and set the code.

"Holy fuck," Rhys groaned. "Does that phone of yours ever fucking stop?"

Rising to his feet, he pulled the offending cell from his pocket and handed it to Rhys. "If you want it to stop, you deal with it."

Rhys snapped his fangs at him and grinned. "Gladly." His thumb danced across the screen. "Eighty-nine emails into the archive box… seventeen text convos set to read… we'll just tap the phone to make that little red number disappear." He swiped to the side. "And we'll jus…" Rhys looked up at him, his brows furrowed and a hint of fear in his eyes. "Who's Highsteaks1403?"

He snatched the phone from Rhys's hand. "I'll deal with that one later."

"No," Rhys said slowly. "Nichol, you better deal with it now."

Glaring at his brother, he opened Highsteaks' message and read it. He squeezed his eyes shut and opened them again, willing the fog in his head to disappear as he reread Simone's text.

Female vampire.

"She's mistaken," he stated, punching the phone icon and growling when it disconnected immediately. "The last one was ended centuries ago and everyone knows the laws regarding the creation of female vampires. Maybe—" He ran his hand over his jaw and started to pace. "It has to be a young one. We'd have heard if a female vamp was created within the last few decades." He fired off a text to Simone. "Anything under four centuries old, and we should be fine."

Boy stilled, his eyes on the front door.

"Rhys, alert Mick and Jagg we may have a rogue female vampire in the vicinity," he ordered, firing off three more messages to Simone. "I want all hauntmates in the communication room in five."

"Who. The. fuck. Is Highsteaks1403?" Rhys demanded, yanking his phone from his back pocket.

Nichol ran his hand through his hair as Stojanovski's text came through. "Simone. And according to Jackson, our presence is required on the grounds in an hour." He looked at his hauntmates. "Bunker. Now."

The males barreled down the ladder.

"Boy, assemble all weapons we managed to smuggle on site. Rhys, I have a bag of burner phones in my room. Plug them all in." He flipped his laptop open, pulled up an aerial view of the compound, and started a video call with his haunt. "I need a list of all known methods of ending or weakening a female vamp," he stated the moment his hauntmates appeared on the screen.

"Decapitation's the only guarantee," Jagger said, his voice tight. "Nichol, man. You guys need to get the fuck out of there."

Rhys returned to the room, kneeling beside him as he laid out the meager weapons Boy had assembled and gave the video feed a tight smile. "Lis, baby. You doing okay?"

He minimized the compound view and tracked potential ambush points. "It's possible our intel is mistaken. Do we have any information—rumored or proven— that any females escaped the culling?"

The Kaius vamps shook their heads.

"Ladies?" he asked.

Bianca gripped Jagger's hand. "None. If there's a female vamp on site, it must be a newborn. A well-hidden one."

He ground his teeth, firing off another round of messages to Simone and snarling when no response came in. "Kaius said Dovidas had an ancient backing him. This female may be unrelated to the current mission." He rubbed his jaw and sat back. "But we'll proceed under the assumption she's working alongside Dovidas and Chen. Possibly an accidental full turning while they were creating those female Deviants last year. Jagg, I've emailed a view of the Stojanovski compound to you. Open it up. I want ideas, and I want them now."

Boy began to arm himself, his blue eyes holding a disarming amount of fear. Nichol passed the remaining arsenal to Rhys. "I have a crossbow stashed in the swamp," he stated before Rhys could protest. "As I see it, we have Dovidas, Chen, the female, and an ancient to deal with in order to put this shit behind us," he said. "We'll work off the idea that the ancient is somewhere close, if not on site."

"Any chance you can get eyes on the ground?" Dominic called out through the mic.

"Working on it," he replied. "I'll go out first and plant the burner phones wherever I can. Jagg, Bianca, I'm going to need you to prime my computer to filter the visuals and record them. Once we have confirmation of a female, Mick, I want you and Audra on the lines alerting every haunt left in the Midwest."

Audra moved closer to the camera. "Retreat," she stated, her cat eyes hard. "Run now, and we'll regroup and attack from a number advantage."

"No can do, sweetheart," Rhys called out, tucking a small stake into his boots. "Females are faster, stronger, and more ruthless by the time they hit a century than most males will hit before their one thousandth birthday. If it's us she's gunning for, there's no running."

Nichol motioned toward the pile of charging phones, pushing Rhys to collect them. "Dominic, I need you and Molly to take over all other haunt operations and business for the night. Answer calls, monitor security, and patrol the premises. Arm yourselves. Heavily." Molly sat up straighter. "Molly, don't sludge Dom tonight, okay? We need him for a few more hours."

She nodded solemnly, earning a snort from Louis.

Turning his attention to the honorary hauntmate, he ran his hand through his hair and clenched his teeth to counter the tingling sensation in his jaw. "Louis, I need you and Lis to do aerial surveillance while I'm planting the cells. Your laptop has a green global icon on it. Enter the Stojanovski coordinates and it'll bring up the compound. I want everything texted to me. Every angle, every movement, every potential hazard. Anything that could slow us, expose us, or end us."

He caught Rhys's eye, a hint of gratitude crossing his brother's face before he resumed testing the cameras on the burners and applying black electrical tape to the bright screens.

"So what's your plan?" Jagg asked, his gaze locked on Nichol's mouth.

He stared at the floor for a moment. "Survive." He leaned forward, his arms resting on his knees. "We could be ambushed walking out of the bunker. We could square off on the grounds. We could be part of the hunt. Without knowing the game, we have no plan." He looked over to Boy. "Boy, you and Rhys will team up. If things go sour, beat it the fuck out of here. I want car keys in your pockets. Now."

"Fuck that," Rhys chuckled. "We're Three Musketeer-ing this shit-storm."

A chorus of agreement rose from the laptop speakers.

"End goal," he growled, pulling the attention back to him, "is survival of the haunt. If we don't put a stake in the threat, a full haunt retreat into the Canadian tundra begins within the hour. And for that, I need as many of you alive as possible. Am I clear?"

Rhys crossed his arms and stared him down, the room still as they held a silent battle of wills.

He dropped his voice so only those in the room with him would hear. "You have the means to release Simone. Your existence takes priority over mine tonight."

Rhys didn't budge.

"I honored your request when it was Lis," he stated, his lips unmoving. "A final request."

Rhys's fangs extended a fraction. "Fine. If our chances drop to zero, Boy and I will start the exodus."

Audra's voice filtered through the speakers, her protests quieted by Mick as Nichol rose to his feet.

"Everyone know their role?"

His hauntmates nodded solemnly.

"Good. Boots on the ground, fuckers."

****

Nichol dragged his duffle bag across the grass, inching away from the electrified fence before he pulled another burner out. He lifted the bottom strip of tape, ensuring the video feed was activated before he propped it against a stone, the camera angled toward the compound's main hall. Louis' text came in instantly, confirming Jagg had visual.

Five to go.

Sliding his phone into his bag to hide the brightness, he fired off another message to Simone.

587OriginalNK: Stay inside. Lock down. Arm yourself. If you see your chance to escape, take it. Please.

He continued to creep along the perimeter, crawling across the dirt on his stomach and using his elbows to propel himself forward. The grounds were deserted, save for the odd squirrel chattering from the forest. He kept one eye on the main building, dividing his attention between the entrance and Simone's window while he made his way through the cattails where his crossbow lay hidden from view.

Louis: movement at the doors

He glanced at the time.

11:47.

Boy and Rhys were set to arrive at the hall in thirteen minutes. He clenched his teeth, forcing his lethargic muscles to move him across the terrain faster as he zeroed in on the trees, creeping as fast as he dared until he reached the outskirts of the woods where he could finally travel by foot under the veil of the overgrown forest.

11:52.

He hefted his backpack over his shoulder and climbed up one of the higher trees, propping a burner among the branches and jumping to the ground. He scanned Simone's preferred surveillance trees for any sign of her, caught between hoping she was safely secured in her rooms and needing to see for himself that she was okay.

11:56.

His phone lit up with updates.

Boy and Rhys were exiting the bunker.

Louis and Lis spotted four figures on the steps of the main hall.

Jagg had ample visual of the grounds.

He lifted his crossbow from his bag and trekked through the woods toward the center of the compound, sliding wooden bolts into his pockets and dropping the duffel among the leaves of an overgrown bush. He gripped his phone, scanning the open field and cursing the moonless night.

Faint movement from the far reaches of the land, two figures sauntering calmly across the land.

Four figures standing motionless on the veranda.

His phone buzzed in his hand.

Highsteaks1403: look up

He dropped his head, his chest constricting as he slowly lifted his eyes to the towering pine.

"Hey, NK," Simone whispered, her face hidden beneath her hoodie.

"Hey, Highsteaks," he replied, his throat tight when he realized there was no way for her to return to the safety of her rooms without being seen. "Here for the show?"

She pushed her hood back a fraction and smiled down at him. "Here for the trophy kill."

He glanced at the field, grabbing on to the tree's trunk to steady his balance as he tracked Rhys and Boy's advance. "Is that Stojanovski at the entrance?" he asked quietly, narrowing his eyes in a vain attempt to make out the features of the shadowed figures.

"I think so."

He zeroed in on the hall, adjusting his hold on his bow. "You need to take him out tonight," he ordered, unable to look up at her again. "Your freedom's your end game, and there's a good chance I won't be around to ensure it. You'll have one chance before your location is revealed and he takes you out. Don't fuck it up, Highsteaks."

He jogged across the field, Rhys and Boy meeting him in the middle. "Ready?"

"Nope," Rhys grinned, turning toward the entrance of the hall.

Nichol and Boy flanked him as his phone buzzed.

12:00.

"Oh, this is going to be fun!" a woman's voice called out from the shadows of the veranda. "Kaius, dear, are you ready?"

Chapter Thirty

Boy flinched as the female's excited voice cut through the night air, his hulking form cowering back a fraction and sending an icy chill through Nichol's veins. Rhys adjusted his stance, stepping closer and side-eying him with confusion.

The female vamp descended the steps, her head tilted while she assessed the trio. "I see the guard dog is still tethered to you," she sneered, her nose wrinkling as she looked Boy up and down. "Kaius. Come. Did you think I wouldn't know you were making your way here? I know everything, mutt. Now stop lurking back there and introduce me to your spawn." She lifted her gaze to the field behind them. "I want to see what your bastard blood has sired."

He kept his eyes trained on the woman, the tendons in his neck straining as he tracked Kaius's steady approach at his back. The female jutted her hip to the side, tapping her foot impatiently until Kai stood at his side, his face expressionless.

"My eldest, Nicholai," he announced, his voice flat. "A skilled linguist and technology specialist." Kai's eyes flicked to him. "My second-in-command and de facto leader in my absence."

The female vamp strode forward until she stood toe-to-toe with him. "He's cute," she murmured, reaching up to cup his chin.

His fangs lengthened at the intrusion, his instinctive reaction earning him a slap that split his skin and chipped a chunk of bone from his cheek.

The female glared at Kaius with disproval. "This one lacks self-control and obedience." She brought one finger to Nichol's open wound and gathered a drop of blood on the tip, licking it off slowly and recoiling in disgust. "Though I suppose he's a passable specimen for a mongrel."

Kai held motionless, sending a quiet pulse of warning into Nichol's head as the vamp made her way to Rhys. She bent at the waist, aligning her eyes with his tattoos. "This one is defective."

"Rhys," Kaius stated, clasping his hands behind his back. "Skilled combatant and globally recognized trainer of quality Tenders."

The female smirked as her long nails scored across an intricate loop, a thin line of blood outlining the detailed marking. "Oh, yes. The Medico della Peste. The Plague Doctor. The Scourge." She trailed her hand across Rhys's chest and tugged at the neckline of his shirt. "Does his reputation hold weight? Is he as lethal as he is pretty?"

Nichol's teeth clenched as Rhys opened his mouth to speak. When Rhys's jaw snapped shut, his muscles twitching in protest, he risked a quick glance at Boy.

The mute male's blue eyes were completely obscured by his hair, his head bowed in a peculiar deference to the vamp while she regarded him with open contempt.

"I can't believe you've kept this animal around," she sneered, stalking around the hulking, blond vampire. She placed one stiletto boot between his legs, kicking his stance apart as she gripped his shoulders and straightened his spine. Her fingers tangled into Boy's long hair, and she yanked his head back. "Show your elder some respect."

Every muscle in Nichol's body tensed.

Elder.

Rhys inched closer to him, his navy eyes locked on the ground and lips tight.

The female resumed her place in front of the Kaius hauntmates, her hands on her hips while she looked at Kai, her black eyes narrow. "Where are the rest of your bastard brats?" she demanded, a perfectly sculpted brow raising. When Kaius remained silent, she pursed her full lips. "Nicholai, is it? Nicholai. Tell me where the others are." She scanned the area. "I was hoping for a more substantial battle."

Taking his cue from Kai, he kept his gaze averted, his mind flipping through every potential outcome for the night.

Death. Final death. Slow death. Quick death.

Inevitable death at the hands of an ancient female vampire.

"Nichol answers to me," Kaius called out, stepping in front of Nichol when the woman moved toward him.

"And *you* answer to *me*," she stated, her fangs elongating as she wrapped her manicured fingers around Kai's neck. "Where. Are. The others."

Kaius's feet left the ground, his arms hanging at his side in surrender.

"Bound for South America," Nichol ground out, his eyes locked on the air between his creator's boots and the grass below him. "We're expected in Argentina in eleven nights."

The female smiled sweetly at him, dropping Kaius and brushing her hands on her leather pants. "See?" she cooed, patting Kai's cheek. "That wasn't worth the fight, was it?" She looked back at the veranda, motioning for the others to join them.

Kaius's head dropped a fraction.

Nichol's stomach sank.

"Dovidas, dear, will you do the honors of introductions?" she sang, taking Kaspars' offered arm and laying her head on his shoulder.

"Gladly." Dovidas smirked, looking the Kaius males over with disdain. "Gentlemen, this is my creator, Khthonios."

Kaius hung his head, his shoulders slumping forward while Rhys swore in quiet shock. Boy moved closer to Rhys, his corrected stance forgotten as he primed for attack.

Khthonios beamed up at Dovidas, giving his arm a light squeeze. "He kept his human family name instead of following our tradition of taking our creator's name." She chuckled. "Sometimes it's best to pick your battles during your child's rebellious phase."

Kaius Khthonios.

Fourteen hundred years barreled across Nichol's hazy mind.

The absences.

The secrecy.

The cryptic comments.

He stared at the back of Kai's head, willing him to turn around and tell him this wasn't true. He'd always known Kai's elusive sire was old and strong, but never had he suspected that the creator who held so much power over Kaius was an ancient female vamp.

They would not survive the night.

They were never intended to survive the night.

Khthonios disengaged herself from Dovidas and turned to Stojanovski. "Shall I explain the game, or would you like to?"

The tendons in Stojanovski's neck tightened. "Perhaps you should," he replied, refusing to meet Nichol's eyes.

With an exaggerated sigh of exasperation, Khthonios turned her attention back to them. "Your mongrel creator once told me he could assemble a haunt capable of ruling the known world," she stated, winking at Kaius. "Such cheek in his younger years. But I decided to indulge him. He's had fifteen centuries. And tonight we'll know if he was successful."

She held out her hand to Kai, her black eyes hardening when he paused before taking it.

"The Kaius haunt against mine." Khthonios pulled Kai to her side. "In the interest of fairness, I won't participate." She laughed. "Dovidas, Chen, and Kaius against…" She scanned them with amusement, "…you." She tilted her head to Boy, a strange expression on her face. "You can keep the worthless guard dog."

Nichol began calculating the age disadvantage, zeroing in on Chen to assess the ancient's coloring.

Rhys stepped forward, ignoring his hand as it shot out to silence him. "What's the prize?"

Khthonios laughed. "Reputation and survival, pretty boy. The only things that matter."

Slapping his arm away, Rhys took another step. "What guarantee do we have you'll allow us to walk out of here after we annihilate your line?"

Kaius didn't react.

Khthonios smiled indulgently at Rhys, her eyes raking over his body. "Jackson will attest to my word," she replied, her attention drifting to Nichol's crossbow. "I was under the impression weapons were not allowed on the premises."

He tightened his hold on his bow. "Fortune favors the prepared."

She nodded slowly, tossing a withering glance at Dovidas before continuing. "You'll receive five minutes to strategize before we begin. The first side to eliminate the other bloodline is the victor." Khthonios clapped her hands together. "This is going to be so fun!"

****

Nichol crouched down, smearing his hand across the dirt at his feet to create a blank slate. He hastily scrawled his plan, meeting Rhys's eyes for approval.

His younger brother read over the message, his lips tightening over his fangs before he nodded, his hardened eyes flicking across the field. "What's plan B?"

He lifted his head and followed Rhys's gaze to the veranda. Khthonios stood between Chen and Dovidas, her wrists lifted to their lips while Kaius remained motionless in the entranceway.

Khthonios's blood would boost their speed and strength, adding decades or even centuries to their abilities.

Nichol was acutely aware his and Rhys's sire stood on the side of their enemies.

Brushing another slate, he scratched out his secondary strategy.

Rhys scanned it over and rose, using his boot to erase their options. "I'm not sure I want Boy at my back," he stated, looking straight at the mute male. "How fucking long have you known Kaius's creator was a female? That she even existed? Because I sure as shit would have remembered if you ever shared that little piece of intel."

Boy dropped his head, his blond hair falling into his eyes.

"Not the time," Nichol interjected as he assessed his bow. "Once we wrap this up, we'll have a thorough debriefing."

Rhys chuckled drily. "Ten-four, boss." He stretched his arms over his head. "How are you holding up? Any tremors?"

He was high as fuck.

He shook his head and counted his bolts. "I'm good," he lied. "We've got this." He texted plans A and B to his hauntmates, sent off a request to Jagger, and looked at Rhys. "Call Lis."

A shot of fear crossed Rhys's face, followed by a stoic resolution as he pulled his phone from his pocket and gave him a pointed look. "Call Simone."

Rhys wandered a few feet away, his hushed reassurances to his sobbing mate laying heavy on Nichol's conscience. He looked down at his own phone, reading over Jagger's text.

—We're with you. I'll get her out.—

He tapped on his messaging app and fired off a message to Simone.

587OriginalNK: Stay alive. Stay hidden. Jagg will get you out when he can.

He turned toward the forest, narrowing his eyes in a futile attempt to see Simone in the blackness of the trees.

"She's smart. She won't give away her presence," Rhys said softly, elbowing him lightly in the ribs.

"Ready?"

"Nope," he replied, forcing a grim smile. He walked over to Boy. "We have your loyalty," he stated without question.

Boy nodded, his attention on Kaius's dark form.

"All right guys," he said as he hooked his crossbow on his back and glanced over at his hauntmates one final time. "Don't fucking embarrass me."

Chapter Thirty-One

The Kaius males stood motionless before Stojanovski while Khthonios led her haunt onto the battle ground. Chen, his movements precise and eyes alert, escorted his creator over the grass while Dovidas sauntered alongside, his fangs fully extended and tinged red from Khthonios's blood. Kaius remained several feet back, his expression locked down as he took his place and locked his gaze on the black sky.

With a hushed word to Dovidas, Khthonios joined Stojanovski and faced the two groups.

"Rule number one," she called out dramatically, flashing a fangy smile to Dovidas. "Stay within the perimeter of the established field. No hiding in closets in the main hall. There's a party in there that we don't want to crash. Yet." She paused to smooth her silk tank over her stomach. "Rule number two, Stojanovski and myself are off-limits for kill shots. That's it. The first side to eliminate all of their opposition bloodline is the victor, and we will head inside for a celebratory meal and a little dancing."

Stojanovski stepped forward, a look of regret crossing his face when he caught Nichol's eye. "The Khthonios haunt will begin two hundred yards to the south, the Kaius haunt two hundred yards to the north. Nicholai, Khthonios has agreed to your crossbow as she has determined it speaks well to your level of preparedness and will serve as a valuable lesson for her own line, but it will be left at the midline until the match begins, available to whoever reached it first. Regroup at your assigned start positions and wait for my countdown."

Nichol stepped forward, his fingers twitching as he released his crossbow and dropped it onto the dirt. Keeping his gaze off his creator, he followed Boy and Rhys as they turned and sauntered toward the trees, the exposing of their backs to the enemy rippling across their muscles. Raking his eyes over the branches concealing Simone, he willed her to remain still and silent while they took their places.

"Kaius is bound to her orders," he said softly in a final effort to erase the betrayal from Rhys's eyes. "To turn on her is certain death."

Rhys grunted. "As you are to his. And you defy orders all the fucking time."

"Kai allowed my defiance," he replied, tapping the bolts in his back pocket. "As he did yours, Jagg's, Mick's, and Dom's." He rubbed his jaw and readied his stance. "He kept this shitstorm from our door until we were strong enough to face it. I suspect he paid dearly for providing us the luxury."

Stojanovski's voice cut across the grounds as the countdown began. Boy crouched down, his fangs extended and eyes blackened.

"Go."

Nichol tore across the dirt, swooping up his bow as Chen's hands grabbed for it. He raced out of the field and into the forest, adjusting his trajectory to lead attention away from Simone's position. He prepped his weapon as he took his place and locked his eyes on Boy as he and

Chen clashed on the grounds, grappling for dominance.

Rhys and Dovidas hit the dirt, fangs and blades flashing in the dim veranda light.

He cocked his bow, tracking Kai's movements along the outskirts of the grass.

The infusion of Khthonios's blood had unbalanced the playing field exponentially, Chen and Dovidas holding their ground better than he'd predicted.

A deadly underestimation.

He squinted while he aimed, the rolling warmth of his high fighting to infuse his mind as he released the first bolt and watched it fall short of his target.

Khthonios's incredulous laugh rang through the air as her head turned toward him. She walked leisurely down the stairs, catching the second bolt in her hand as she strode across the plains.

He fired another three rounds, drawing the amused female to him while she snatched his bolts from the air.

In his peripheral, the quiver of Simone's crossbow came into view.

"Go!" he snarled, cursing loudly when another arrow landed at Khthonios's feet.

"I can hit her," Simone whispered from above.

He released another shot and slammed his hand into his pocket, tossing his spare car keys into the bushes. "Stojanovski is your assignment," he ordered, cocking the bow. "Do it and get out."

Her crossbow remained in position, her pack of bolts landing within his reach.

He closed one eye, refocused, and shot, Khthonios catching it mid-air when it flew past her. Her black eyes zeroed in on his position.

"If you hit me, you'll be breaking the rules," the

female vamp called out, dropping her collection of bolts and splintering them with the heel of her boot. "Not a wise move."

He tracked Kaius's movements, his creator's advance toward Rhys and Boy slowing when Khthonios's back turned from him.

Rhys was losing to the younger vampire.

Boy was monitoring Kaius, battling Chen, and booting Dovidas's feet out from under him at every chance.

He reloaded.

Khthonios's arms rose, her head tilting to expose her throat. "You can end the game now," she smiled, arching back as he peered through his scope. "If you end me, every part of my line falls with me."

He froze.

Khthonios laughed and closed her eyes. "I can smell the stench of that animal's blood in you," she sang, walking in a circle before she resumed her position. "The moment that arrow embeds in me, you will die. Your creator will die. Your brothers will die." She turned her head toward Simone's tree and scented the air. "She will be spared."

Khthonios pointed directly at Simone's position. "Smart girl, avoiding the blood of my bastard child's line," she called out, placing her hands behind her head and smirking at him. "Blood manipulation, dear. Care for a demonstration?"

Before he could reply, a peculiar sensation ricocheted through his veins, his hands and feet weakening. His attention shot to Rhys, stomach knotting when his brother stumbled to his knees, giving Dovidas the clear advantage while Boy leapt to his feet and stared

Khthonios down, opening himself to Chen's attack.

"All I need to do is will your deaths with mine, my little mongrel," she purred, a feral smile on her face when Boy was tossed to the ground. "The games just became more interesting indeed." She licked her lips as the feeling returned to Nichol's hands. "I truly do love games, Nicholai. One well-placed arrow, and all the games I want to play will be over. So tell me, mutt. Is it worth the gamble? Do you believe you can end me before I can destroy you all from the inside out?"

Faces flashed across his mind.

Audra. Bianca. Molly. Lis.

He lowered his bow.

Plan B.

Khthonios dropped her arms and sauntered back toward the main hall. "Wise move, young one," she laughed before her attention was drawn to Kaius. "Get your worthless ass in there and finish this."

He watched while Kai hesitated before he gripped his head and fell to his knees.

"I didn't ask," Khthonios stated, her stiletto boots clicking on the stairs as she returned to Stojanovski's side.

Kaius rose to his feet and scanned the battle, ignoring Nichol and zeroing in on Rhys and Dovidas.

Nichol launched himself from his position, barreling unsteadily toward the others as Boy and Chen fell to the ground and Chen gained the upper hand, Boy's movements almost sluggish. He shook the haze from his head and lifted his bow, pulling Chen into his scope.

"Don't fucking move!" he hollered, releasing the bolt when Boy went still.

Chen fell back to the sounds of Khthonios's

disappointed chastisement, his body disintegrating into sludge across Boy's boots.

Khthonios took a step forward, her hands gripping the railings of the stoop as she hissed. "Don't you dare let my baby fall, you useless bastard," she snarled at Kaius as the haunt leader tackled Rhys to the ground, freeing Dovidas from Rhys's fangs.

He yanked another bolt from his pocket, hooking his toe in the stirrup and lifting his weapon. He aimed and Dovidas launched at him, his fangs embedding in Nichol's shoulder while he fought to draw Kai into his scope. Boy's long arms snatched Dovidas from him and tossed him aside, taking a chunk of his shoulder with him.

Weaken Kai.

"Rhys!" he barked to Boy, taking aim at Kaius and pushing all thoughts of what he was about to do from the forefront of his mind as Dovidas latched back on to his throat and a small blade pierced his side.

He felt Dovidas fall behind him, his body reduced to a sludge drenching his cargos and seeping into his boots. Rhys's confiscated blade remained lodged under his ribs, nothing more than an irritating remnant of Dovidas's failed attack.

Cursing Simone inwardly to the sound of Khthonios's rage, he forced his vision to clear as Boy leapt onto Kaius's back and ripped him from Rhys, exposing Kai's chest to Nichol's scope.

Weaken, don't kill.

He adjusted his aim, squinting as Kaius's lower body filled his scope and his haunt leader stilled, providing him with a clear shot.

Aiming for Kaius's hip, he fired, his blood high

sending a tremor through his body as he released the arrow.

The crossbow fell from his hands, and he watched in horror as his bolt embed itself in his creator's chest, the wooden tip pushing through his ribs to his heart.

A clean hit.

A clean, final hit.

Kaius dropped to the ground.

Boy fell to his knees at his side.

Nichol stood motionless and braced himself for his creator's body to disintegrate, Khthonios's approach barely registering as he took in Boy's labored movements. The mute male eased his arms under Kaius's body, stumbling to his feet while Rhys inched away, his navy eyes locked on Kai in confusion.

"The game isn't over," Khthonios snarled, snatching his crossbow from the ground and slamming it against his chest. "Finish it."

A low growl erupted from Boy as he exposed his back to Nichol, shielding Kaius from another hit. Kai's limbs jerked and twitched, the arrow still lodged deep in his body.

He looked down at his bow, wrapping his fingers around the barrel as realization sank in. "Kaius's bastard blood," he said slowly, taking in Boy's broad back hunched protectively over Kai's spasming body. "I… it was a clean hit. I ended him."

"All you did was eliminate my contribution to your maker's Deviant, repulsive existence," Khthonios growled as her lip curled in a sneer. "That rabid beast was nothing before I completed his transformation."

Rhys rose to his feet slowly, his steps unsteady as he made his way to Nichol's side. "Then we fucking won," he snarled, his confused gaze locked on Boy and Kaius while he unceremoniously smeared Chen's remains from his boot onto the grass.

Khthonios's lips pursed, her thin fangs extending to her chin. "What says the referee?" she called toward the veranda, her words clipped.

Stojanovski descended the stairs and stilled. "By your own admission, your bloodline was effectively eliminated from the battlefield, regardless of the continued animation of the body," he replied. "The game is over."

Her head dropped back in annoyance. "Fine." She knelt down, running her fingers through what was left of Dovidas thoughtfully. "You're going to have fun with the fallout of this," she sighed, rising to her feet and wiping the remains onto her pants as she glanced toward the trees where Simone sat. "You live tonight only because these mongrels were smart enough to have their most effective weapon watching their backs. And I respect preparation. But aligning yourself with mutts is a foolish pursuit, little girl. I will not forget your scent."

With the flick of her tongue over her fangs, she began her trek toward the exit of the compound.

Rhys's mouth opened, snapping shut when Nichol raised a staying hand, his attention wholly on Boy.

The mute vampire's grip tightened on Kaius as Khthonios walked away, stilling the increasingly violent spasms pummeling through Kai's body. He dropped his head for a moment, squared his shoulders, and sprinted ahead of Khthonios. Falling to his knees, Boy held Kai's limp form toward the female.

An offering.

Khthonios crossed her arms and lifted her toe,

nudging Kaius's jerking arm. "I fixed your mistake once, you conniving little runt," she sneered, drawing her leg back and booting Boy across the face. "Never again."

Boy's head bowed but he maintained his position, blood dripping from his cheek.

Khthonios looked to the sky in exasperation. She reached down and yanked Nichol's bolt from Kaius's heart, holding it in the air while the physical indicators of a Deviant mis-turning wracked Kai's body. "You want your trophy?" she laughed, tossing it behind her toward him as she side-stepped Boy and continued on her path, reaching the gates and waving. "Let your hauntmates live with your failures and your secrets, dog. Mommy fixed your broken toy once. I won't do it again."

Mommy.

As Khthonios vaulted over the fence and disappeared into the night, Boy drew Kaius against him, opened his wrist, and allowed the misshapen Deviant fangs to latch on.

Chapter Thirty-Two

Nichol's feet remained anchored to the ground as Rhys walked past him and bent down to retrieve the blood-soaked arrow. His brother ran his hand along the length and held it out to him, his arm wavering from his immense blood loss. "Take it. We'll put it in the trophy case to represent the night you saved our collective asses. Again."

He continued to stare at Boy and Kaius, his throat tightening when Kai's limbs twitched with the telltale jerk of a Deviant. "Boy," he said quietly, accepting the blood-soaked bolt from Rhys and slipping it into his back pocket. "We're going to get Kaius into the bunker. We'll regroup from there."

Boy's blue eyes lifted to his, the trademark vacant stare replaced by a combination of remorse, sadness, and fear.

Dropping to one knee, he hoisted his crossbow onto his back. "We'll figure it out." He ran his hand through his hair and shook his head as Kaius's newly deformed fangs snapped at him. "All of it."

Rhys and Nichol flanked Boy when he rose to his feet and adjusted his hold on Kai, keeping his wrist within reach of the misshapen fangs. The group began making their way to their bunker, Nichol's nostrils flaring when he picked up Simone's scent. She joined them silently, receiving a brief nod from Rhys as they crossed the field, Stojanovski meeting them on their path.

"Back to your room," Jackson ordered, his jaw muscles flexing when his gaze fell on Simone.

Nichol stepped forward. "Not tonight."

He stared Stojanovski down, daring him to argue.

Jackson looked to Kaius. "She returns to me after she's debriefed," he stated, his eyes widening when Kai tore a chunk from Boy's wrist and spat it on the ground. "You have my silence." He backed up, allowing the group to pass. "No charge."

****

Simone flattened herself against the wall as Boy descended into the bunker, the snarling blond vampire tossed over his shoulder and held tight. Nichol lowered the hatch and set the code, keeping his eyes purposely averted from hers.

"So, apparently that's our creator," Rhys announced, sliding his back down the door and hunching over his knees. "We love our Deviant daddy."

"We've met before," she mumbled, her eyes on Nichol when he visibly flinched, his lips tightening across his fangs. He pulled his phone from his pocket and wiped the screen clear of blood.

"We're going on speaker," he stated, his voice flat. "Simone, I'll be alerting the others to your presence, but I would appreciate it if you didn't participate in the debriefing until asked." He tapped an icon and set the cell on the floor, slumping against the wall and closing his eyes as the phone rang.

A familiar voice she couldn't quite place answered immediately. "All present."

Nichol's lips turned up briefly. "Same here." He

opened one eye. "We have a former trainee here. She'll be participating in the debriefing, since she was the one who took out Dovidas. Say hi, Simone."

She glanced over to Rhys, rolling her eyes when he gave her a thumbs-up. "Uh, hi?"

A familiar voice came over the speaker. "You did well, Simone."

Audra.

"Thanks," she replied, crossing the room to sit on the bed.

Nichol rubbed his face roughly and straightened his back. "I'll report. Tomorrow night, we'll open the floor to questions and observations." He looked over at the hatch, a strained look crossing his face when a howl erupted from the bunker. "I assume there'll be a fuck-ton of questions."

"Can we do this over Skype?" someone called out.

"Nope," Rhys replied. "Computer's in the bunker. And there's no fucking way we're going in there right now."

There was some muttering before the voice returned to the speaker. "Talk slow. Bianca's going to repeat it for Jagg."

Nichol stretched one long leg across the floor, his nose wrinkling as red flakes of Dovidas fell off his cargos. "Will do. I'll keep it short, and we'll fully review once we arrive on site tomorrow night." He looked over at Rhys and lifted his wrist to his mouth. She watched in fascination as he opened his vein and held it out to his brother. Rhys inched over, took Nichol's arm, and wrapped his lips over the wound.

Her heart clenched.

"The female vamp is Khthonios," Nichol began

slowly, his eyes closed and head dropped back against the wall.

****

Nichol allowed his statement to sink in before he continued. "You probably had a better view of the events than we did, but there's a lot of audio we need to cover. Dovidas, Chen, and Kaius were all sired by Khthonios." He flattened his hand across the hardwood. "And, from what I understand, Khthonios is Boy's sire as well."

His hauntmates fell silent, the only sound coming through the speakers being a collective gasp from the women.

"Boy's a little busy right now, so I'm lacking some relevant intel," he continued. "But from what I can surmise, Boy is older—significantly older—than Kai and was Kaius's original sire. Except the turning didn't take and Kai—" He clenched his teeth and ran his hand through his hair, unable to go on.

"Instead of turning to sludge like he should have with a true hit, Kai has gone Deviant. Which is technically impossible given what we know about the human to Deviant to vampire transition," Rhys stated flatly as he unhooked his fangs from Nichol's wrist. "But here we are. Boy has Kaius contained downstairs in the bunker and our sire is basically nothing more than a rabid animal."

Ignoring Rhys's harsh words, he massaged his own neck in a futile attempt to loosen the lump that had formed. "I suspect Boy screwed up the turning process centuries ago and instead of becoming a vampire, Kaius went Deviant. And although Boy should have ended him then and there, he asked Khthonios to, I don't know, fix Kaius? Complete the process? Redo it?

Given Khthonios's statements on the battlefield, I think some of Boy's blood remained concealed somewhere in Kaius's body after Khthonios vamped him properly and it's that blood which is now keeping Kai from disintegrating. Rhys can attest to the change in Kaius's scent. Although there's the strong sour smell of Deviant, Boy's bloodline is now recognizable and Khthonios—our bloodline scent—is no longer detectable. I'll need to do more research on it since I didn't even know it was possible to try to turn someone again after they went Deviant the first time, but there has to be a physiological reason Kaius went Deviant under Boy but managed to become fully vamped under Khthonios. And the fact my hit eliminated only Khthonios's blood is proof Boy's blood has been somewhere inside him all along."

Silence stretched out until Molly spoke. "You're saying Boy is Kaius's biological dad and Khthonios was essentially a blood donor?"

Hanging his head, he closed his eyes. "I'm sure we all remember Dovidas's comments. Bastardized blood. Mongrels. Mutts. It would appear there's more truth to that than we anticipated."

He grunted as he shifted position, leaning his elbows on his knees. "Bianca, I guess you were right when you said there was something in our genetics making us Kaius vamps emotionally stunted. We're part Deviant." The absurdity of his statement rippled through him. "Holy fuck," he groaned as more reality hit him. "Boy is technically family."

"Shit," Rhys muttered, Bianca's quiet voice repeating everything for Jagg in the background. "That silent asshole we've been treating like our personal bitch for centuries is blood. Ancient blood. Older than Kaius level of ancient blood."

A chorus of shocked curses streamed through the speakers.

Mickey let loose a string of words Nichol hadn't heard combined before. "I don't know what you're all freaking out about. I've been calling that ancient fucker on for, what, over a year? Sweet fuck, Audra. How many times have I told him I'd stake him in his sleep if he so much as looked at you again? And you're telling us he's not only older than Kai, he's basically our goddamn grandfather?"

He looked over at Simone to see her eyes wide, her hand over her mouth. He picked up his phone and flipped over to his messaging app, firing off a quick text.

587OriginalNK: enough family drama for you?

While his brothers took a moment to unwind from the tension of the night, lamenting over who had treated Boy worse over the years, he sat back and watched while Simone pulled her phone from her pocket and read his message.

Highsteaks1403: this is better than cable tv
Highsteaks1403: you ok?
587OriginalNK: Nope

His speaker continued to pump out a din of noise, his hauntmates decompressing while they dissolved into an insult war with Rhys periodically joining in as his strength improved.

"Enough," he finally called out. "We're going to pack up and wrap up a few loose ends here. We'll be on our way at dusk tomorrow." He touched the edge of the hatch. "We'll need a secured cell in the quarters for Kai and Boy until we can figure this out."

Bianca's soft murmuring preceded Jagg's voice. "We're on it, Nicky," he said. "You did well."

He snorted, Kaius's howls still reverberating through the tiny house. "I staked our sire."

"And we're all still here," Rhys stated. "Kaius included."

Khthonios's warning echoed in his head.

All who ingested my line will fall with me.

"Yeah, we'll have to add that to the list of things we need to discuss when we're back on home territory," he muttered. "I'll text you when we hit the road tomorrow."

He disconnected the call and slumped back against the wall.

****

Simone paced the small house, listening as the ladder leading to the bunker creaked under someone's weight. The hatch opened and Nichol crawled out of it, eased it closed, and set the code.

"Is everyone secure?" she asked, joining him as he sat beside the hatch, one hand absently running along the tight grooves.

"For now," he replied, checking his phone. "Rhys is barricaded in his room. Boy has Kai subdued for the time being." He brushed a chunk of Dovidas from his leg. "You should have taken Stojanovski out when you had the chance."

She smirked. "Yeah, well, I kind of like the ego trip I have from saving your old ass."

Nichol snorted and covered his face with his hands, rubbing his temples. "And now you're trapped here."

She leaned her head on his shoulder, her stomach knotting when he shifted away from her. "Talk to me."

He rolled his shoulders out and stretched his neck

back. "You were there," he mumbled, running his tongue across one fang.

She closed the gap between them again and captured one of his hands in both of hers. "Yeah, I was. I don't need a debriefing. What I need is to know how you can sit there and beat yourself up when you managed to keep your entire bloodline intact. Against a female vampire. An ancient female vampire."

"Intact," he scoffed. "I was aiming for his fucking kidneys, Simone. Looking for the hit to weaken him enough to buy us time to do, I don't know, something." He ran his tongue over his fangs, shaking his head. "I figured Boy would take him out if it came down to it. I did…" He gestured to the hatch as a low snarl erupted from the bunker. "I did that." He looked over at her, his hazel eyes tired.

"Tomorrow night, I have to walk into the haunt and tell everyone I was too fucking high to aim true. I have to explain to my brothers our entire existence may be tied to Khthonios's continued existence, and the lives of their mates may now forever be tied to hers as well. That she wants to see us eliminated but we can't fight back. I have to lock my creator in a cell like a rabid dog and feed him through the bars." He stared at the door. "And all I can focus on is where I can score a vial or two to tide me over for the next couple of days."

She turned Nichol's hand over in hers, running her fingers over the deep creases of his palms. "But you have the time to do it," she said softly. "You're still here. Rhys is still here. Boy is, too. Maybe if you'd been straight tonight, you'd have hit Khthonios and none of you would be here."

Nichol snorted. "I was never intending to take her

out. I intended to draw her out. Keep her attention on me long enough for Boy and Rhys to establish where Kaius's true loyalty lay." He flexed his fingers, glaring at her when she tightened her hold on his hand.

"You didn't intend to survive," she stated, running her thumb over his.

"Nope."

"Are you angry that you did?"

His brows furrowed, his freckles dancing across the bridge of his nose. "I'm just angry in general." He looked back to the door. "And we need to get you back to the hall before dawn." Nichol rose to his feet, assisting her up. "You should have taken him out."

She grinned, leading the way out the door and onto the grass. "Stojanovski is going to be watching his back around me for a while after tonight," she laughed. "I think I've bought myself at least a month of calling the shots."

They crossed the field, Nichol's eyes flicking to the fading ash in the middle. As they approached the exterior doors, he slowed.

"I'll be passing your contact information on to Jagg and Rhys," he said, stopping short of the entrance. "Be nice when they message you, and download a decent spellchecker."

Leaving.

The reality of his impending absence began to sink in.

He was leaving. She was staying.

And he was stepping back from her, literally and figuratively.

"What are the chances you'll respond when I text you?" she asked, easing his hand down to his side.

Nichol glanced behind him, scanning the plains as he backed down two stairs. "I'll be out of commission for a while. Lay low for a few weeks. Alert Rhys if Khthonios makes her way through here again." He took another step back and shoved his hands into his pockets. "You did well tonight."

He turned, and he left, the light of his phone visible as he retreated through the dark compound to his bunker.

She eased her own cell from her pocket, opened her messaging app, and tapped on Nichol's chat icon.

User does not exist.

Chapter Thirty-Three

Nichol stood at the junction, leaning against the hatch of the SUV. "I assume nothing I say will convince you otherwise," he said, staring across the empty highway. "You'll report back frequently?"

Boy nodded, his slouched form partially hidden by his own vehicle as he watched Kaius buck and fight against his restraints in the back seat.

He kept his eyes averted from the thrashing Deviant snapping his fangs at the window where Boy's exposed arm was visible. "Khthonios—" He hesitated, not certain he wanted to know.

Tapping a quick message on his phone, Boy angled the device toward him.

She lost her game and her own code of honor will not allow her to punish you for it. But I guarantee you she is already planning a rematch.

"So no immediate retribution for us? How about for you?"

Boy shrugged and shoved his phone back into his cargos.

"We owe you more than we probably know."

With little more than a frown, Boy stared him down.

Stretching his arms out, he arched his neck back to release the tightness building in his throat. "Okay. Go. But I expect nightly updates until you hit your destination, and if you need anything, it'll be taken care of." He opened the passenger side of the car and roughly nudged Rhys's knees aside as he searched the glove box.

"Here," he said, tossing a small leather case at Boy. "Spare phone, charger, cash, and a credit card linked to an emergency fund. I'll top it up as needed, but there's a few hundred thousand in there to get you started."

Boy clutched the case in his large hand and nodded as he opened his door and folded himself into the seat. He set the pack down beside him and reached into the back, contorting his body to provide Kaius with access to his wrist.

Nichol looked away.

"Anything," he repeated, opening his own door. "Pay off who you need to pay off, buy what you need to buy. Call in favors. We have a lot outstanding. Use them."

Revving the engine, Nichol turned back onto the highway.

"Where do you think he'll go?" Rhys asked, opening one eye.

He shrugged. "Europe? Asia? Maybe stick to the Americas to avoid boat travel." He glanced in the rearview mirror and watched the red lights of Boy's car as it disappeared in the opposite direction. "How are you holding up?"

Rhys groaned and sank further into his seat. "I'm hungry. I'm horny. And I just sent a text to Lis that probably earned me a week sleeping on the sofa." He swiped his thumb over his phone and paused to read the response. "Yup." He tapped out a short message and dropped his phone into his lap. "We made it, Nicky. We survived a run-in with an ancient female," he grinned, closing his eyes again. "We are fucking *gods*!"

"We are fucking behind schedule," he corrected, speeding up to close the gap between them and home.

And to put as much distance as he could between himself and the woman occupying his head.

****

Nichol folded his detailed notes in half and placed them on the table, each point neatly checked off and of no more use. "Questions?" When his stunned hauntmates remained silent, he pushed away from the table and rose to his feet. "I'll be available for consultation as needed and will continue to work online behind the scenes. Rhys remains de facto leader until..." He paused, glaring at the floor. "Just follow his word unless he says something stupid."

He tucked his laptop under his arm, winding the charging cord around his palm as he exited his office and made his way to his bunker to pack.

"You should have told me."

Slowing his steps to allow Audra time to catch up, he grunted. "I was busy."

Her cat eyes narrowed. "Obviously." She kept pace with him until they reached his room. "Dammit, Nichol. You should have talked to me."

He opened his door and strode to his closet, pulling a small duffle from the top shelf. "I'm in as much a talking mood now as I was before I left here," he muttered, shoving a few changes of clothes into the bag and adding a comb to the pile. He eased his computer on top and carefully pulled the zipper closed.

Audra stood at his door, her arms wrapped around herself. "Nichol."

"Audra."

She breathed out slowly. "I'll be coming to see you

in the cells. Whether you like it or not."

He fixed her with a dead stare. "There's a DVD player on the bottom shelf in the com room. Under the spare gaming system. If you're going to annoy me with your psycho-babble, you could make yourself useful and bring a few movies by."

She hugged him tight as he inched past her. "I'm so mad at you."

"That makes two of us," he grumbled, unfolding himself from her grip and stalking toward the former bloodslave quarters.

Once he was properly established in the cell he would be inhabiting for the foreseeable future, Rhys swung the door open and sauntered over in, checking the restraints around Nichol's ankles. "Keys," he ordered, holding out his hand.

He passed the lock keys over, testing the strength of the chains a final time before making himself comfortable on the small cot. The tremors were only beginning, the tightness in his muscles building at a steady pace.

Rhys pulled a chair into the small cell, leaving the door wide open. "So how do you see this playing out?"

Running a hand over his neck, he looked to the ceiling. "One week of physical withdrawal. A few months of mental." His eyes traced a small crack in the cement. "I set the restrictions on my laptop, but will need you to set a password."

Rhys held out his hand for the laptop, sneering after his first password choice was rejected. "This is fucking stupid," he snarled, his fingers tapping out a new one. "I know how secure I want my code. Who's this dumbass program to tell me otherwise?" He sat back triumphantly. "There. All yours."

Setting the computer on his bed, he looked at Rhys. "What's the general feel up there?"

Rhys draped his long arms over the back of the chair. "They're fucking worried."

He ran his hand through his hair and clenched his teeth. "You're a capable leader and Boy assured us Khthonios won't hunt us down for revenge. They shouldn't be concerned."

"About you, fuckwad," Rhys countered. "General consensus is I'm an asshole for allowing you computer access so you can keep working. Audra's already started a sign-up sheet for responsibilities." He rolled his eyes and dropped his head on his arms. "Lis signed me up for laundry duties."

He snorted. "I don't do laundry."

"No, but Audra believes we need to establish—what the fuck did she call it—a gender-neutral division of haunt duties." Rhys pushed himself out of the chair and exited the cell, heaving the door closed slowly and coding the lock. "You sure you don't want me to hang out for the day?"

"Go," he replied, reclining on his temporary bed. "I have better shit to do than entertain your ass for the next fourteen hours."

****

Better things to do.

Nichol swatted at his laptop as he paced by it and squinted at the screen.

Nineteen hours.

The cement below his feet held a strange shine to it after nineteen hours of relentless prowling back and forth in the small cell. He needed to move. Needed to stretch.

Needed to run.

Needed to calm the fuck down.

He slumped onto his bed and tossed his arm over his eyes. Every muscle in his body was wound, the tautness creating a peculiar ache in his bones and sending involuntary spasms through his nerves.

He checked the computer screen again.

Nineteen hours, two minutes.

He got back on his feet and focused on isolating one muscle group at a time, methodically releasing the tension in a circuit until Rhys arrived, blood bags in hand.

"Eat," Rhys ordered, flinging the cell door open and handing him the bags. "Chains still holding?"

"If they weren't, you'd know." He kicked one leg out to unhitch the loops before he continued his prowl across the tiny space.

Pulling out his phone, Rhys leaned against the bars and began reciting updates, pausing periodically to fill in the incomplete reports. As he wrapped up the evening's intel, he shoved his phone back into his pocket and crossed his arms. "Stojanovski isn't budging on Simone," he stated, eying him closely. "I've offered a triple buyback, but so far he's done everything but tell me to go fuck myself."

He stopped pacing and stared at the floor, flipping through every angle his agitated mind could conjure. "I assume you've examined the traditional failings," he said, distracted by the slight unevenness in the concrete. "Nutrition. Accommodation. Abuse."

Rhys nodded. "Even attempted to run with the injured ankle. But since Simone was actively hunting on her own accord on our final night, long-term strain was pulled from the table."

"She doesn't want to be there," he grumbled, resuming his walk.

"You know that doesn't matter," Rhys replied, his voice quiet. "I've got nothing, man."

He flexed his hands out, rolling his shoulders back. "I fucking told her to take Jackson out. She should've listened. Isn't that what you trained her to do? Follow orders?" He ran his tongue over his fang and grabbed a bag of blood. "Your training methods are defective."

Rhys grinned. "So I've been told. Repeatedly." He extended his hand, taking the empty bag. "I'm out for the day. You sure you don't want someone down here?"

"Positive." He stepped aside as Rhys exited the cell and locked the door. "I'll top up the contractor accounts and get those training dates approved before I hit the emails."

His younger brother stared at him through the bars for a moment, navy eyes narrowing. "We can cover it."

"And I need to do it."

****

"Stay. The fuck. Back." Nichol stalked to the cell door, wrapped his bloodied fingers around the bars, and bared his teeth at Rhys. "Leave the bags and walk away."

Rhys adjusted his stance, widening his feet and crouching in instinctive preparation for battle. He lowered the bags of blood to the floor and nudged them forward with his toe, the unappealing sloshing of the liquid bouncing off the cement walls and pounding through his skull.

"I'll return tomorrow," Rhys stated, backing away as he pulled his phone from his pocket. "This is peak, Nicky. We make it past the next few nights, and you'll be golden."

He slammed his palms on the bars and turned his back, listening for Rhys's retreating footsteps through the empty halls of the bloodslave quarters.

This is peak.

Peak fucking hell.

Every cell in his body was suffocating, straining to latch on to those last remnants of ancient blood clinging to his veins. His vision had pin-holed, his mind focused on a hunt with no viable prey in sight. Each movement took an exorbitant amount of effort, but his body couldn't remain still.

This is peak.

He sunk to the floor, dropping his forearms over his knees and lolling his head back against the cold metal.

Five nights of restless hell.

His brain alternated between foggy disconnection and debilitating shocks as the damaged synapses in his head misfired in an unrelenting loop before easing him back into his haze.

It hadn't been this intense last time.

But he'd had his sire's blood on tap to ease him through the worst, to strengthen him both physically and mentally.

Five days of sleepless purgatory.

He inched his arm through the bars and dragged the warm blood closer.

This is peak.

****

Nichol opened one eye, the blinding light of the quarters searing his retina.

"He wakes."

Rolling onto his back, he sluggishly eased himself

up onto his elbows and forced both eyes open to look at Audra. "What are you doing here?"

"Watching you rest," she replied, waving her notebook in the air. "Tracking movements. Deciphering speech."

He fell back on the mattress and reached under the cot, tapping his computer to life.

She crossed her legs. "It's Thursday."

Grunting at Audra, he checked for himself.

Thursday.

Nine whole nights lost.

She rose to her feet, remaining a respectable distance from the cell bars. "How do you feel?"

Desperate.

"Hungry," he mumbled, sitting up and rubbing his face as Audra fired off a quick text. "Tell Rhys to get down here ASAP and fill me in on the past nine nights."

The cat eyes locked on him narrowed. "There's time for that tomorrow," she stated. "Tonight, you're getting a meal, a shower, and, if you think you can handle it, a run outside."

Her voice brokered no argument. And he didn't have it in him to try. He nodded slowly. "How's Mickey holding up through this?"

Audra smiled at him and began tapping in the cell's lock code. "He and Louis have been boosting his control through blood-sharing since Kai… since the last mission ended. He's fine. You're our top concern."

Kaius.

Boy.

Khthonios.

Sanctuary.

Deepfryers.

"There are bigger issues at play," he grumbled, bending down to pull his boots on.

Audra placed her notebook and pen on her chair, repositioned a bobby pin in her hair, and tugged the chain keys from her pocket. "According to you, maybe. Lucky for us, your opinion doesn't matter right now. Double-knot those laces."

****

"We don't need you adding any more shit to this dumpster fire."

Nichol looked up from his laptop as Rhys's voice filtered through the bloodslave quarters.

"No one's adding anything. It's there. And I think it's been there for a long fucking time."

Mick.

Closing out the haunt's investment portfolio, he sat patiently while two pairs of heavy boots clomped through the hall toward him. Rhys's eyes were black, his fangs fully extended. Mikhail trailed a step behind, his shoulders slumped, and lips drawn tight.

He got to his feet and stretched his arms over his head. "What fresh hell is being served up tonight?" he asked, anxious to add something distractingly different to his monotonous nightly work.

Rhys looked to Mick and crossed his arms. "Spill."

Mickey mimicked Rhys's position, his eyes locked on the floor. "There's a problem with Simone."

"That would be Rhys's concern, not mine," he replied, his flat expression masking the sudden spike of fear blasting through him as his sluggish mind flipped through every potential danger she may have come across.

Khthonios ranked at the top of the list.

Rhys motioned for Mick to continue, his attention on the wall behind Nichol's head.

Mickey's hands shoved into his pockets, his posture worsening. "No, this is your concern." He looked to Rhys for help and was met with a sullen glare. "So remember when you just kind of gave up sex? For like, no reason?"

His expression morphed to match Rhys's.

Mickey shifted his feet. "And, uh, remember when you started getting laid a few weeks back?"

Images flashed across his mind, only to be shoved aside. He took a step toward the bars of his cell.

Mickey backed away a fraction. "I shouldn't have been able to track that as clearly as I did, what with Louis being around and all. So it took me a bit to wade through things. Date checking, probing, that kind of thing."

Rhys kicked his foot out, booting Mick in the shin. "Fucknuts over here has determined you're connected. To Simone."

Connected.

Vampire connection to a human was an intense biological imprinting, one which left the vamp irrational and borderline rabid when he was separated from the unlucky recipient. When Dominic connected to Molly, the poor bastard needed to be chained up in the haunt's cells when she was sold to Dovidas. He was a disaster without her and an overprotective guard dog with her.

The mere suggestion he was connected to Simone would be laughable if there weren't a million other things he needed to focus his energy on.

He ran his hand over his jaw and turned his attention to Rhys. "Did you bring down the latest blueprints for the low-rise on the east side?"

"Right here." Rhys passed a hastily folded paper into his cell. "They're ready to break ground once they receive the okay from you." He waited for Nichol to open the creased drawing. "Adding a second exit to each dwelling initially shot the price up, but the approved amendment to the window requirements for every bedroom has almost balanced it out."

Pointedly ignoring Mick, he examined the blueprint for issues before passing it back through the bars. "I'll sign off on this before sunrise."

"The timing matches up with Simone's birth records," Mickey interjected, moving forward.

Rhys swiped his thumb across his phone. "We'll be needing line identification for the two vamps who arrived three weeks ago. They've been paired with older ones in the modified northern accommodations, but Jagg hasn't been able to get in touch with either of their creators to corroborate their statements."

He focused on the bars around him. "Add it to the list."

Mick continued to press on, his hulking form closing in on the cell. "Jagg confirmed a few European cases of connections dating back to the birth of the human."

Passing his phone into the cell, Rhys followed his path of avoidance and tapped open a video. "Jagg and Dominic have begun training the vamp cops in shifts. We should consider a weekly review session as part of the contract."

"I'll add it in and adjust the payment schedule to reflect the additional time," he muttered, watching in fascination as his hauntmates stood alongside armed men and corrected their form. "We'll need to establish a training rotation lead team on our side as well."

"If you weren't such an asshole all the time, we probably would've figured it out sooner," Mickey stated, rapping his knuckles on the metal bars. "Ignore me all you want, Nic. You're a connected male and there ain't shit you can do about it."

He fixed his younger brother with a dead stare as Rhys took his phone back and yanked Mick's arm.

"We're out of here for the night," Rhys called, dragging Mickey toward the stairs. "I'll be back tomorrow at dusk with updates."

****

Nichol remained hunched over his laptop as Rhys approached the cell.

"I know you've been struggling with no phone," Rhys opened, pushing a small shopping bag through the bars. "I had Molly pick this up for you during the day."

"Would this be why it's been two nights since I last saw you?" he grumbled, snatching the bag away and lifting out a brightly-colored plastic contraption. He frowned, flipping back the cover and flinching when canned electronic music blared from the item. "What the fuck is this?"

Rhys grinned, stepping out of his reach. "It's a baby phone. Push one of the buttons."

He pressed down on one of the large numbers and was greeted with a cheery song about playing with his friends, sung by a high-pitched voice that pierced the back of his skull. He carefully replaced the cover. "What is wrong with you?"

"Don't smash it," Rhys warned as he moved to drop the offending item to the floor. "Louis booted the other one Molly grabbed, and it took us an hour to find the right size of screwdriver to get the batteries out to make it shut up." He smirked when Nichol's expression went flat. "Vamp strength has nothing on toys made for babies."

Wrinkling his nose at the toy, he placed it gently onto his cot. "Waste of resources," he stated. "Report."

Rhys pulled up a chair, the smile disappearing from his face. "It's been three weeks," he said slowly, scratching at his arm. "How much longer do you need down here?"

A year.

Two.

A decade.

He draped his arms through the bars. "Why."

"We—" Rhys's dark brows knotted, his gaze locking on the wall behind him. "We don't have the time you need."

Adjusting his stance, his muscles tensed at the thought of returning to the freedom of the haunt, a freedom he wasn't sure he could deal with yet. He'd managed a few supervised runs outside and one walking tour of the grounds to appease his obsession with the haunt's security, but each stint was short-lived and under the watchful eye of Audra, Jagger, or Rhys. "Why."

"The calls. The emails. The research. Approvals for this, re-reading that. Training schedules. Orders." Rhys ran his hand through his hair. "No Kaius. No you. No Boy. We're holding on by sheer fucking luck right now, Nicky.

"There are massive gaps in security coverage. The list of calls I need to return is insane. And those are the ones deemed urgent." Rhys looked at him, his eyes worn. "The learning curve's too fucking steep. Every detail you just know, we're wasting hours researching."

He glanced pointedly at the plastic phone. "Yet you have time for that."

"I forgot to put in a grocery order. Molly picked it up as a joke while saving my ass from a horde of hungry women." Rhys's fingers dug into his tattoos. "I'm drowning. We all are."

Drowning.

Apt.

Turning to his cot, he carefully unplugged his laptop charger, winding it around his hand. "Topside we go."

Rhys lifted a hand, staying his preparations. "Before I unlock the cell…Simone."

"You found a loophole?" his inquired, his voice holding enough disinterest to almost fool himself.

Rhys assessed him for a moment. "Is Mick on to something?"

He grunted, refusing to dignify the question with anything more.

Rising to his feet, Rhys punched in the code. "You sure about this?" He swung the door open. "There's one other small issue that's arisen over the past three weeks."

He leveled Rhys with a flat stare. "What."

Rhys rubbed his neck, the muscles across his shoulder blades visibly knotted. "Reports are trickling in across every continent. It seems something has opened the door to a shit-ton of untethered and uncontrolled Deviants." He started down the hall. "Male and female Deviants. And they aren't going down easy."

Chapter Thirty-Four

Nichol collected the stack of warm papers in the printer tray, ever conscious of the wary silence of his hauntmates at his back. He leaned over his laptop and tapped open the most current map of occupied haunts remaining in the country. "We offer bounty money," he stated, printing off the map and cross-referencing Deviant sightings with the haunt locations.

"Jagg and Bianca, you two can coordinate responses in North and South America where the highest concentrations are currently. Dominic and Molly, I'm tossing Europe, Africa, and Asia at you. Australia is untouched as of tonight, but I'm monitoring the situation. I'll create two separate bank accounts you can access for online transfers."

He quickly added the number of Deviant sightings in his head. "Deviants turn to sludge at a decreased rate compared to fully turned vamps, so we'll start at one million per photographic proof of elimination and adjust from there. Go."

Audra's arms crossed, her cat eyes narrowing as the first four vacated the com room. "You shouldn't be up here. It's too soon. You've only passed the physical addiction, Nichol. You haven't even begun to address the mental."

Opening the security camera feed, he scanned the visuals. "Mick, you and Audra need to team up and close the gaps between the eastern quadrant and the south." He jotted down the log in information and password. "I'm adding the icon to both of your laptops. Once that's done, I want a visual check of each camera and the wiring. Go."

Audra glared at him as she accepted Mick's hand and rose to her feet. "We're discussing this at dawn," she threatened, her heels clicking angrily down the hall.

He closed up the video feed and straddled his chair as he opened his emails. "Louis, I need you to touch base with Jagg and assemble a temporary schedule for vamp cop training. One which rotates us through in pairs." He pursed his lips. "If Jagger approves, add Bianca to the rotation. She can provide throwing star techniques we aren't as skilled to teach."

"On it, boss," Louis replied, saluting him on his way out the door.

He kept his back to Rhys and Lis, frowning at the disorganized email folders Rhys had created in his account. "I need you two on international relocations. I want to know who's gone, where they are, and what route they took. Any vampires who are in-transit need to be warned about the Deviant issue and should be prepared with secondary and tertiary escape routes."

He looked over to Lis while she twisted her fingers in her lap. "Compile a detailed spreadsheet of identification requests from the emails I'm forwarding now. I'll be sending you the passport and license layout I use, and you can take it from there."

Lis's eyes flicked to Rhys. "I'll get right on it," she said, standing and straightening her back. Rhys slapped her ass as she passed him on her way out, earning a stern glare.

"I appreciate you involving her," Rhys stated,

leaning out the door to watch Lis walk away. "She's still trying to make amends around here."

He forwarded the slough of emails from masters and Tenders requesting assistance, renaming the folder before he moved on. "I don't give a fuck about her motivations," he stated, scanning the news. "I give a fuck about her completing the job."

"She's smarter than I am," Rhys grinned, pulling his chair up beside him and looking over his shoulder. "You sure you can do this?"

Bookmarking a new propaganda site for later review, he returned to the scads of unanswered emails. "You have six hours before I expect a report. Fuck off."

****

Nichol swung the door to his bunk open, hastily assembled reports tucked under his arm as he flicked the light on and groaned. "Shouldn't you be in bed?"

Audra's brows rose a fraction. "You mean as you should have been three hours ago?" She watched him while he bent to unlace his boots. "That wouldn't be more work you're holding, would it?"

Aligning his boots with the wall, he tossed the stack of paper onto the coffee table and sat down beside Audra. "That would be what happens when I don't have a phone to receive updates. I end up deciphering Jagger's chicken scratch and piecing together Rhys's notes from the forty pages he managed to scrawl across."

"You shouldn't be up here," she reiterated, the accusation gone from her voice. "You aren't ready."

Picking up the first report, he leaned back on his sofa, the softness of the seat a huge improvement from his accommodations of the past three weeks. "I'm fine," he grunted, lifting his feet to the table. "I understand you've been Boy's contact since I've been out of commission."

"I have," Audra said slowly, pulling her phone out. "He and Kaius are holed up outside of a northern Alberta town in Canada." She handed him her cell as Boy's clipped texts loaded on the screen. "He's refused to reply to my questions. Just location updates."

He scanned the messages. "That's all we require right now," he murmured absently, passing the phone back. "Alert me whenever he makes contact."

Audra nodded and sat back, getting comfortable. "Mick mentioned something interesting to me last night," she stated casually as he side-eyed her, his shoulders tensing. "You and Simone—"

"There's no 'and'," he growled, redoubling his attention on Jagger's sloppily-penned report. "Mikhail is mistaken. The hybrid is Rhys's concern now and I have work to get done before I get to sleep on a mattress that doesn't send springs into my ass every time I move."

Audra rose to her feet and patted his knee. "I'll let it go tonight, but I'll be touching base with you tomorrow." When he didn't move from his place, she bent down and hugged him tight. "Don't scare me like that again."

He grunted, stilling until Audra's awkward display of affection was over. "Go away."

****

The com room emptied quickly, Nichol's barked instructions sending the hauntmates out the door with little hesitation. He turned back to his computer and began transcribing the previous nights' report, entering the relevant information into various spreadsheets and documents.

"Hey," Rhys called, reentering the control room and

waving a familiar device in his direction. "You think you're ready for this?"

His fingers twitched on the keyboard. "About time," he grunted, extending one hand to accept the phone.

Rhys rolled his eyes. "You've been topside for twenty-four hours, you fucking junkie," he snarked, freezing as the words left his mouth.

Nichol tapped the cell screen to life, ignoring his brother's unintentional slip. "See this?" he demanded, turning his screen to Rhys. "This is how you organize your calendars and lists. Not," he paused to hold up the crumpled paper Rhys had handed him the night before, "this."

Rhys leaned against the door frame. "Just jumped right back into the grind, hey?" he asked, glancing around the room. "If it's too much—"

"I'm fine," he huffed, his thumb flying across his phone as he fired off a text to the Denver mayor.

Rhys's navy eyes appraised him. "And if you're not, you'll let me know, right?"

He nodded, flicking through his unanswered messages and deleting those he deemed unnecessary. He kept his head down until Rhys rapped his knuckles on the door frame and sauntered down the hall, leaving him alone.

Keyboard needs dusting.

Electrician needs keys to the western property.

Jean-Michel took out two Deviants outside his property and requires payment.

Loading the haunt's bank accounts, he placed his phone face-down on the desk.

And clicked on the small messenger app icon on his computer.

He stared at the reactivation page, his fingers hovering over the keyboard.

Not on the to-do list.

He clicked it anyways.

The messages loaded on his home page, Highsteaks peppering his feed.

She was alive.

She was bored.

She was online.

587OriginalNK: hey

Time crawled as he waited for a response.

Any response.

Highsteaks1403: he lives

587OriginalNK: He does

Highsteaks1403: call?

Nichol looked at his phone.

587OriginalNK: can't. safe?

Highsteaks1403: yeah

He typed a quick message, deleting it as the last letter appeared on the screen. Another. Another. He slumped into his chair and ran a hand through his hair.

587OriginalNK: I miss you. I'm sorry

Highsteaks1403: you apologize a lot

587OriginalNK: I fuck up a lot

Highsteaks1403: lucky 4 u I don't #DovidasKill4TheWin

A small grunt of amusement echoed in the com room. He glanced at his phone again, debating the stupidity of hearing Simone's voice again.

He didn't have time for senseless phone calls.

During night hours.

587OriginalNK: can I call you after dawn?

Highsteaks1403: i've waited up for you plenty of

times. once more won't kill me

Minimizing the chat screen, he attacked the banking with renewed energy until Mickey's voice punctured his concentration.

"You're happy."

He arched his head back as he confirmed an email money transfer. "What?"

Mick stood in the doorway, his blue eyes narrowed. "Nothing." He crossed the room and set a pile of opened boxes on the table. "Mail delivery."

****

Nichol paced the floor of his bunker, his phone tight to his ear. "I don't give a single flying fuck how busy your creator is, if he doesn't sign off on your contract, you're out of Denver at dusk."

He flung his phone across the table, cursing as it bounced off onto the floor.

Where the fuck is she?

Five days of calls, a tentative peace building between himself and Simone, and then nothing.

No texts.

No calls.

Nothing.

He slumped onto his sofa and closed his eyes.

Top up Boy's account.

Email plumber with new specs.

Update security settings on former bloodslave monitoring apps.

He rubbed his jaw, forcing the grinding of his teeth to stop. Scooping his phone from the floor, he dove into his list, pushing both of his cravings from his mind.

He couldn't afford to be distracted.

****

Nichol eased off the gas as he approached Denver's city limits. He glanced at his buzzing phone and tapped the green answer button. "What."

"When the hell is your sorry ass getting here?" Rhys asked, the sounds of construction filtering loudly through the cell's speaker.

"I'm five minutes away," he replied, turning off the freeway. "I got held up with another detained Tender in Newark."

Rhys swore, relaying his response to Mick. "I told Finnea to fly her out of Philadelphia. Did she manage to board?"

He grunted. "After a ten grand payoff to some asshat manager."

"Send Finnea the tab and triple the amount for stupidity," Rhys ordered. "Is that you pulling in?"

Hanging up, he brought his car snug alongside Rhys's and hopped out. He slammed the door shut and backed up to scan the building. "How long do they anticipate the final touches will take?" he asked as Rhys sauntered over.

"One week. Eight suites are already loaded and occupied. Another six are expected within the month."

He frowned. "I have seven suites listed as occupied," he said, pulling his phone out to check his spreadsheet. "Who's in the eighth?"

Mick stood in the doorway, his large form hunched to avoid cracking his head on the entrance. "Probably a squatter."

"Fuck that," he snarled, pushing past Rhys and storming into the building. His hauntmates followed as he made his way through the halls, comparing his notes to the closed doors as he passed. "I have no vamps listed under suite eight."

Rhys shrugged. "Guess you better deal with it then."

Glaring at his nonchalant hauntmate, he banged his fist on the door, listening as a strangely familiar code was punched in and the door opened.

"Hey, NK."

****

Simone looked to Rhys, her eyes narrowing. "You didn't tell him."

Rhys grinned at her, his fangs on full display. "Must've slipped my mind, angel. Mind if Mick and I have a look around?"

She stepped to the side to allow the vamps to pass, her attention back on the one standing perfectly still in the hall. "You coming?"

Nichol's jaw twitched, his hazel eyes regaining their recognition. "Yeah."

He skulked past her without another word, taking care to avoid brushing against her.

She closed the door and set the code, leaning on the frame while Nichol prowled through her new apartment, his biceps flexing and relaxing rhythmically.

"I thought I requested white caulking," he grumbled from the bathroom as Rhys sidled up to her.

"Why didn't you tell him?" she hissed.

Rhys smirked and craned his neck toward the bathroom where Nichol's feet were visible as he hunched over the bathtub. "He had a lot going on."

"Have," Nichol barked, exiting the bathroom and making his way toward them. "I have a lot going on and now I have a fucking caulking issue to deal with." Mick and Rhys exchanged a strange look of exasperation and wariness as Nichol pushed past them and tapped in the code. "Good to see you got out, Simone," he called over his shoulder as he stormed down the hall.

Her mouth fell open, her stomach sinking when Nichol turned the corner and disappeared.

"What the hell?" Mickey whispered beside her, his blue eyes wide.

Rhys's face was locked down, his fangs lengthening. "What are you getting off him?"

She looked to Mickey, confused.

"It's there," Mick muttered, shaking his head. "The connection is even more intense than it was for Dominic when we had to chain him in the bloodslave quarters and hold him down for feedings. I..." He looked back down the empty hallway. "I don't know how he's still walking right now."

****

Nichol swung his chair around and sat at his computer, his priorities set during the drive back to the haunt.

He had shit to do.

His phone continued to buzz incessantly, turning into little more than white noise while he pulled up the building specs and began running down the list of approved supplies.

White caulking.

Highlighting the order, he fired off an email to the builder.

Hey, NK.

He continued down his list, checking off each item and adding new ones as more came up. Simone's voice looped in his head while he plowed through emails and blueprints, schedules, and requests. The incessant buzzing of his phone became less demanding as the night wore down, the inconsistent vibrations pulling his attention more and more while the hours ticked by.

He opened the haunt accounts and began scanning the transactions as Rhys entered the com room, his lips drawn tight across his fangs.

"That was a dick move."

He flipped to the next account while Rhys stepped further into the room.

"Simone's taking over the vamp cop training effective Friday," Rhys continued, crossing his arms and widening his stance.

"She's well-suited for it," he replied, sitting back in frustration when he couldn't locate what he was looking for. "Where's the payment to Stojanovski?"

"He arrived at the compound three nights ago."

Nichol paused and looked at Rhys. "Who?"

"Louis."

****

Simone rose up on her toes and looked through the peek-hole at the slouching vampire in the hall, his head bowed and hands shoved deep into the pockets of his cargos as he spoke to the door. "I fucked up. Bad."

She dropped her forehead to the wood and sighed. "Dammit, NK," she sighed, entering the lock code and opening the door. "Come in before the electricians open the side doors and fry you."

He slunk into her suite, stepping aside while she entered the code again and pushed the door closed. He kept his eyes averted, his weight shifting from foot to foot as he ground his back teeth.

"Take off the boots before you walk on the carpet," she warned, padding across the room and sitting on the sofa. She drew her legs up to her chest and watched him bend down to untie his laces, his movements hesitant. He lined his boots up against the wall and straightened, hazel eyes locking onto the floor. She unfolded herself and reached across the new coffee table, grabbing a game controller, and holding it out to him. "Sit."

His face relaxed slightly as he approached her and accepted the remote. "What are we playing?"

"We're racing for glory," she said, turning on the console and settling into her seat. "Rhys said you're off the blood."

His jaw twitched, his face locking down again. "Yeah."

"Good." She went quiet while he selected his character. "He also explained Mickey's theory to me."

His attention on the screen, he wrinkled his nose when she chose the battle mode. They played in silence, a small shudder traveling through Nichol as the sun rose. By the eighth round, she set her controller down.

"You can crash on the couch today," she said softly. "I don't have internet yet, but most of the games I have in there can be played offline." She laid her hand on his knee as she rose, the muscles hardening under her touch. "Night, Nichol."

She crawled into her new bed, the sheets still crinkly from their single night of use.

Old.

Everything about Nichol looked old. His posture. His movements. His eyes.

Old and worn and tired.

Rhys hadn't prepared her for it. He focused all his warnings on Nichol's busy schedule and the strange connection theory Mickey pushed adamantly. He'd said nothing about Nichol's incessant grinding of his teeth, the minute twitch of his right eye every time the phone buzzed, or the muscle knots in his shoulders which were visible through his shirt.

She rolled onto her side and listened to the faint sounds of her game console whirring to life.

'Off the blood and back to normal', Rhys had stated resolutely as he sat beside her the night before, lifting his phone to forward a series of emails to Nichol.

Back to normal.

Even through the door, she could hear Nichol's phone going off every thirty seconds. She could hear the game pause as he spent his early daylight hours attending to a barrage of emails and texts while his hauntmates were resting. Could hear his hushed responses while he paced the carpeted floor and provided a safe route to a stranded vamp, the video game long forgotten.

She got out of bed and cracked her door open, watching silently as he hunched over his phone, his thumb flying across the screen.

"The internet will be up by noon," he stated, frowning at his cell. "Caulking won't be replaced until next week."

She pushed her door completely open and leaned against the frame. "Neither of those are life or death," she said quietly. "You need to get some rest."

He grunted in response.

She crossed the floor and looked over his arm at his phone. "What language is that?"

"Slovenian," he replied, typing out a response in words she couldn't begin to read.

Waiting until he was done his message, she wrapped her hand around the phone and eased it out of his grip. The tendons in his neck tightened as she held her thumb over the power button, turned it off, and set it on her coffee table.

"This is a no tech zone as long as you're in my suite."

His hazel eyes flicked between her and his phone. The grinding of his teeth became more pronounced as she approached him and placed her arms around his neck, drawing him tight to her. She laid her head on his chest and nudged his arms with her elbows. "Hugs are a lot more effective when the other person doesn't stand there like a gargoyle."

His arms rose to her waist, his hands locking together behind her. The minutes ticked by, the gnashing of his teeth slowing to a stop.

His brain fires differently when he's near you.

Mickey's hesitant words from the previous night echoed in her head and she tightened her hold. Nichol tensed against her, his arms locking in place a fraction away from her body, but she held position and waited, her heart stuttering when his chin lowered to the top of her head and his hands unclasped. He wrapped his arms around her, clinging to her as the tension in his shoulders released and his body began to relax.

Chapter Thirty-Five

Nichol could feel the incessant pressure on him drain out as he clung to Simone, the looping lists and demands in his mind being boxed up and set aside while the scent of her three-hundred dollar shampoo filled his head. The ever-present tightness in his throat eased when her thumbs drew small circles on his back and her heart rate slowed.

Big. Fucking. Mistake.

Big. Fucking. Mistake.

He tensed. "What were the terms of your release from the Stojanovski compound?"

She sighed, her warm breath cutting through his shirt and searing his skin. "If you're asking if you're my new assignment, no."

He released his grip on her and stepped back. "The terms."

With obvious exasperation, she turned from him and knelt beside one of the boxes still peppering her suite. She hunted through it, setting several books and shoes to the side before she stood, a neatly stapled contract in her hand. "Here. Read them yourself."

Taking the stack, he scanned the document.

The Hybrid will be provided with accommodations and a sustainable living allowance for the period of two years from the date of signing, in the city, state, and country of her choosing.

The Hybrid agrees not to directly or indirectly disclose any information attained throughout her training and subsequent employment within the vampire community without the signed written consent of Rhys Kaius.

Simone waited patiently beside him as he flipped through the extensive non-disclosure agreement and scanned the supporting articles for signatures.

"This was adapted from the official Former Tender contract I created a few decades back," he said as he handed the forms back to her. "Providing you adhere to the clauses, you're well-protected and your freedom is guaranteed from vampire society."

She flipped through the document, silently pointing to a single clause.

The Hybrid is released from all duties relating to vampires with the exception of those she elects to pursue of her own free will.

His shoulders knotted. "Fuck," he grumbled, snatching his phone from the table. "I shouldn't be here." He started to the door, powering his phone on. "I'll have Rhys send out a document outlining compensatory damages."

She laughed.

Hard.

"Hot damn, Nichol. You're so wound, I'm amazed you haven't spontaneously combusted." She followed him to the door, kneeling in front of him as he crouched to pull his boots on. "I've chosen to hole up in this freezing city when I could be in Paris or Athens. I've signed on to train vamp cops alongside your annoying brothers. I've resigned myself to having a hideous brown sofa, comfortable as it is."

His brow furrowed.

The sofa was functional, with a nondescript color palette that could be paired with a variety of decors.

Her hands cupped his chin as she spoke slowly, enunciating her words. "I elect. To pursue you. Of my own free will." She brought her lips to his forehead. "Is that clear enough, or should I re-enact it with hand puppets?"

Her fingers caressed his jaw and her lips traveled across his temples, flitted over his cheekbones, and settled on his mouth. He released his laces and dropped his hands to the floor to steady himself.

Or bolt.

"Don't even think about it," she whispered against his mouth, her fingers drifting from his jaw to the back of his neck.

He turned his head. "You have options," he stated, ducking out of her grip and rising to his feet, the rhythmic buzzing of his phone centering his racing brain.

Simone snatched his cell from his hand and flung it across the room. "What the fuck, NK? Haven't we danced past this yet?"

"Past what?" he snarled, running his hand over the back of his neck to erase the sensation of her fingers on his skin. "I don't have time for this. For you." He began pacing, circling the small space, and cursing himself for not adding an extra eighty square feet to the blueprints. "Everything is fucked up. The things that aren't? They will be. And the biggest fuckups of the year have been mine." His hands flexed, the familiar tightening of his throat graveling his voice. "The blood. Kaius. Boy. Louis."

"I was a call girl for four years."

He stopped his pacing and turned toward her. "I know."

She lifted a hand in the air, counting down on her fingers. "I dropped out of university in my second year because I couldn't afford tuition and coke."

Recalling the quick history search he'd performed on her when her bloodslave shipment had arrived on site, he glared at her. "I know."

She bent a third finger down. "Stole three thousand from my mother's boyfriend and broke up the only stable relationship she'd had since I was seven." A fourth finger. "Threw up during the ceremony of my best friend's wedding because I was hung over." A fifth. "Slept with, well, almost every boss I've ever had."

Rhys flashed across his mind, and he winced as a shot of jealousy rippled through him. "Thanks for the reminder, Highsteaks," he grunted, unable to rid Rhys's smirk from his head. "What the hell's your point?"

"My point," she said, tilting her head and wiggling her fingers, "is I fucked up bad, too. A lot." She placed her hands on her hips. "You wanted me back at Stojanovski's. Knowing how much I've fucked up over the years, do you still want me now?"

"What I want is irrelevant," he stated, holding his ground. "I don't have the time."

She shrugged, scooped his phone from the floor, and walked into her bedroom.

He watched as she pulled her shirt over her head and tossed it aside. Her yoga pants were next to go, shimmied down her thighs and kicked into the corner before she slipped his phone under her pillow and climbed into bed.

Holy. Fuck.

He began running fight scenes in his head, his eyes

locked on the swell of her hip under the blanket.

He took a step forward.

Another.

He crossed the floor in four strides, gripping the door frame to hold himself back.

"I thought you were busy," she said, rolling onto her back and placing her hands behind her head. "Or are you here for your phone?"

He shook his head, not trusting his brain to reply.

Another step.

"Oh, no you don't," she sang. "Not another inch closer until you answer my questions."

His gaze trailed down her covered body, his mind filling in the visual of what was underneath. "Question one," he grunted, his vision narrowing as her scent began to overtake him.

"Do you want me to stay in Denver?"

He took another step. "Yeah. Two."

She stretched her arms up, purposely arching her back and slamming Nichol's mind with memories. "Would you be willing to spend one night a week here, just you and me? And…" She held up a finger. "No. Phone."

He stalked forward, a strange trickle of warmth worming its way through his body. "Yeah. Three."

She licked her lips. "Will you stack my game arsenals enough to take you down?"

He zeroed in on her tongue. "Fuck yeah." He stepped within reach of the bed. "Four."

"Are you connected?"

He drew back a fraction.

It was a ridiculous claim, completely unsupported by facts. Aside from his self-imposed celibacy, he had spent the past thirty years as he had the first fourteen hundred.

Annoyed.

Frustrated.

Fucking busy.

"N…" He paused.

The constant tightness in his muscles waxing and waning for the past three decades was gone. The incessantly evolving lists looping through his mind day and night were just out of reach, barely accessible in his head with her proximity. The constant craving whispering seductively from the corner of his subconscious was silent.

"Fuck," he barked, running his hand through his hair and locking his gaze on the ceiling. "This is a waste of time. I should be pissed. There's a list a mile fucking long I should be getting on. I can't even… I can't even think of what's on the list right now, but it's there." He rubbed his temples, assessing every muscle in his body for the tension he always carried. "Fuck, Simone. I don't even care what I could be getting done right now," he snarled as he ran his tongue over his fangs. "You're playing games, and I'm not pissed. I need to call Mikhail." He frowned, patting his back pockets. "I need to apologize to him."

"So that's a yes?" she asked, her blue eyes morphing from flirtatious to unimpressed as he retreated back a step.

He dropped his head. "I'm sorry. I think so. Yeah."

She sat up and pursed her lips. "And your first reaction to this realization is to call your brother," she stated. "Seriously, NK? I'm right here. And practically naked."

****

Simone bit her lip when Nichol finally looked at her, his hazel eyes completely blackened as he advanced on her. He reached for her blanket, tugging it off slowly onto the floor.

"I can't change what I am," he warned, running his hands up her calves. "I need you to be okay with that. I can't. This is it."

Her stomach clenched as her own words pounded in her head.

Biter.

Your kind.

If I'd known what you are, we would never have talked.

She sat up and leaned forward, trailing her thumb over his lower lip. "I'm sorry," she whispered, grazing one long fang with her nail. "I'm so, so okay with what you are. Everything you are." She laid back again and stretched one leg toward him, nudging his hand with her knee. "Every snarky, obsessive-compulsive, miserable, stubborn part of you."

Those lethal fangs of his lengthened, sending an unexpected thrill through her body as he continued to trail his fingers up her legs.

"You call me out on my bullshit," he stated, gripping her hips and sliding her toward the foot of the bed.

She closed her eyes as he hooked his thumbs in her neon orange thong and dragged it down her thighs with excruciating slowness. "There's a lot of bullshit to call out."

"You have a tolerable sense of humor," he continued, kneeling between her knees and trailing his tongue from her ankle to her hipbone.

She inhaled sharply as his teeth grazed her across her stomach. "And you have no sense of humor," she retorted, her back arching instinctively when his large hands traveled up her ribs and his thumbs brushed against the cups of her bra.

His tongue traced loops on her skin toward her center, his grip on her ribs tightening. "You have a strategist mind. Even if your spelling is atrocious."

"Are you trying to convince yourself of something?" she asked, whimpering when his tongue flicked across her nub. She ran one hand through his hair as he lightly teased her, her hips lifting to him when he refused to increase the pressure.

"Just informing you the connection is the last reason I'm here," he murmured before he took her hint and ran his tongue through her folds, sending jolts of pleasure up her core and into her fingertips. "Fuck, you have a beautiful taste."

Her eyes rolled back in her head as Nichol worked her with his tongue and fingers, bringing her to the brink and pulling back time and again until she dug her heels into his back and growled. "I'm going to take matters into my own hands in about thirty seconds."

In less than ten, she was a moaning mess, her hands tangled in his hair as she tugged him up her body.

****

Nichol buried his head in Simone's neck while he reached behind her to undo the orange bra he was slowly warming to. She slipped her hands under his shirt and ran them up his spine, the contact doing absolutely nothing to alleviate the pressure of his cargo zipper against his erection. He ground his hips against her as he finally unhooked the stubborn bra, desperate for the friction regardless of the damage the metal teeth of the zipper were probably doing.

"Damn, that's warm," he gasped into her skin as the heat of her center filtered through the fabric between them.

She pulled his shirt over his head, licking her lips as he sat up and tossed the tee across the room. He watched her fingers snap open the button of his pants and ease the zipper down, relieving the intense strain.

"Lose 'em," she ordered, dropping her knees from his hips so he could slide off the bed. "Lose 'em slowly," she amended when he stood.

He shoved his cargos off and kicked them aside, his boxers impatiently following suit. "Nope." He crawled back on top of her, his attention wholly consumed by the incredible breasts inches from his lips. He circled his tongue around one hardened nipple while his fingers reached between her legs and slid through her wetness.

Her small hand brushed against his as she gripped him. "You close?"

Stilling his hips, he nuzzled the soft skin of her breast. "For eighteen minutes now," he grunted as she pumped him. He pushed himself up and glared at her. "I'm not making it to nineteen minutes if you don't stop."

Her blue eyes glinted as she sped up. "You've got all day and a recovery time of, what, a minute?"

He dropped to his elbows and buried his head in the crook of her neck, his body tightening despite his pathetic attempt to hold out by envisioning electrical blueprints. When she guided him into her heat and pushed her hips up in one smooth movement, he lost the fight and released, his hand slamming against the wall to steady himself as he held his aching fangs far from her throat.

His vision hadn't even returned before his body began reacting to the slickness surrounding him. He stilled while she rocked against him, holding off until he regained control over his senses.

Until he was confident he wouldn't bite.

****

Nichol toed off his boots and held them in his hand while he crept down the garage stairs into the main halls of the haunt. Rounding the corner into his office, he slipped into the dark room, carefully closed the door, and flicked on the lights.

Fuck.

Mickey spun around in his chair, a shit-eating fangy grin spread across his face. "Tell me I'm right, Nicky. And enunciate it real clear for me to enjoy."

Lining his boots against the wall, he stormed past Mick and powered his computer to life. "You been touching my stuff?" he growled, frowning when the desktop appeared, the basic black background replaced with a close-up photo of Mick with his tongue dangling out. He turned and glared as his younger brother struck the same pose. "You're an idiot."

"Maybe so," Mick sang, frantically firing off a text. "But I'm a right idiot."

He latched on to his chair and ripped it out from under Mickey. "That you are. Now fuck off."

"We're both fucking off. Jagg's doing a quick review of the vamp cop techniques downstairs. We've been waiting for you, loverboy."

Deciding ignoring was better than debating, he stormed out of the com room and down the hall to the weapons training room, Mick hot on his heels.

"About fucking time, Casanova," Rhys called out as he entered. "The Hybrid better be able to walk by Friday."

He crossed his arms and looked to Jagg. "I don't remember adding a training review to the night's schedule."

Jagger lifted a small blade into the light and turned it slowly, assessing the trueness of the steel. "I made the call at dawn," he said, closing one eye and repeating his motions. "But by the time I tried to run it past you, Mick was ripping through the haunt crowing like a rooster about being right." Jagg gave him a cheery smile. "I've slated in an hour after this for Dominic to run through some connection lessons with you. He's prepping his notes right now."

When Mickey tossed his arms in the air victoriously and began a slow strut through the room to the sound of his brothers' applause, Nichol locked his eyes on the ceiling.

Totally fucking worth it.
****

Simone adjusted her aim, raising her bow to align the scope with her target. "Your margin of error is wider than you think for the initial hit," she called out, closing one eye. "As long as your arrow strikes between the head and the heart, you'll have time for a second attack." She released the first bolt and reloaded, firing off the second instantly and hitting the dummy square in the chest. "If you miss on the second, you're done."

Nichol stood in the entrance of the training room and scanned through the last of his incoming emails, responding to the most urgent as the trainees stepped up beside Simone and raised their own bows. He kept one eye on her while she wound through the group, correcting form under the watchful eye of Rhys who crouched silently in the corner, his lips turned up in approval.

Bolts flew toward their targets, all of the second attempts missing their marks completely.

Rhys smirked.

Simone hid her smile, clapping her hands together. "We'll work on the double-shot more next time," she announced, bending to collect the failed bolts from the floor and tracking Rhys as he stalked across the floor.

"Nichol Kaius will be reviewing all body-cam footage in the event of a weapon draw. He's arranged for the vamps settling here to pony up a security deposit of sorts." Rhys sauntered among the men, his fangs on full display. "Any of them get caught breaking the sanctuary laws will be detained, their deposit forfeited for donation to local schools should they be found in violation." He caught sight of Nichol and smirked. "All right, guys. Beat it out of here. Simone has plans."

The men filtered out of the room and past him, acknowledging the old vampire with a quick nod before they disappeared down the hall.

"Nothing makes me prouder than watching one of my girls kick ass in front of a group of men," Rhys stated, snatching his bag from the floor.

"She's not one of your girls," he corrected, distracted by Simone as she adjusted the foot pull of a new bow.

Rhys feigned a heavy sigh. "Not anymore, she isn't," he huffed, side-eying him as a smirk formed on his lips. "But you know, she was mine first. And as I always say, women never forget their first vamp."

He hummed in agreement. "Speaking of that, Mick and Lis are on security detail tonight." He paused. "Alone."

The younger vampire's eyes narrowed as he pulled out his phone. "You're a dick. Enjoy your date, Romeo."

While Rhys dialed Lis's number and stormed out the front door cursing Mickey's name, he leaned in the gym doorway and powered off his phone.

****

The clerk gave Nichol a deadened stare, taking his keys from his back pocket and dragging his feet toward the display case. "So it's a no to the five games I already pulled out, then?"

Simone squeezed between the kid and the glass door, reaching up to grab the latest role-playing game and scanning the back. "Will this work on my old system?"

Nichol pointed to the newest console. "Add two of those and whatever games she wants," he ordered, biting his tongue to avoid smiling when she broke out in a spastic dance of excitement. He leaned against the counter and waited as the clerk begrudgingly opened two more displays for her to rifle through until she made her selections and the kid could ring them up.

"You're, like, the seventh vamp in here this month," the clerk said, running his credit card without glancing at the signature. "Never knew you guys were gamers. You should check out the convention next month. Lots of cosplayers and demos for upcoming games."

He grunted in response as he lifted the thin plastic bags and gave them a slight shake to ensure the bottoms wouldn't tear out. "Talk to her," he said, placing his credit card into his wallet. "She's the RPG addict."

Twenty minutes later, he dragged Simone and the video games to the SUV.

She smiled at him as he tore out of the parking lot. "We're going to that convention."

He snorted.

She ran her hand up his inner thigh, stopping just short of his crotch. "And we're going in costume."

He adjusted his hips and sped up. "We'll see."

Content with his reply, she grinned and looked out the window, squeezing his leg periodically until he pulled up to her complex. He hefted the consoles and games into his arms, not trusting the flimsy bags to survive the short walk to Simone's suite.

"Phone," she demanded, punching in her lock code.

He held it out to her, mildly amused when she disappeared into her bedroom with it and came back empty-handed. "Middle drawer on the left side," he stated, setting the consoles down and prying the boxes open. When she leveled him with a flat stare, he shrugged. "It's a safety concern. Should the need arise, I may not have time to look around." He continued to unwrap manuals and carefully realign her existing consoles to avoid stacking them while he ran cords between the gaming systems and the television. "I'm placing an order for a larger TV tomorrow," he grumbled. "And a few splicers."

She got comfortable on the brown sofa and handed him her new game expectantly. He sliced open the plastic wrap open with his fang and passed it back.

"Let's see how good you are at a game where your platinum card doesn't win the game for you," she taunted, getting comfortable.

Handing her a control, he sat on the opposite side of the couch and snapped the stiff cord of his own remote. "I have superior reflexes, superior memory, and superior experience."

She smiled sweetly at him and pulled off her sweater.

Three hours of low-cut tank top distraction later, he set his feet onto the coffee table and tossed his controller aside. "This game sucks."

"Too bad you don't," she grinned, finishing off a rival before saving her progress. She crawled across the sofa and straddled him. "You're staying the day, right?"

He nodded, her proximity sending a warm rush through his veins. "I'm not due back until ten tomorrow night."

It felt odd to vocalize.

A complete break, an entire twenty-five hours blocked out of his schedule.

He was pulled out of his head by her movements, one hand easing her curls from her neck. She had a nervous anticipation in her eyes.

"I'm good," he replied, refusing to look at the smooth skin of her throat as he realized her intentions.

She tilted her head, further teasing him. "You fed off me several times during my training," she stated, narrowing her eyes as she assessed him. "Why not now?"

He pushed back the images of her offered wrist in the com room with the small punctures from Kaius's fangs still visible. He refused to delve into the resentment her blue eyes had held as she stood silently beside him, her arms held in his hands while he continued to transfer deposits and sell stock holdings. He shoved back the memories of Simone waiting, ignored, in the corner of the room until he finished reviewing Jagger's reports.

"You're thinking up an excuse," she said, crossing her arms. "It better be convincing."

Fuck.

If he had his phone, he could text Rhys for advice. Text him, and do the opposite of what his punk-ass, couch-sleeping brother recommended.

He placed his hands on her hips. "I hate thinking about it," he said slowly, his thumbs drawing circles on her skin. "Your training. How you got there. Why you got there. Rhys. Stojanovski. I need to keep the now and the then separate at the moment." He ran his thumb over the scar on her ribs. "Even if Rhys and Mick like to bring it up as often as they can." He gave her a tight smile. "Besides, Audra suggested feeding wasn't a first-date activity."

Simone ran her hand through his hair and rested her forehead against his. "We've known each other for nearly two years, NK. Longer, if you count the haunt. First-date rules don't exactly apply here."

Inching his hands up her sides, he closed his eyes. "Yeah, well, none of my date research mentioned fangs either."

Soft lips brushed over his brow. "Research?"

He hooked his fingers into the straps of her tank top and eased them off her shoulders. "I read a lot about appropriate activities, but most involved extended periods in public settings open during daylight hours." He arched his head back as her lips traveled down his face. "I also learned about bases."

Simone laughed into his neck. "What base are you hoping to reach tonight?"

"Second."

****

Simone's grip on Nichol's shoulders weakened as he continued to thrust up into her at an excruciatingly slow rate. She draped her arms over the back of the sofa, cursing when his mouth latched on to her breast. "This is definitely past second base," she panted, inhaling sharply when he adjusted his hips and changed his angle.

One of his hands wove through her hair, pulling her lips to his. "I'm an over-achiever."

Over-achiever was an understatement.

Nichol had kept her on the cusp for over two hours, every leisurely movement bringing her closer without pushing her over the edge.

After the second hour, she had stopped threatening to stake him.

He was just too damn good.

She wrapped one hand around the base of his neck and looked down at his closed eyes.

Closed eyes flickering rapidly behind his lids.

"What on earth are you thinking about?" she asked, her thighs tightening around his hips when he hit a particularly sweet spot.

His eyes snapped open, the blackened irises elongated. "Sparring." He grabbed onto her hips to keep her in place. "If I didn't, this would've been over one-hundred, twenty-eight minutes ago." When she laughed, he tightened his hold. "You're not helping."

She swiveled her hips against his hands, smirking when his eyes squeezed shut, and he inhaled sharply. "I'm going to be as unhelpful as I can." She trailed her tongue over his lobe and lifting her wrist to his mouth. "Bite me."

His entire body tensed, his fangs lengthening

slightly.

She nuzzled against his jugular. "Like this."
****

If Nichol had been handed a surveillance video and instructed to identify the timeline of events, he may have been able to determine what came first: his bite, Simone's, or the freight-train orgasm that ripped through his body, shooting his leg into the coffee table and shattering the glass.

But in the moment, all he knew was he was fucked. Epically fucked, and ravenous for more.

Her head was tucked under his chin, her unruly curls tickling his face as her breathing began to even out. He tightened his arms around her and closed his eyes, examining the corner of his mind her existence had exploded into.

Content.

Secure.

Hungry.

"Highsteaks," he whispered, angling his head to keep her hair out of his mouth. "Up."

"No."

Funny.

She thought she was funny, and he could feel her amusement in his own mind through the link she inadvertently caused through their shared bloodletting.

He adjusted his hold and pushed off the sofa, dodging the shards of glass peppering the carpet as he carried her to her bed. "Stay."

He wandered into the kitchen, opening cupboards and the fridge and glaring at the collection of white Styrofoam boxes. Opening one, he sniffed the pizza inside for spoilage.

"Is that the pizza? Toss it into the microwave for a minute," she called to him, her hunger becoming more amplified.

He obeyed, quietly cursing the appliance when his first three attempts failed.

"One, zero, zero, start."

"Yeah, yeah," he grunted, glaring at the pizza until the microwave dinged. He returned to the bedroom with plate of pizza in one hand, a glass of water in the other, and sat on the edge of the bed as she ate.

He could feed his mate, dammit.

Mate.

He stood, mentally reviewing the suite inventory for a vacuum.

"Don't even think about it," Simone ordered, patting the bed. "I'm full, I'm tired, and I want to cuddle."

****

Nichol was vaguely aware of the sensation of warmth ghosting across his chest as he woke from a dead sleep.

Warmth and metal.

He remained motionless, tracking the intruder as it skimmed the cold steel across his stomach, the heat of a hand trailing behind it. Once he was certain he had determined the angle of attack, he cracked one eye open a fraction, ready to pounce until turquoise nail polish caught his attention.

Turquoise nail polish holding a small blade.

"What the hell are you doing?" he demanded, pushing himself up on to his elbows and earning a hum of appreciation from Simone as his stomach muscles tightened.

"Just looking," she smiled, tightening the blanket

around her bare chest before she reached across him to set the knife on the bedside table. "Checking out the goods and all."

He glanced over at the weapon. "With that?"

"Rhys suggested you may not react well to waking with a woman in the room." She smiled at him brightly, her rainbow curls a mess. "I was going to stab you in the thigh if you panicked."

"I—" He looked around the room to orient himself. "That was wise."

"I know."

He reclined back in the bed for a moment, probing her corner of his head and finding her happy and relaxed.

Rhys suggested.

"When did you talk to Rhys?" he asked, cringing internally at the hint of jealousy and possessiveness that had crept into his voice.

Simone continued her assessment of his torso, tracing the lines of his abs with her pinky. "Around eleven."

He frowned. "What time is it now?"

"One."

One.

He quickly calculated the hours he'd rested. "I was out for ten hours."

"About that."

Fuck.

Easing his way out from under her, he bolted from the bedroom and began snatching his clothes from the floor. "I need my phone." He yanked his cargos over his hips. "There's a shit-ton to get done tonight."

"Rhys said take your time," Simone called over from her bedroom door, completely calm despite his rising tension. "He said as long as I check you aren't dead every hour or so, he'll hold down the fort until you arrive. So relax."

He tugged his shirt over his head as he crossed the room to grab his boots. "How did you check that?"

She glanced at his crotch and then looked up at him, a Cheshire smile on her face. "I have my ways."

Ways his now-awake body was apparently wishing it had known about an hour earlier, judging by its traitorous reaction.

She disappeared into her room for a moment before she joined him, skirting the glass shards on the floor as she handed him his phone. "I expect a text or call when you get home."

He powered his cell on and nodded, kicking himself for not taking care of the mess before he went to bed. "I'll send a cleanup over before dawn," he said, adding it to his list and opening his contacts to find a number.

Her hand covered his screen and she brought it tight against her chest. "I'll get on it the moment you walk out the door."

Her heartbeat pounded against the back of his hand, the calm, steady beat centering him. He glared at the mess one last time and bent down, brushing his lips against hers. "I'll have a new table sent over right away then," he murmured, reveling in the softness of her lips. "Lock the damn door."

He stepped into the hall, breaking into a jog as the lock code engaged and the vacuum whirred to life.

****

587OriginalNK: here

Highsteaks1403: miss you already call me later

Nichol glanced over his shoulder to ensure his

brothers hadn't yet spotted him.

587OriginalNK: miss you too :*

He crossed the field, kicking the remnants of a minor snowfall from his boots as he approached Rhys. "What the fuck is going on?"

Rhys smirked at him. "The gigolo lives."

Tossing a well-placed elbow into Rhys's ribs, he scanned his hauntmates. "The blade was a wise suggestion."

"Yeah, well, I figured the last woman to wake you was probably your mother."

He didn't argue. He *couldn't* argue.

Rhys motioned toward the makeshift sparring ring. "We're rotating two-on-ones. Dominic and Mick are piling on Jagg right now. You're up next."

Jagger eventually went down, the two youngest brothers coordinating an attack from both sides and managing, through a combination of luck and determination, to hold Jagg down on the damp grass.

Nichol stepped into the ring, Rhys following suit.

"Finally decided to join us, Rico Suave?" Mick asked as he passed, dodging his arm when it swung in his direction.

Dominic laid a hand on his back. "I know the separation from your connected is hard. I hope you'll come to me whenever you need a shoulder to cry on."

He glared at his smart-ass youngest brother. "Don't you have a report due on my desk yesterday?"

Jagg called the fight to order, outlining the parameters and touching up the boundaries with his boot while scuffing a secondary, smaller square into the terrain. "Nicky, you're confined to this area. Rhys and I have full range. Go."

The round went on for well over an hour, Jagger and Rhys coming at him from all angles, their fists and fangs drawing as much blood from him as he did from them. Dom and Mick sat on the sidelines, cheering the younger brothers on as they attempted to take down the eldest.

Rhys spat a mouthful of dirt on the ground and straightened up, hooking his thumbs in his cargos. "Anyone who's seen Nichol's connected naked, hands up."

As Rhys lifted one arm in the air, a territorial snarl tore through Nichol, and he lunged at Rhys. Jagg yanked his feet out from under him and toppled him to the ground. Rhys pounced, restraining his arms with his weight while Jagg wrapped around his legs.

"You know," Rhys grinned, easing his grip when he relaxed into defeat. "You once told me if you ever made that sound, I was supposed to walk you straight into the Deepfryer. Still want me to hold you to that?"

He got to his feet, brushing the wet grass from his legs. "Fuck. Off."

****

Nichol glanced down at the dried grass at his feet, making a mental note to add more brooms to the haunt's next grocery order. He closed out the stock holdings and began working his way through the plethora of emails filling his inbox.

"Here's the number," Jagg called out, pulling up a chair and sitting beside him. "Louis said to call any time."

Using his phone to snap a quick picture of the number, he pinned the small paper to his note board. "I haven't seen Louis's service contract cross my desk yet," he said, ensuring he was facing Jagg before he spoke.

"Any clauses I should know about?"

"Not that I know of," Jagg replied, pushing his hood down. "He wrote his own, so you'll have to ask him." He pulled another paper from his pocket and handed it to him. "Bee made a list of the things she'd like to see tweaked on The Rising website, as well as a few security requests. Audra and Mick asked the vamp cop site be styled in the same way and the two linked, so it provides an illusion of being allied."

"It can't be just an illusion," he stated, scanning the crumpled page quickly. "This is doable. I'll have both up and running by Monday."

Jagg smacked him on the back as he stood. "I know we've been on your ass about Simone, but don't take it hard. We've all gone through it over the past few years." He paused. "There isn't a single male left here right now."

He grunted and pinned Bianca's neat writing to the board. "Probably why you Neanderthals have been more tolerable as of late." He smirked. "You've been house-broken."

"Smack-talk all you want, little vamp," Jagg called over his shoulder as he strode from the com room. "But don't come crying to me the first time Simone puts you in the doghouse and you need a plan of escape."

He snorted as he entered Louis' contact information into his phone.

He'd already researched the doghouse thoroughly and had compiled a document on effective methods to avoid it.

Pulling out his phone, he fired off a text to Simone.

587OriginalNK: what would put me in your doghouse

Highsteaks1403: cheat on me

Highsteaks1403: bite another woman

Highsteaks1403: screw with the sensitivity settings on my console

His brow knotted.

587OriginalNK: maybe don't use your PC until I come by next Friday

Epilogue

Louis stretched his arms along the back of the ornate sofa and watched as the visiting vampires disappeared onto the Stojanovski grounds, eager for the hunt.

Jackson flopped onto the opposite couch, smoothing his suit jacket while he leaned back. "Not participating this evening?"

"Still good from last night," he replied as he rested his booted feet on the table. "Anyone of concern I need to speak with? I didn't see any new faces on the floor."

Stojanovski tugged his phone from his jacket pocket. "No new reservations passing through until next week. I'll email you the names I want checked out once they confirm." He looked pointedly at him. "Any more news from the Kaius haunt?"

"Denver's open suites are filling quickly. The vamp cops are actively patrolling the city boundaries now." He glanced down at his own phone, flicking open Jagger's latest update. "Deviant hunting has been approved and payments are being transferred to those able to supply Nichol with proof."

"And my hybrid?"

He smirked. "Nichol's hybrid has had two dates with her connected vampire and is doing well."

Stojanovski sighed dramatically. "I suppose it was a decent trade-off. I sure didn't need to be harboring the vamp-killer responsible for ending one of the Khthonios line."

His buzzing phone in hand, he pushed himself off the sofa. "Text me if you need me."

He exited the main hall and made his way across the grounds to the small bunker he was now calling home. Engaging the lock, he dialed Nichol back and turned on his TV.

"What."

He chuckled. "You called me, you miserable asshole."

"Right." There was a rustling of paper. "I received the copy of your contract with Stojanovski. You're aware of the non-disclosure clause in section eleven?"

"Yup."

"Any communication you have with our haunt will require Stojanovski's signature if it relates to any information gleaned from guests on the property," Nichol warned.

He changed the channel from a cooking show to a hockey game. "Paperwork's already been prepped and printed for those situations. How's Mick?"

Nichol grunted. "Somewhat more temperamental in your absence, but maintaining." The sound of boots on hardwood echoed through the phone before a door closed. "I appreciate your sacrifice for Simone."

Brows raising in surprise, he turned the volume down on his television. "No sacrifice, man," he said. "Fresh meals, access to intel, and a private bunker. I think I made out a shit-ton better in this deal than you did."

The old vampire went quiet for a moment. "I owe you."

****

Nichol revved the engine of the SUV, allowing it to lurch forward a foot before he slammed on the brakes.

"I'm coming, I'm coming!" Audra jumped into the passenger side and flung her purse to the floor. "Oh my god, Molly can talk a lot. Okay. Let's go."

He tore down the driveway and onto the empty highway, his foot heavy on the gas. "We're going to be late."

She laughed and patted his arm. "I'll tell Simone it's my fault. Don't worry. I called Mick already and let him know to keep her distracted until we arrived on site."

He eased off the gas a fraction. "Did he say how training was going?"

"Simone took down eight with the rubber arrows during the mass attack exercise."

Snarling, he upped his speed again, the lights of Denver growing closer. "I didn't approve her involvement in that," he growled, his temper rising. "In fact, I specifically forbade Simone from participating in any exercise pitting her directly against any of the men."

Audra looked at him, her feline eyes deadened. "And we all see how well that turned out for you."

He opened his mouth to respond before snapping it shut, slicing his lower lip on his left fang.

His traitor of a BFF grinned. "And when Simone tells you all about it, which she will, you'd be wise to avoid mentioning your edict. Tossing in a 'nice work' would probably be smart, too."

Slowing to exit onto the freeway, he mulled over Audra's recommendations. He caught sight of his eyes in the mirror, their blackened irises giving away his frustration over Simone placing herself in harm's way.

She laid her hand on his forearm. "Just pass it off as

horny. It's been a week, after all. What's in the back seat?"

"Electric piano," he grumbled, tilting the rearview mirror to ensure the box hadn't tipped. "My research says acknowledging anniversaries with a gift is important."

A keyboard was an insufficient token for the month of sanity Simone's presence in his head had provided. A month of delicious anticipation building for six nights every week until he saw her again.

A month of the peace her proximity pushed into his mind and through his veins, easing the blood-high whispers rippling in the back of his head.

She squealed, earning a glare from him. "That's so sweet! I'm so jealous."

"I'll forward my relationship notes to Mikhail tomorrow." He pulled into the training center lot and parked. "Three minutes late."

Hefting her purse onto her shoulder, Audra exited the car and waited for him to lock it. "No one's even coming out yet. You're fine."

Fine.

He was fine for twenty-five hours a week. And three minutes of those twenty-five hours had already ticked by.

The pair entered the building and waited in the lobby as Mickey and Simone wrapped up their lesson, their spirits high.

Prodding Simone's room in his head, he relaxed.

She was happy. Excited. Unharmed.

And craving something.

He probed deeper as she hung the bows on the wall. *Craving him.*

He fired off a quick text to Rhys before he powered his phone off.

—*I'll be back on site at 10:03, give or take a few hours.*—

A word about the author...

Katja Desjarlais is a teacher by day and a romance writer by moonlight. She is an unapologetic music addict and has an obsession for bad Bach puns despite her irrational aversion to Baroque. Her favorite words include 'plethora' and 'dapper', and she is physically repulsed by the word 'moist'. Katja's interest in the paranormal can be traced to her early childhood film choices and to the revolving book collection on her phone.

Desjarlais lives in the Okanagan Valley with her husband, three children, and three cats. Her ideal summer vacation is spent traipsing through the United States with her family and attending heavy metal concerts.

katjadesjarlais.wordpress.com

Thank you for purchasing
this publication of The Wild Rose Press, Inc.

For questions or more information
contact us at
info@thewildrosepress.com.

The Wild Rose Press, Inc.
www.thewildrosepress.com